Luna
A traveller's tale

KEN ELPHINSTONE

COPYRIGHT © 2022 KEN ELPHINSTONE
Published by Compass-Publishing UK 2022
ISBN 978-1-913713-84-3

Designed by The Book Refinery Ltd
www.thebookrefinery.com

A CIP catalogue record for this book is available from the British Library.

Prologue

I sometimes remember the beginning: the start, the errors, the great extinctions. I remember learning from my mistakes and adjusting. It has taken over a billion years to coax these simple beings to edge toward other worlds.

However, when considering it all now, I see a new beginning; a chance to go beyond this place they call Earth.

While I have pushed these creatures to develop to their current phase, and towards the brink of the next stage, I cannot communicate with them, merely coax. It is they who must learn; it is they who must seek the next window in this universe's development.

The latest of my many manipulations flies below me now, trying to make sense of her growing awareness. But I am patient; she is still only a child.

But where is Luna? Where is this caterpillar turned butterfly? Where is this infant stumbling to find who she is without a mentor to guide her way?

Let's see. Ah! she is there, taking her first steps... about to go Travelling.

1
Where to?

A shiver of consciousness stirred within her psyche. Something had stimulated her; she didn't know its source, but it awakened in her a need to move. She found the energy to break from her body, and her spirit-self rose. Pausing, she turned back, seeing her body lying on a white-sheeted bed, looking very young among the surrounding, white-coated observers.

As instructed, a need to travel far from where her body lay was her driver.

Remembering her task, Luna began throwing off her lethargy as if emerging from a series of heavy blankets. Again, looking back at herself, she urged her spirit out the closed door. Now she was drifting down a wide, polished corridor with intermittent, well-groomed flowering plants and stacked hospital wheelchairs. A window revealed a sunlit landscape of occasional buildings and green fields. At first, she paused; then her spirit-self passed through the closed window and floated above the rooftops, feeling the need to move faster.

Quicker now, roads and fields rushed past as she gained speed and height. Patches of fields grew smaller as she approached the hills beyond the last of the houses. Fields,

"My name is Luna. Who are you?" Then, in a spiky tone, she demanded, "Why do you question me?"

The voice's tone changed, as if trying to generate a mindful and tactful connection with her. "Ah yes, Luna! You were here before but are now changed. It's as if you've taken a fresh path in your thoughts, from cub to hunter."

Without knowing how she had changed, Luna had grown and evolved in her last sleeping hours—as if walking for the first time, forgetting she could only crawl before. Her mind had taken a major step-change, one of many yet to come. Unaware of her past, she could not respond to the voice, knowing only that the voice couldn't help her any further. She became hollow, needing to think, asking herself, "What now?"

Once more the voice returned, in an almost pleading tone. "Luna... I, too, am the spirit of someone. I agreed to help people like you, but I'm lonely. Please stay." Then, allowing the quiet to build before he began again: "Please stay with me. There's no one here to pass the time with." Luna allowed the quiet to build further before the voice returned in a softer, resigned tone. "But then, I know you can't."

"I want to go back!"

With minimal redirection of her senses, she started off again, with only a passing reference to the land and sea. She was back in her white-walled hospital room. She looked down at her body below, lying on the bed as if dreaming; but now she saw the others in the room in detail.

The group of white-coated Directors surrounded her bedside Artificial Intelligent module. Together, they commented upon the multiple dancing AI displays, with only her brain activity seeming to show an energetic bobbing movement. A phone rang, and Senior Director Sniphle slid his hand into his top pocket to answer his mobile. He turned away, gripping the phone to his ear, and said sharply, "Talk!", prompting the others to be quiet. A moment later, he switched his snarl to a smile in an almost sneering way. "Good," he said, "we got a Green. She did it. Ariel and Arche report she met with the spirit. She obeyed our directions."

The other directors gathered around her bed, nodding to each other, smiling. Luna watched them, no longer prepared to be directed by these people. But, despite her reservations, she re-entered her immobile body with its tubes and wires, waited a moment, and slowly opened her eyes.

Gauges flickered at the AI console near her bed, prompting Director Ranghan to reach down to adjust the screen's aspect. Sniphle approached the bed. "Luna, good, well done!" Stretching forward, he touched her shoulder. "After you rest overnight, we have another task for you. We need you to go off-world. Think about it, explore the possibility, then rest."

Luna felt weary and ignored his words, but mused to herself, *Maybe I will, maybe I won't.* Bristling with defiance and a new self-assurance, she allowed sleep to overcome her.

2
Hiccup

Unnoticed and unknown, Luna's mind was evolving beyond her physical form. She slept, passing from shallow to deep sleep and back as dreams arose and washed out.

An unrelated incident occurred while she slept. As if by divine intervention a localised lightning storm caused the local electrical power supply to fail, affecting all power supplies in the Director Organisation building. This resulted in the automated back-up power supply kicking in. To the human observer, there was a momentary flicker to room lighting, but Luna's AI machine blinked, almost as if from a cough. Gauges flickered momentarily before its systems restored themselves to their factory pre-sets and continued their soothing hum. But Luna's dreams now found a new direction, spurred by the AI hiccup, providing her a different chemical boost. As if a new door had opened, she became aware. She felt stronger, more alert, her mind actively striving for a new adventure.

She rose out of her body and looked back at herself, seeing the wires, tubes, machines, and subdued lighting, with nurses busying themselves around her. She went as she did before: through the door, along the corridor, and out the window. She flew high across the fields, but slower this time, noticing the leaves rustling in the trees and branches, resisting the wind's occasional gust. It was evening; the sun had fled over the horizon, but the dusk was pleasant and soothing. She liked this time of day. The retreating sun turned its golden horizon darker, reflecting the clouds from a yellow tinge to orange, then darkening still to reds and purples.

As with the sky, so too did her feelings darken with the sinking sun; but consciously breaking away from her mood, Luna travelled faster, catching up with the sun, beaming to herself as she understood how fast she was travelling to bring the setting sun back from its slide over the horizon. "Ah, there again, I see the reds, changing back to orange and yellows, and now the sun itself. Wow, a thousand miles an hour!"

Pleased with herself, she understood the changing aspects and dynamics of the sun rising in the west instead of the east. But her mood swings brought her back, and she became less interested. Luna realised now that once she understood a process, she no longer needed to experience it. Slowing, she stopped, and staying a little longer, smiling once again, waved the sun and its many colours a fond farewell.

Then a thought struck. "Why look down? Why not up?" Her penetrating vision gazed in wonder as she saw first the planets and the layers and depth of stars receding into infinity. "What did Sniphle say about going off-world?... Perhaps I should wait a little longer for that. But what else on this world?"

Time passed as she drifted over the green land. She remembered her body still lying on the bed, thinking to

When she reached the building, she made her way to her room and assumed a stationary position above herself once more. She looked down, contemplating herself for a while, unenthusiastically accepting her situation. "Is that bed with the tubes my home? Is the body of the adolescent girl lying on it really me?"

She wearily entered her still body. She accepted it was time for sleep and rest, thinking enough for now, wanting nothing else to fill her mind. Slowly but surely, like stepping into a bath, she settled into herself once more, soaking back into her physical form, only now feeling her itching tears rolling down her cheeks.

3
A Different Dosage

The tear-stained Luna lay on the bed, apparently asleep, the AI monitor bleating a regular loud, pulsing tone. Looking up as the door opened, the senior nurse turned it off as the thin-faced duty Director arrived at the bedside. "What's the matter with her?" he asked, the panic in the Junior Director's voice rising in alarm.

Senior Nurse Michael, speaking up, said, "She has been like this since last night, when I came on duty. Apparently, the senior sister reported her condition to the Chief Director around midnight. But we've had no guidance. If you look at the records starting at 4 pm yesterday, you'll see she was going through some normal passages of REM sleep lasting ten minutes. Then at 8 pm last night it became constant. At one point, she smiled and began murmuring, but nothing understandable. Then, at 7:45 am this morning," he looked at his timer, "12 minutes ago, Luna began screaming. That's when I rang you, because you're on the list as duty director."

The Junior Director, Ranghan, not fully understanding what was being said, asked, "What else has happened? You said on the phone it worried you?"

Nurse Michael looked at him, now understanding that this so-called well-educated but inexperienced man had very little idea of what was going on. Michael gave an answer Ranghan might understand without landing himself in trouble. "Just look at the charts, sir. It shows all I've been trying to tell you. The dream sleep has become constant and has lasted a very long time. It's now almost 8 am, which tells me she's been in this constant agitated REM sleep for the last 12 hours. It's exhausted her. REM sleep, dream sleep I mean, should normally last no longer than an hour at a time. Look at her heart-rate figures; look at the breathing rates; look at the AI brain activities graphics."

Out of his depth, Junior Director Ranghan bowed to the nurse, equally junior in years, and hesitantly said, "What do you recommend?" Michael knew better; others had warned him earlier never to recommend anything regarding the health of the Specials. Taking pity on Ranghan, he said, "You could report the situation to your senior."

Ranghan, weighing this up for a few moments and looking repeatedly into the face of the now-calm Luna, nervously reached for his communicator and began dialling.

A very disgruntled Senior Director, Dr Vernon, barged through the door, having had his breakfast interrupted. Irritably, he stared down at his nervous junior colleague and barked out, "Ranghan, did you check her medications?"

Ranghan ceased his incessant pacing back and forth between the AI and bed end and replied, "Err, I assumed the AI would have seen to that. I can't overrule its directives without some very senior signatures. Although I was on duty last night, the senior nurses contacted Director Bennon. She said to monitor Luna's situation, as the Special had rest time over the weekend."

With a pinched expression, Director Vernon turned back to the junior director and barked at him, "Director Ranghan, don't divert blame somewhere else. Consider yourself on report. I will bring this matter up in the next meeting of seniors, and we will deal with your misdemeanours. You will hear from us." He stopped his tirade for a moment and, with a grim expression, called to the retreating junior. "Dr Ranghan, don't make any plans for the future."

Vernon picked up the records and, with a clenched jaw, tabbed through Luna's history logs. He stepped through the physical categories, noting the out-of-limits pointers. Oblivious of other staff, he assessed Luna's breathing rates, BP, physical convulsions, body temperature, rapid eye movements, and important time scale before these events occurred. Next, he ventured into the inputs and outputs reports. Liquid in, liquid out, perspiration rates at the differing events of the REM spikes. He then reviewed the medication dosage being administered, noting values being dispensed by the local AI unit. The intense Director Bennon had pinpointed drugs used to keep Luna sedated, plus those used to promote her psyche abilities. He noted the Twilight and Direction Travel doses recommended for her, which, compared to other Specials, were unusually low. Alarmed, he also noted that the AI had delivered much higher doses, close to those he considered the higher normal for other Specials. All this seemed to begin just over 12 hours ago.

Regarding this matter, he asked the staff to bring him up to date as to any anomalies with Luna's AI monitor. A member of the laboratory services staff confirmed that there had been an odd lightening strike, giving a brief and, under supervision, to wander along the corridors. It was there she looked out the windows and caught glimpses of the world outside. It confirmed to her that the dreams were true. She had travelled through these corridors, through this window, and out. She knew all her carers and the Directors, but the corridors also gave her glimpses of other rooms with people lying on beds as she had done. They also being ministered to by carers.

While thinking through what had happened to her, she reaffirmed her determination of not being used further by the Directors. On gaining strength, and with a furrowed brow, she told herself, *If I travel again, I will remember. I will have a purpose.* She halted her thoughts of the others in the white rooms, and those dark-minded controlling directors. Becoming frustrated, she wondered, *Why am I here? My body is getting stronger. If I'm bodily impaired, it's not manifesting itself. Does this mean I'm mentally scarred?*

The physical excursions exhausted her, and she slept true sleep, dreamless sleep. Her mind relaxed; so too her body, for the only time it could recall. On waking, her limbs felt heavy and there was an aching pain in her muscles, but it was something pleasing, telling her she was alive and happy.

Sometimes Directors came to see her, and she remembered each of them from when she was observing from above. Some of them had sympathy for her; others were questioning, driving, and reluctant to allow her to rest. Suspicious now during these visits, she did nothing nor say anything that let on she knew them or had any inkling of them during her induced sleep. In particular, Senior Director Sniphle remained in her thoughts as someone different, someone to be cautious with. She had known of him in the background of her life for as long as she could remember, but now she had a new understanding about him. Her developing senses could see that she troubled him. *He's dangerous. I'll have to keep this man under watch. I'll also have to tread wisely in anything I say or do. It seems he's the one who drives the chemical mixes they give me.* With this, her physical body slumped almost into a faint. "Oh! why am I here?" she moaned aloud.

uncovered a common theme, an ancestry of folks with similar tales from aunts, grandparents, and even further back. These were told and retold as family tales to eager children who passed them on to their own, the truth being watered down all the while. It aligned the stories to certain families, many with Celtic backgrounds, although many disputed this. Another factor was red hair colouring, but again this was contested, despite the high percentage of subjects compared to the general populace. Then came DNA comparisons, where it was found that a higher-than-normal percentage of Neanderthal ancestral DNA was present in these families."

"It was Director Sniphle who told me that the deciding factor for many studying the phenomena was that when close communities intermarried with families having similar histories, it was here that the ghost stories were strongest."

Jillian was hooked and hadn't noticed the server approach with a pad in hand. It startled her when the woman asked, "Do you want anything else, girls?"

With a look of authority, Wendy looked up and offhandedly said, "We're off duty, so a glass of the house red for me and the menu, please. How about you, Jillian?"

"Yes, the same as you," was the quick answer.

Once the server had taken the order and gone, Wendy continued. "Where was I... oh! Yes. The red-haired thing. They pointed the phenomenon out to a successful business executive displaying red hair, who himself had his own family tales. It was during follow-up meetings with him that an eager college fellow convinced the executive to fund a two-year research program. The results were as predicted by the fellow and many other intrigued colleagues. There *was* a family connection between them all, and there was a common mutant DNA 'G' factor resident. Just as the 'ginger gene' paper was to be published, the executive funding the study forbade the release of any documentation, and instead requested the help of dubious laboratories to see if they could isolate and enhance the errant code for these Outliers, as they called them then."

At that point, the attendant arrived to lay the table.

Wendy, seeing a natural break in her story, stopped and looked up. "Let's stop there while we have something to eat. I'm starved."

The junior nurse already knew part of the story from her mother, and pleaded for the senior nurse to continue, but Wendy declined. She leaned close and said quietly, "Listen, if you're interested, I can bring you up to date with the rest of the story, as it involves Director Sniphle, your mother's sister Salena, and others. But it'll have to be while we're away from here. I think the server is showing an interest, and we do *not* want them to know we're talking about the early days. So, if you don't mind, let's call it a day. I'll fill you in with all that I know later."

With a wide grin, the excited Jillian said, "Okay, let's eat!"

6
Red Hair

After making their way via different routes, the two nurses, Wendy and Jillian, met again, this time at a coffee shop on the top floor of a shopping complex. Wendy looked up from the menu as the young nurse approached and said, "Hi Jillian. Were you followed?"

As she slid into her seat, Jillian replied, "Hi Wendy! No, I don't think so. I took precautions, doubling back on separate busses, and no one else got off and on again."

The senior nurse seemed eager to continue her story as part of a cleansing of pent-up memories and settled back into her seat to resume her tale. "Good, let me continue. Where were we—ah yes, the experiments! As they taught us in school, building a new person was almost easy compared to what was to happen next. They say that when an engineer is tasked to design, build, or replicate an object, their inbuilt ingenuity will, given time and sometimes standing on the shoulders of giants, achieve their goal. Most engineers love the challenge and will work until they've achieved the prize. Then, like most engineers, they return repeatedly to polish their baby."

A frown of uncertainty crossed Wendy's mind. She paused, turned her head at an angle and asked Jillian, "You did DNA Theory during your studies, didn't you?"

Jillian nodded, taking a sip of her cooling cappuccino while thinking back. "Yes, of course. Wasn't it achieved long before the middle of the 21st century? They taught us in class—the first of the manufactured DNA-shelled clones was the completed body of an adult, but without a soul." She frowned and asking said, "Didn't they find these grown DNA-shell bodies lacked personality, intellect, and purpose to move?"

Wendy could see the young nurse had studied well and said, "Yes—it didn't have any personality. It needed experience; it needed exposure to life. Its brain synapses needed filling. The engineers found that without all these, the body was just an empty vessel, a shell."

Jillian, nodding in agreement, added, "That's as far as they taught us."

Satisfied, Wendy said, "The budding Dr Frankenstein's were just left with a body of parts. However, the engineers continued to hone their creations. The result was individual chromosomes played with repeatedly for those able to pay. Stronger hearts, better eyes, replaceable lungs, livers, and kidneys. They built machines to stimulate and exercise muscles, and resistance training to strengthen their bones. This provided brain and muscles with a physical memory of movement. But the problem of a completed, fit body with a blank hippocampus remained."

Wendy smiled a little, finished her Americano, and was about to continue when Jillian leaned her head forward and, eyes sharpening, looked side to side. In a rush of eager anticipation, she asked, "Where does Director Sniphle come in all this? I heard he was a pathfinder with the technology?"

Wendy ignored the question, smiled, and said, "Remember, I told you about the rich donor. Well-hidden among the forgotten archives of first-generation patron 'ginger gene' experiments was the hidden key. They had kept the refrigerated cells in a secure condition, waiting for the next tranche of funds to take the research further. But the rich man had fallen foul of outside forces and had lost the ability to continue to fund his pet project. In good faith, the laboratory kept the frozen cells safe from the occasional management clean-outs. Even then, a little luck kept the packages safe, with the small parcels having slipped from their nesting shelf, left hanging underneath their earlier location. Relentlessly, the years passed, until fate allowed an intense researcher, just keen enough to persist in his search, to hunt down the package. The researcher found the frozen samples and grabbed the opportunity of 'dealing' with them after a major clear-out. Newer techniques eased his sequenced search through the three billion base pairs, allowing him to direct the search to the unnatural DNA segment he was looking for." She stopped, as if thinking about what she was revealing, took a deep breath, and asked, "Guess who the research student was?"

Jillian shrugged her shoulders. "I don't have a clue."

Wendy shifted forward in her seat, eager to tell. "It was none other than our boss, Director Sniphle... back when he had hair." She half-laughed, bringing a smile to Jillian's face. "His after-hours undercover research had no restrictions. He delved farther than he appreciated. He uncovered unpublished data from Cold War files of telepathy experiments in both old Soviet and US records. Here, he homed in on the test subjects and their progeny, getting DNA samples required by the current government authorities. Without restraint, he began cutting, splicing, embedding, manipulating, and occasionally toying with the DNA codes. Soon the engineered genes were taking him onto paths he no longer understood. They lost him in a forest of data beyond his abilities, and he didn't understand what he had created. But pressures from colleagues at the laboratory were showing raptor's interest, and he knew he had to act before being uncovered. He planted a copy of his work into the offspring of a paying customer who was looking to have a tall, artistic, intelligent, athletic child—a boy."

"How do you know all this about Director Sniphle?"

Coyly, Wendy hesitated, as if fending off the question, then unconvincingly answered, "Easy. I was dating one of his classmates who used to tell me about him. Oh, and that's another story you may need to know, but not now. I'll give you the dirt on him later." She continued, "So... the red-headed child did all requested from its genetically engineered body design, although he was a slight surprise to his parents, given that both she and her partner were olive-skinned and dark-haired. But the child, named Triton, shined—on the sports field, socially, and in class. Privately though, his parents worried about his constant nightmarish dreams."

"So, what happened to Triton?"

"Enough for today. I'll let you know later; it's too complicated in a oner."

7
Instructions for Elara

Luna ended her third day of full consciousness, exhausted because of her exertions from walking through the corridors on the pretence of exercise. She was really fact finding. She saw the other Specials, each in their own rooms, all looked after by the kind and caring nurses. On one occasion, the door window was closed, to which Ngoosi, who was accompanying her, told her the Special Charon was in "transition," as the Directors called it. During these times, they only allowed Directors in the room. While noting this, Luna and Ngoosi moved on, passing two rooms where they glimpsed two more Specials, Mimas and Rhea, who appeared to be sleeping, with only a nurse in attendance. Farther along the corridor another group of Directors were busying themselves around another Special, Elara.

A shocked Luna grabbed at Ngoosi's arm and, after a quick intake of breath, said, "Ngoosi, what's happening to her?"

"She's in what they call the Twitch Stage. It looks like they're readying her for transition. It normally takes two hours for the chemical doses to take effect, as someone individually administers them. Once proved to be effectual, they then introduce the next stage. Once this has happened and all is stable, they call for the Senior Directors to bring in the..." She stopped, raised double fingers on each hand and continued, "Travel Stage, as one director once joked."

"How long does this take?"

As if gauging whether to answer, Ngoosi looked into Luna's innocent face before replying. "Usually it takes about three hours before they get to the last stage. It looks like they're about midway through at the moment."

A dizziness gripped Luna, as did the need to escape this place before her body displayed the realisation of what was occurring. In shock, her eyes bulged; and she knew she must escape soon. She reached out and said, "Ngoosi, please take me back to my bed, I don't want to be here." There was no immediate movement from the nurse. "Please take me back... now," she pleaded, looking up to Ngoosi with an insistence in her eyes, and as an afterthought said, "I don't like whatever's going on here."

Ngoosi did as bid. She reached for an emergency wheelchair and helped Luna get seated. The return journey didn't take long, and a worried Ngoosi helped the silent Luna onto her bed. Reaching for the nurse's hand, the empathetic girl, on seeing her concerned carer, assured her, "Don't worry, I was just a little shocked when I saw the process. There's no need for anyone to know about this episode. Really, it was just a shock to me, that's all."

The nurse seemed content, weighing up the repercussions of reporting the incident, before smiling reassuringly at Luna and saying, "I'll get something to settle you."

"No, no, don't worry. Let me rest for a while. Give me an hour, and we can go for another walk this afternoon." With that, the concerned nurse seemed satisfied, titivating the bed and dimming the ambient light before leaving.

Luna settled herself, relaxing, making sure there were no pressure points that would disturb her while she readied herself. *I must travel and try to talk to these others*, she told herself. *Now if I can, I'll do as I remember, but this time without the injection they give me. I just have to remember what my mind drives me to do.* She relaxed further into her bed. *I must calm down further and block everything out without the medicinal help.*

Luna, calming into a Zen state despite minor distracting sounds from singing birds, blocked out any outside interruptions. Only a brief time passed before she realised, *There, I've done it. I see myself now, only a metre away.* She rose above her bed and, looking down on herself, turned and headed out through the door, then swiftly along the corridor to Elara's room and through the closed door.

The duty doctor noting the graphic readings of Elara's brain functions on the AI screen. He then looked up as the attending Director nodded to him, raising both eyebrows as if asking the question. 'How's it going?' The doctor nodded back in a satisfied way. "Good, let's give it another couple of minutes, and she should be ready for the Travel Stage."

Luna hovered to one side, viewing the outwardly sleeping girl, then spoke to Elara by projecting her thoughts. "Elara, Elara, can you hear me?"

There was a flicker in the sleeping girl's eyes, and a slight response on the AI clinical display, but luckily, the doctor was no longer watching that function. Steadily, the graphical blip unhurriedly clicked its way towards the edge of the screen to disappear.

Again, Luna said, "Elara, can you hear me?" Once more, the graphic blipped. "Elara, I can see you can hear me. Can you talk to me?" Again, the graphic showed above the normal reading, but this time it was continuous, becoming a low bouncing norm. "Don't worry. I'm just like you. I know you can hear me. Talk to me inside your head, otherwise the doctors may know I'm here. They may get suspicious, and we shouldn't allow them to know we can speak together..." a pause, "just yet."

Luna waited a few moments, staying quiet while watching the low-dancing AI graphics. "My name is Luna, and I'm just like you." She waited again but saw only the graphic continue its dancing march across the screen. "Elara, I'm alone. I don't have anyone to talk to. Please talk to me." Without voice or facial expression, she did her best to insert feeling into her pleading emotions.

With an almost tingling sensation in her head, she heard, "Luna... it is a pleasant name, but where are you? Ah, there you are near the foot of my bed, but it is strange... I can see through you. But wait, though you are translucent, I can also see you smiling."

The curious Luna then said, "Elara, what are they doing to you? Why are these people around you? They're not like the nurses; they're pushing for something. What do they want?"

Elara responded, "I've been here many times. I have watched them; they are preparing for the next stage. Sometimes I can see them... they are waiting for the package. Then the man without hair, I think his full name is Director, Keno´ T. Sniphle. He inserts a phial into the intravenous tubes, then I travel. I go wherever they send me! As if a passenger, I just fly to wherever they want me to go. Where to, I'm not always sure, but I try to observe it all."

In the physical world, Director Sniphle raised his bald head and asked one of the other attendees to check Elara's graphics. The young man promptly glanced at the monitor, and said, "They seem to be in the 'Norm' range, sir." His snappy reply came quickly, knowing Sniphle was a fierce, bad-tempered authoritarian who had no time for pretty young men.

Elara, in an urgent tone, as if frightened, said, "He's done it! I can feel it coming—it's with me now!"

Alarmed, Luna at once said, "What's happening? What are they doing to you?"

Elara had been in this place before and knew what was about to happen. "He will give me another phial, and I will have to travel. I have tried to stop it, but it happens, and I cannot resist. Look, he is inserting the last phial into the intravenous drip now; I can feel it flow. It's not hot or cold, but it's almost a relief that it's here." She expressed an increasing urgency in her tone. "It's with me, almost warm and numbing, its liquid lightning through my arm, now into my body towards my head. It is flushing up to the back of my head now." There became a panic and a resignation within her words as her mind emptied itself of anything other. "Luna, I must go."

"No, don't go. We need to talk. We need to understand."

There was a panic growing into Elara, her spluttering words short and uneven, "I have to go, it's drawing me, I can't stop it."

Elara was unable to resist, even though she clearly wanted to stay, to talk, to understand. Here there was someone else like her. But the content of the phial had a drive. It directed her away, much as a rushing torrent meeting a meandering stream. Gauges flickered only briefly above the Norm level before it swept her away to fulfil the role chosen by the Directors.

Luna saw her new friend rise from her still body briefly, glance back, and sped through the door. Luna waited, eyeing the few strands on the bald Sniphle's head with contempt, knowing he was the reason they took her new friend. She was alone again. Luna noted the others in the room making up the Directors team: Sniphle, the doctor, and two young junior Directors. She noted them, logged their faces into her memory. *"I've been there as Elara is doing now, and I don't enjoy remembering it. They direct me while I'm immobile. I hear them, their words piling up into my psyche, and I resent those unseen voices. Without my physical form, there's little I can do... but, I will find a way."*

She turned. Nothing more here. She went back to her room to rest.

8
Triton Captured

Jillian was eager to get her next instalment of the "Director Organisation" story, but it was almost a week before she and Wendy met again. As soon as both nurses settled into a quiet corner of the mall's top floor café, Jillian jumped in with her pent-up questions. "Wendy, what happened to Triton... and what's Director Sniphle's story?"

Wendy smiled a little, her eyes sparkling with intrigue, then jumped in. "Let me first bring you a bit of gossip about our leader. I'm sure you'll hear about it from someone, but just in case, I'll give you the truth. Director Sniphle and I had a fling together for about a week, but there was something wrong between us, and I broke it off. But we remained okay friends with each other, and I still think he has a soft spot for me—perhaps that's why I got the senior nurse promotion."

She sat back, nodded, and started again. "As you know, he began the company way back, but it was really his own errors that enabled him to start the Director Organisation."

Jillian settling back into the soft chair said, "Go on, I'm all ears."

As if getting a load off her chest, Wendy relaxed a little and began her story. "Well, the gossip is that one of his aunts 'groomed' him as a child. As you can see by his appearance, he's not the most elegant of men. When he was a youngster, barely into his teens, he was a very gangly boy with a wisp of a moustache. His black hair was thin even then, which he tried to disguise, growing it long, combing it in different ways, or by dying it. The thirteen-year-old kids in his class disliked him, which kept his outsider paranoid personality heading towards being a complete outcast. His only friend was his Aunty Beth, who seemed to take him under her wing, bolstering his confidence.

"In the next couple of years, his confidence grew, although not so far as being part of the tight inner group of students in his class year. Most of this confidence came from Aunty Beth's regular invitations to her bed. Sniphle, though, wanted acceptance by all the other students, and while they were developing their own early teen relationships, Sniphle bragged about his relationship with Aunty Beth, even showing secret photos."

In a frustrated shake of her head and with a sigh of disappointment, Wendy said, "The news of his deeds got out, and his liaison with Beth made local and eventually national news. The poor, devastated boy fell deeper into his outcast persona as authorities charged Aunt Beth with being a paedophile and later sent her to prison for a brief term. Sniphle took the prison sentence as his fault."

Wendy became serious, remembering him telling her the tale, but continued, "From then on, he has trusted no one, and as far as anyone knows, apart from me, he has never had a partner. For whatever reason, it seems to have formed him into the Gollum-like person he now is."

Jillian felt for the imprisoned aunt and asked, "What happened to Aunt Beth?"

Wendy looked away, frowned a little, then answered as if not wanting to. "When she got out of prison, she died suddenly. Although there was an inquest, they concluded she had poisoned herself. However, many of her friends hotly disputed this."

Both nurses remained quiet for a moment or two, reflecting on the sequence of events, before Wendy contemplated the interest her story was exerting on the young Jillian. Jillian, tied up in the story but wanting closure, said, "What about Sniphle? Surely he would feel her loss?"

Wendy, reluctant to tell more about her own opinions of the director, said, "Knowing him as I do, I think he's clinically paranoid, possibly with psychopathic episodes. He should undergo some serious counselling, if not some heavy medication. But the place would collapse without him."

Jillian looked worried for a time, remembering her lessons on paranoid cases while trying to match the symptoms to her boss. His darting eyes, the speed of his movements, his sudden bouts of anger under that frozen smile when he put the younger Directors down in conversations... But him being psychotic filled her with a dread, making her shy away from further thought about him and the fate of Aunt Beth.

The senior nurse knew she had disturbed Jillian and changed the direction of her story back to the origins of the Director Organisation. "Our bald boss was a sloppy record-keeper when he was employed at the DNA laboratory. It was this that led to his dismissal at the first lab he worked at."

Jillian settled a little, her worried expression diminishing. Buoyed by Jillian's interest, Wendy felt better and continued her tale. "Sniphle's attention to detail was superb, but documenting his codes into a repeatable filing system was his failing. I was told about the years that followed. His employers found out about his wanting record-keeping, and he was quietly let go, so as not to cause a public stir." She stopped, ensuring she had Jillian's full attention. "Listen to this! He had made copies of those special DNA parcels, and he had surreptitiously placed them into twelve more unsuspecting mothers. We later found out that although Sniphle could monitor the resultant babies from afar, he didn't understand what he had created."

Jillian broke in. "So how did he get where he is today?"

Wendy smiled. "Fortune favoured our Dr Sniphle with his own wealthy parents. They were proud of their clever son, even though they didn't understand why he'd left his job. All they knew was that his efforts didn't bring in a fortune. They rejoiced in his pioneering DNA work, telling their friends of his ground-breaking research without understanding it. They were so enamoured with his words, they funded him to start his own laboratory." Wendy smiled, looked to Jillian, "The Director Organisation."

She bent forward and spoke quieter. "Away from the new twelve, the first of Sniphle's 'fruits,' Triton, continued his progression into adulthood with his continuing and growing hidden problems. To all but his parents, the developing Triton was the outgoing centre of his peers, who strove to meet his standards. He was their leader and tipped to rise to the top of whatever avenue he chose."

She stopped before confessing, "Listen, I got this piece from your Aunt Salena. She told me she had heard from him that continuing through his teen years, the vivid dreams steadily became more real. However, he told her his self-preservation was a match for his night-time demons, but he began having a growing dread of his dreams, which at first, he hid as best he could. But they grew, until not only his parents but also the occasional bed partner, often awoke to his night horrors. To Triton, these were not always horrors. Occasionally there was an escape, as he exercised his innate ability to flee and hide. He puzzled to himself many times, when questioned by worried witnesses, about whom he was escaping from. Who was it chasing him in his head, and what and how many were in his head to cause his nightmares without him having experienced or witnessed any horrors in his life so far? To Triton, it was a mystery, and blessed with an enhanced IQ directed towards puzzle solving. He committed himself to finding his tormentors. However, the years passed, and his persecutors continued their unrelenting torment."

"The death of his favourite grandfather was the key to unloading the nightly weight, which was causing him a reluctance to enjoy the pleasures of bedroom activities. In time, he noticed a familiar soul among the tormentors, a kindly menace, not there to chase but to travel with him in his dreams."

Wendy continued her story, her head forward and in a secretive manner. "Unfortunately, Sniphle had monitored Triton and his parents from the early days and had regular contact with the family from his inception. He knew all about the troubled nights of his first concocted DNA brew."

Secretively, Jillian likewise bent forward, similar to Wendy. "You mean Director Sniphle knew all about Triton's problems and didn't help in any way?"

Nodding, Wendy went on. "Although surprised, Director Sniphle became interested in some side effects; this clouded his assumption that all was well because of Triton's other outstanding traits. With the night-time horrors catalogued, Sniphle became intrigued. Was there something else there? He surmised. Was it just Triton, or were the other twelve experiencing similar horrors in their sleeping hours? He later asked one researcher what else was happening to Triton that they had missed. What else had the cutting, grafting, and blending introduced into his new fruit?"

Wendy's face reddened; and, looking down, she said, "Um, the thing is, I also had a brief fling with one researcher who told me a little more. Brian, the researcher, he told me that when the innocent Triton reported his unknown companions during his dreams, Sniphle reached out to the boy with 'Let me help you' words. He then targeted the blameless family with his malice-stacked thoughts. Our bald boss contacted the worried parents and hinted to them he might find a cause, saying, 'Perhaps I can help. Please visit me at my clinic. Let us do a sleepover and run some tests.' His scheming mind was racing back to what other pieces he had added to the DNA mix that could cause this symptom."

Jillian interrupted, "From what I've heard of Director Sniphle, he wouldn't do that for free. Triton's parents must have been expecting a large medical bill."

Wendy abruptly sat back in her chair, looked to her companion with wide eyes, and said, "Jillian, listen, I was in the room and could see that his parents, Charles and Cynthia Taylor, were at first hesitant until the scheming serpent saw the boy's father's downcast eyes. Then made his offer. He told them he'd known of them since before Triton was born, 17 or 18 years before. He told them he would let Triton stay over for an extended weekend, all at his expense."

Jillian, straightening up, broke in. "I can't believe he would do that! He's such a penny-pincher."

"You just don't know how much he wanted the research done on his creation," Wendy replied, and went on with her tale. "Sniphle continued, crushing any resistance from them. He said to them, Charles, Cynthia, you have always been closest to my spirit of life. Triton is like family to me. The weekend will be at my expense."

The gushing enthusiasm of the white-coated, balding Sniphle overwhelmed Triton's mother. "Yes, that would be wonderful. Let's try to sort out these nightmares once and for all." Triton, though, had reservations, and torn between his innate distrust of the man and his own dread of the nightly terrors. His father, seeing the reluctance in his son but buoyed by his wife's enthusiasm, lent his weight to the decision. After glancing briefly at Triton, Charles turned to Sniphle and offered an enthusiastic handshake. "So, when and where can we send him to your place then, Director Sniphle?"

Wendy lowered her voice further, and staring into the junior nurse's eyes, reported, "Salena told me that with the decision taken from Triton, the relief of his concerned parents overwhelmed his reservations. When the family left, Sniphle called his trusted compliant chemist, asking for compounds that could make his special fruit reveal all. Sniphle planned the entire weekend, selecting staff obedient to his command, instructing them to appear sympathetic to the young visitor. He knew also that the young man was in the throes of teenage hormonal urges, and so selected his nursing staff with this in mind." Wendy smiled a little, glancing up to Jillian, and said, "This is where your aunt comes into it."

"Oh, so this is how Aunt Salena knew so much!"

"Yes, you've got it! The adolescent was exceptional, with a sharp mind. However, the compounds they fed to him diminished any resistance to what Sniphle was doing, and instead tied him to a reliance on them. During the in-depth psychological sessions, aided by the dubious chemical mixes, Triton revealed he could achieve out-of-body experiences to the incredulous staff. He then proved it by demonstrating how he could read the notes of those attending the session while his body lay on a couch, eyes closed. Sniphle at once ordered the session closed while injecting a sedative to keep the boy from using his powers any further. The only request from Triton was for more of the compounds that had originally subdued his spirit, but provided a euphoric hit. While quietly studying the boy, Sniphle noted with satisfaction the keen interest he was also taking in the nurse. Your Aunty Salena." The senior nurse saw that Jillian now understood the role Salena had played.

"Sniphle then told the research staff he had the boy 'hooked.'"

The server arrived and took the order before Wendy finished her story. She then moved on. "My researcher friend told me at the time that Director Sniphle asked if anyone in the team had any ideas of how the boy travelled outside of his body? Was it the compounds or the boy himself, or indeed, both? If it were, could they isolate one from the other, then blend and replicate the situation? Better though, could they control it? He told them, 'But first, let's keep him here; and should he want to return to his family, let's give him reason to come back here again and again.'"

"Your Aunt Salena knew her strengths, and she was quite something. She was no longer an inexperienced girl, newly aware of her breasts, hips, and thighs. She was now confident of her body, honed by years of gym work bringing muscular legs, jutting buttocks, and breasts that needed little support. Salena told me she had noted movement from the lad's bed and knew he was recovering from the induced sleep Sniphle had the doctor prescribe."

"It was here that your aunt flaunted her beauty. She told me how she remembered Triton's first reaction to her. Salena told me she just acted as naturally as she could and allowed the waking boy to observe her almost unconscious movements. She told me she just stood up from the chair and bent forward over to the monitor, appearing to be oblivious to his watching eyes. Salena enjoyed his gaze and playing with his teenage mind. She allowed her breasts to hang forward a bit as she reached to change the monitor screen aspect. Without hurrying, she turned her head and watched as his eyes followed her until they caught her looking at him." Wendy, smiling, then said that Salena said to him, "So, you're waking up, are you?"

Hurriedly, he turned away, aware of her gaze. His normal confidence evaporated. But then glanced back once again to catch her smile of encouragement. "Don't be embarrassed. Most guys can't help themselves, and I know you mean no harm. I'm here to look out for your needs while you're here, so just relax, and we'll both enjoy your stay."

He smiled in acknowledgement and, with returning confidence, said, "What's your name? There were so many at the introduction, I didn't catch it."

9
A Trip to New York

Luna forced a smile as Ngoosi entered her room, asking, "How are you feeling now? I was a little worried after you asked to return from our walk along the corridor."

Her pale-faced shock after watching Elara drawn away had Luna speechless until Ngoosi's question. Forcing herself to calm down, she said, "No, I'm fine. I think it was seeing the other Specials, as you call us, lying in their beds. Tell me, is it often that we get out like I am now?"

In a show of personal pride, Ngoosi gave a white-toothed smile and said, "Oh, it happens, but not too often. Usually about once a week, us nurses take you to the gym room. There, we attach you to a stimulating exercise machine, and the AI takes you through routines for an hour to keep you physically fit. Some of you stir a little, but mostly, you seem to sleep through it. I think you wouldn't have the strength to have been able to go for our walks down the corridor otherwise."

"So, how about you, Ngoosi? How about you? I feel you're not too happy at the moment. What's bringing you down?"

Without restraint, Ngoosi replied. "It's my Mum. She's in New York now with my sister, and I haven't heard from them for a month. It's not like them." Ngoosi explained the extreme lifestyle New Yorkers had now that lower

Manhattan had become mostly inundated by the changing sea levels over the past years. Although she knew their last address, she couldn't contact them; life in NYC was no longer as it had been in the past.

"Maybe I can help. Give me their last address and something I can recognise them from. Let me try; you've been so helpful to me. I think of you as a friend, not my nurse."

The sceptical nurse only needed someone to unload onto, not help her, but she went along with the young girl and told her the address and showed her a picture of her mother. With that, Ngoosi said, "Listen, it's nearly time for your lunch. Let me arrange it, and I'll be back in an hour. In the meantime, do you want to read or watch a media program?"

"No. No, just let me rest a little longer." With that, the kindly nurse left.

When she had gone, Luna settled herself down to a comfortable position and closed her eyes. When concentrating, she went within herself, darker, deeper, until she found her trigger point. *There, within the darkness, light. Let me concentrate a little deeper and closer into the centre of the circular speck of serrated colour in the middle, like an eye looking back at me. I remember, from before, the background light straining to get around and beyond.*

Without understanding its threshold, she stepped through.

She understood her new state though, and saw her body from above. *There below me, my body, with almost a smile on my face; but I must get out of here and across the sea to Manhattan, to that last address of Ngoosi's mother.*

The first part was always slow, out through the window and detect the direction; now speed, and more speed. The sea had come so fast, and the coast already. There: The Statue of Liberty still standing, with the sea lapping around her base. Luna began searching the lower east side, West 73rd Street. With her hawk-like vision, she took in the waterlogged scene and considered the erosion. *It looks like all the streets are in danger, with the sea lapping between the buildings.* The many structures cushioned each wave, but throughout the area, she eyed the ripples etching the sand away from the concrete on these once-lit buildings.

Almost breathless, remembering where she was to go, she asked herself, *I wonder if Ngoosi's mother is still at the address. Let me try… Ah, no, it's a notice saying, "Property Evacuated."* But she followed the stairway leading up to the second-floor apartment, 202. She read an attached, neatly handwritten notice that directed the reader to another address in another city, Newburgh. She knew the city was to the northwest, not far. *Just a hop, and I'm there. The Lapetus Building, fourth floor, Apartment 403.*

When she arrived and passed through the door, Luna wondered to herself upon seeing a seated, middle-aged woman in uniform, *Is this her sitting watching her screen? How can I tell? The photos on the wall. Is it Ngoosi's mother?… Yes, it must be.* There in one of them was an unmistakable teenage Ngoosi, holding hands with mom and another younger girl, smiling with her front teeth missing. Mom looked weary, but she was smiling at the camera.

Satisfied, Luna began scanning the rest of the apartment. A bedroom, small living-kitchen area, small shower plus toilet room. There, faded areas on the wall where pictures had hung in the past and were no longer there. These were not hers. Luna realised now that Mom hadn't been here long; it could be she'd just moved in and away from Manhattan a short time ago.

The seated woman stirred from her tablet, unsteadily getting to her feet, bringing Luna to wonder what next. She hovered to one side, waiting to see if there was anything else to take back to tell Ngoosi before noticing Mom putting on a coat over her uniform and checking her bag. Luna could see Mom was preparing to go out, but where to? Then, looking at the clock, saw it was 7:45. Then remembered it was still morning on the US East Coast. To herself she thought, *Possibly she's going to work; I'll follow her.* Luna felt an affinity to the older woman, as if their minds could feel one another, but weakly.

Gilda felt a shiver of goosebumps as she closed the door, sensing something invisible beyond the dimly lit corridor. She looked behind her several times before doubly locking the door. She decided on the stairs instead of the lift. Gilda knew something was there, but she wasn't sure, wanting to eliminate all but her own feelings, thinking the elevator would somehow cloud her senses.

Even the few steps on the sidewalk to the bus stop, and the four-stop journey, did not relieve Gilda's feeling that somebody was there, watching her.

As Gilda stepped off the bus, Luna could see the reason for the woman's uniform. This was a day-kindergarten, and she must be here as a nurse. Young kids greeted her while other recent arrivals for the day's activities started jumping up and down with excitement while parents offloaded their children for the day. They all seemed to like her, some gripping hold of her for comfort as their parents bid hurried farewells.

Eye widening, Luna felt an unexpected shock as something blocked all her senses, almost physically. Without a bodily form, the shock expressed itself as a sudden blankness. Again, she felt the impact. Struggling to fathom what was happening, she understood she was being drawn away. Gilda had gone. In less than the blink of an eye, Luna travelled back across the ocean to her room, hovering above herself once more.

Concerned, leaning across her bed, a nurse, Margret, was gently tapping Luna's shoulder. To one side stood a junior Director. On feeling her physical senses returning, Luna knew she must re-enter her body and wake.

Margret called to her, "Luna, are you okay?"

Luna knew it was time for a little play-acting; she opened her eyes and acted surprised at them being there. First, a fuzzy wake-up before she said, "Oh, Margret, you gave me a start! I was having a dream."

"Tell me what the dream was about!" said the junior Director, asking in a way that angered both Luna and Margret, who rounded on her and reminded her Luna was under her care at present. In mock defence, the cold Director said, "Oh, I meant nothing. It was an innocent question," she lied. Luna, though, had her answer ready. "Oh, my dream. It was something about a bitchy little she-dog getting beyond herself. But it's fading already. Sorry, that's all I have."

Without understanding that Luna's words were directed at her, the young Director announced the reason for her visit. "I'm here to check that you're okay and to remind the nursing staff that you will come under our care in three days' time."

Both Luna and Margret remained silent while exchanging glances, before returning their gaze to the Director, who was becoming uncomfortable under their stare. The junior Director, wanting to reassert herself, unnecessarily announced, "Well, Luna, Director Sniphle and the rest of the team will meet you on Monday morning, and hopefully take you to the next level. I'm sure you will love it." With that, she turned to Margret. "We shall leave Luna in peace now."

The Director, turned, made for the door, opened it, and stepped through, not bothering to catch the door as it closed in front of the following nurse. Margret took hold of the door handle before turning towards the expressionless Luna and said, "We'll try to help you all we can, but there's little we can do about them." nodding her head towards the departed director. "Ngoosi will bring you your lunch in about 10 minutes. Is there anything I can do before that?"

Luna thought for a while, a little shocked by the announcement of the events planned in three days, then just shook her head.

Ngoosi arrived, as Margret had said. "Pansit," she announced. "It's a light, savoury noodle dish from East Asia. I quite like it. Anyway, there's a fish dish this evening if the Pansit isn't to your liking."

Luna forked in a mouthful and nodded approval before she started eating. Bright-eyed and with a hint of intrigue, she said, "Ngoosi, I saw your mother today. She's okay and seems to be happy." She looked into Ngoosi's eyes and paused a little. "She's living in Newburgh; it's about 100 km from Manhattan."

Ngoosi's brow frowned with a pained expression. She turned to her patient. "Luna, what are you talking about?"

Luna took down another forkful of the Pansit and answered Ngoosi's sharp question. "I visited her. She moved from the waterlogged apartment block in Manhattan and now lives in a small place in Newburgh."

Annoyed at what she perceived as senseless chatter, Ngoosi snapped back, "What? How would you know this? How *could* you know this?"

"Ngoosi, listen to me. I can travel outside my body when I'm sleeping. It's what the Directors make us do. But I can do it on my own; I can do it without their drugs. I also think it may help if you don't tell them I can do this without their direction. I don't trust them." She paused to see if the nurse was still understanding what she was saying. "I travelled out of my body to the address you gave me, but I found her evacuated apartment block and a notice on her apartment door with a new address. I went there, and she was just getting ready for work." Looking into the sceptical nurse's face, she said, "Listen, when I was there, I saw a picture of a younger you with your mom, and a little girl with missing front teeth." An uncontrolled broad smile with flashing strong teeth spread across Ngoosi's face. Tears filled her eyes as she remembered first the photo, and then back further to the time, and who had taken it. Enthusiastically pulling a chair forward, she whispered, "Tell me how she is. Where is she? Have you got the new address? Tell me everything!"

10
When You Die,
You Are Not Dead

The teenage Triton remained optimistic, but Salena kept him at bay with just enough encouragement to allow him hope. She had her instructions to encourage him to return to the clinic time and again. In this way, Director Sniphle could continue his investigations while slipping an addictive additive into the drugs he was feeding the teen. The chemical mix was achieving results, and slowly the team drew out hidden characteristics of Triton's abilities. They discovered he could reliably achieve out-of-body travel. They also gave him tasks to conduct while he was travelling as proof of his claims. Mostly, it was easy for him—usually reading messages at progressively distant locations and behind locked doors. Indeed, it was all too simple for him. On one occasion, they instructed him to travel to multiple city locations in Europe to see how fast he could manage it. On another, they jokingly instructed him to travel around the world, reporting weather as proof of the locations he passed over. The major shock to Sniphle's team was the speed with which the boy could achieve these tasks. In less than five minutes, he travelled around the world and gathered the evidence.

Now, beginning a deeper understanding, Sniphle's team identified the effects of specific combinations of chemicals and dosages they prescribed. They discovered they could subdue Triton's spirit and to direct him to almost any location they wished. The team treated Triton's abilities like a game, sending him on data gathering missions for their own amusement despite reports from the nursing staff of their effects on Triton. With prompts from Salena, Triton realised this was for Sniphle's team's benefit, not to help him achieve the initial purpose of his visit—solving his continuing nightmares. It was here that Salena stepped beyond her primary responsibilities. At first, she felt sorry for the young man as he returned to her care, more tired than on earlier occasions. She saw him, too, with the start of a craving. With her pity, there also began a growing appreciation of him as a man. Only in his eighteenth year, yet fully grown and confident of his physical prowess, he maintained a boyish enthusiasm that appealed to her. But as mostly happens, there began a series of plateaus, in which each became more comfortable with each other before stepping to additional levels. For one so young, he had an inner, deeper intelligence that appealed to her. Most men she had known hadn't grown mentally much beyond their early twenties, and treated her as just another body. She knew it wasn't until they were into their forties that men grew up at all. Yet here was an inexperienced young man just approaching eighteen who accepted she had a brain and was not just tits and arse, as some men had spoken of her.

As Salena and Triton mounted the higher steps of their relationship, he grew more confident in admitting his fears of where Director Sniphle was taking him. She accepted his growing concern and confirmed that it was not for her to tell the Sniphle team what Triton had shared with her. But she told him that perhaps Sniphle should know of his concerns about the drugs that were being used on him. She argued it would be better if the Directors didn't know about their relationship.

But Sniphle had planned it this way. He had chosen Salena to keep Triton returning to the clinic until the addictive chemicals had kicked in and the boy had been hooked. Triton was aware of his body being drawn to the addictive drugs, so he tried to resist—but an extra push from the directors quashed his resistance.

Sniphle, although aware of Salena's draw on the young man, was unaware of her strengths, only of her physical attributes. She got Triton to remind the psychiatric doctor of his primary reason of being at the clinic, to investigate the sleeping trauma. Despite Sniphle's pressures, the D.O. team made headway into the young man's problem. With the help of psychiatric drugs, they could induce Triton into a state whereby he could slow down his agitation during sleep.

Eventually they made a breakthrough and could get Triton to converse with one of the spiritual fellow travellers on his out-of-body journeys. As he'd suspected, the one kind figure who travelled with him claimed to be his grandfather. Together they talked, and to Triton's amazement, the old man claimed to be still alive in spirit. He argued he knew his body was dead and wasn't sure why he was still aware of the lives of the living. "At the end of my life and the start of my death, I found I was still conscious of the surrounding people. Seeing the family grieve, but not too much, I saw the relief of some at my death. I wasn't aware of the strain my last illness was causing on the rest of the family until I looked down on myself."

Triton saw his grandfather as he first remembered him when he was a young boy, but with an absence of colour; he was translucent. In a sombre tone, Grandfather said, "Please tell them I'm sorry. I didn't mean to be so tiresome; I was just thinking about myself and the pain of knowing I was dying."

In a show of sympathy and understanding, Triton nodded to the old man and replied, "There are others, aren't there?" Then, looking for confirmation, he continued, "They're... not nice to me. They've frightened me for as long as I can recall."

Unable to put an arm round the boy's shoulder in a show of comfort, but pleased with his grandson's acceptance of him, Grandfather said, "Yes, there are others. They're not looking to scare you or cause you harm or distress. They're afraid. So am I. When we die and are aware we're dead, though our spirit lives on, we cannot communicate well with others, like you and I are now. We... perhaps I'm making a generalisation. We know the actual end is coming, as the energy of our spirit selves ebbs into the realm of Dark Energy. It's only when we're no longer remembered by the living that we fade and pass into the dark."

Triton, attempting to understand, asked, "But I've heard of spirits in old buildings and ghosts still dressed in clothes of the past."

The old man nodded. "Yes, we know of these. For some reason, some of us recently dead don't fade away into the dark energy and disappear completely. Some stay in this half-world we're in now."

Triton saw his grandfather was becoming saddened by his words as he continued, "I've seen others like myself fade. They're no longer able to communicate with anyone. I see them become sad and sometimes angry. It is these who have frightened you in the past. I'm lucky I found you. I can follow you in what you do, just like the others with their living loved ones. But you see me and are aware of me, and now I have a purpose." He paused before he said, "The others are looking for a loved one who can see them, just as you do me. Most get frustrated they can't communicate and become angry."

Grandfather waited as if time was irrelevant and just looked at Triton, taking in the family features he recognised—seeing features of his own mother in the way Triton's hairline formed a slight widow's peak, the dimpled chin of his own son... and there he saw his own heavy eyelids on the boy.

"Grandad! I have little time! What about the others... what happens to them?"

The old man seemed to sigh, repeating his understanding of the place he was in. "Remember why they become angry. They fade when people who are still alive start forgetting them. When those who are alive die or forget, it is then that the spirits go into the dark." He waited a few moments, looking into the boy's eyes to see if he had a question, then said. "Maybe... Probably! People who are still alive and can see our dimension report them, us, as ghosts."

Triton remembered ghost stories and said, "But not everyone can see a ghost; it's only an old wife's tale. Right?"

The figure of the old man changed a little, his features blurring, becoming slightly younger, then said, "Yes, you're right! Most don't have these senses, and by the time they're past their childhood, they've mostly lost this skill."

Triton thought through what his grandfather was telling him; and, seeing a bigger picture, asked, "When I travel to other places, do you always come with me?"

Grandpa's eyes showed a misty smile before he said, "Sometimes you're too quick for me. I'm not sure what you do to be in this state. Maybe it's the surrounding doctors who do something. On these occasions, I don't know where you go. Then you travel exceptionally fast and return to those who send you. But when you're like you are now, without the doctors, you seem to be more aware of us spirits."

Grandpa waited a little and seemed to hang his head to one side as if listening, nodded, and began again. "Sometimes I can hear the others like me talk, but it's almost like a whisper, almost out of reach. As a result, we're all mostly lonely. We have no one as we fade into nothing." Grandpa looked down with a sadness Triton had not noticed before.

The mood had changed, and Triton, fearing a breakdown between them, blurted, "Grandpa, it's time for me to go. I'll be back though. You've helped me to understand some of my fears, and I'm not so afraid to return here now."

The old man nodded as if giving his blessing and said, "Yes, until next time, then. Perhaps you and I can travel together, talk to others like me. And maybe, without you being pushed by the doctors."

With that, Triton looked once again into his grandfather's eyes, then straight through them as he faded from that place.

11
A Meeting of Minds

Luna planned, but knew it limited her time. With only two days before she could implement her plan, she knew it would be difficult. Following her secret travel to Ngoosi's mother to help them reconnect, Luna knew she now had a friend who would help her if asked. She remembered Elara's example; she knew she had to escape while she still could. Her body would need to be strong enough to travel to wherever she wanted without tiring. Therefore, she should get the nurses to push her harder on the regular AI-stimulated exercise sessions when the Directors placed her in the dormant stage. Next was the need for outside help; but she didn't know at this stage who it could be. She planned further, remembering Ngoosi, but knew that asking her for help or having her plans overheard or revealed was a danger.

Where should she try next; where should she venture? Then an idea struck. Maybe she should try talking to the other Specials, though this would entail out-of-body travel while the nurses and Directors didn't notice. She thought through the possibilities, and she knew it had to occur on the night-duty stint when everyone was sleeping.

After her supper, Margret helped Luna make herself comfortable and bade her good night. Timing herself,

Luna gave it an hour before settling back within herself and reaching for her trigger point. In due course, she looked down on herself from above, noticing for the first time her cropped red hair, thinking to herself. "Why do the nurses have long hair while I don't?" but without thinking of a reason, she put it out of her mind. She turned and was through her door and down the corridor in a moment. Rhea and Mimas looked to be engaged by the Directors, but luckily Elara was alone, asleep. Luna sailed through the door, noticing the cropped red hair on her, too. "Elara, it's me, Luna. Wake up, wake up." There was a slight movement from the bed, and Elara's semi-snoring stopped. Luna repeated her plea a few more times before Elara was awake.

At first, it pinched wrinkles tight on her concentrating face, but as Luna's thoughts penetrated the mist of Elara's, Elara understood, releasing the tension. At first, she voiced her words: "Is that you, Luna? Where are you? I can't see you. I hear you inside my head, but can't see you. Am I dreaming?"

Luna remembered that the last time she'd been in contact with her new friend, Elara was being readied to travel. She looked into the girl's eyes and said, "Elara, try to talk again inside your head; otherwise, the others may hear you if they're passing."

Elara tried again. Concentrating, she said, "Luna, try listening for me in your head again."

There was quiet before Luna began homing in on a vague notion invading her mind. The shadow of a voice became stronger while she focused harder. Almost at once, it became clear what Elara was saying. "Yes, it's coming. I understand you."

The joy of mentally conversing with each other was almost too much for the pair. Both realised that without their physical forms, they couldn't give each other the hug that both desperately needed. But for the next hour, the pair chatted back and forth. When Luna asked how long Elara had been in her room, there was no believable answer until the question of age came up. Elara said, "I'm just coming up to my 33rd birthday." Then a thought struck her, and Elara asked, "How old are you, Luna?"

It came as a shock to Luna as she delved into her memories. "I don't know!"

Elara, feeling the silence from Luna, gave the girl something new. "You've only been here in this wing for about three months. The rest of us have been here for as long as I can remember. The first time I saw you was when I was being taken to the exercise room one time, and there you were, looking very young. From my limited memory, you look to be in your early teens, possibly as young as 12 or 13. I can't really tell from the limited time I saw you. You could ask the nurses; they'll have the records."

"What about the others," pausing, "the other Specials? How old are they?"

"We're all about the same age. I think Rhea is the oldest; she's two months older than me. Charon is the youngest—I think about three months younger. I heard two of the nurses saying one time that there are others like us, boys. But no one talks about them. There's also a door at the end of the corridor near Sniphle's office that they allow only some nurses in."

Luna narrowed her eyes and frowned, asking, "Elara, do you ever talk to any of the others?"

"No, I can't travel outside without the drugs they give me any longer. I did when I was younger, but they knew, so they withheld the wonderful stuff I enjoy until I stopped. Now I can't do it anymore, although I've tried from time to time."

Intrigued, Luna said, "What wonderful stuff are you talking about?"

Elara's wispy aura shimmered a little as she thought, then said, "Oh, it's a combination of things. They give me a shot of something that puts me into a pleasant mood, where I feel overly sensitive and feel I want to be touched. Then the Directors massage me to bring me to climax over and again." Elara remembered its tingling pleasure, which Luna picked up as a vague feeling of joy. "Sometimes I can't get enough of it, and they know it. I know I'm trapped and do as they direct, but on the whole, they take care of my needs." She stopped a moment before adding, "The nurses don't like what the Directors do, but I can do nothing about it."

Luna then asked, "Have you ever spoken to any of the others, or have they tried to talk to you at all?"

Elara said sadly, "No, none of them." She stopped for a moment in her memories. Then Luna picked out something else Elara was resurrecting. "There was something some time ago, something beyond here that seemed to fill me, but it was brief. It was as if someone or something was watching me, but it was like a shadow I couldn't chase. The Directors give me the potion that points me to where I must go. Any deviation is impossible." She stopped again for a moment. "I still get that feeling of the outside shadow from time to time, but it is only a shadow."

An awareness of a physical movement brought Elara to withdraw, breaking the pair from their mixing of minds. Luna knew instinctively to leave, and upon retreating, saw a nurse bending over the bed. She watched as the nurse, Margret, straightened the covers on the bed and saw Elara wake from sleep. "Oh, sorry did I wake you my dear? I'm on my last rounds, checking you all. You looked to be so deep in sleep I felt tucking you in wouldn't bother you. Anyway, unless there's anything else I can get you, I'll say my good nights to you."

With eyes sparkling in uncontrolled happiness, Elara stretched her arms wide and said, "No thanks, Margret, I was just having a wonderful, wonderful dream. Good night!"

Luna knew that would be it for the night and vowed to try the others another time as she withdrew back through the door and paused, looking along the corridor towards Sniphle's office before turning back towards her own room. *It's time for rest, so back to my room... for today.*

12
Redder Than Red

The junior nurse, Jillian, took to her added responsibilities with more interest now. She was aware of her charges' backgrounds. But she was still unsure of the role and whereabouts of young Luna, and how she came to be part of the Specials. At their next meeting, she knew where to point her next questions at the senior nurse. "So, Wendy, how did Luna come into the Specials family?"

Wendy looked up, and a memory passed across her mind, bringing a smile before a sadness flooded it out. "It's difficult to say. I know most of the story, but there are parts I'm not sure about." She sat back in the seat and looked away, the sadness filling her more.

Her face blank, the story rolled out almost as a relief as she relayed the events. She ignored the coffee as it arrived, instead telling the tale as if it were a confession, not caring who was listening. "It all started so innocently. We all knew when we joined the laboratory that young Mr Sniphle was selling his new DNA fixes, as he called them. People applied to his laboratory to get a fix for whatever they perceived as a problem. For example, if you wanted blue eyes instead of brown or green, he could chop and change different parts of your DNA to trigger you to have blue eyes. That one was quite a winner for a time until critics pointed to the negatives of having blue eyes in bright sunlit countries. There were people wanting stronger muscles, longer legs, whiter skin, browner skin, some wanting blue-black skin. It became a fashion accessory to have what you wanted to enhance the style of the day."

Jillian broke in and said, "But the authorities put a ban on all that because of the harm it was doing to the children down the line."

The senior nurse nodded and said, "Yes, they it made illegal... but as usual, lawyers always seem to find a way of leaving a door open when writing legislation. Some laboratories bypassed the laws and guess who?... our Director Sniphle found a way." She looked up at Jillian with an odd expression to see if she understood. However, not seeing an animated response of understanding, she went on. "But, to continue the story of your Aunt Salena... She was a stunning beauty with dark hair, but the style for those few years was auburn hair. Salena somehow persuaded Sniphle and the lab techs to change her MC1R gene to red, asking them to make it redder than all others."

Again, Jillian broke in and said, "How can you have something redder than red?"

Wendy, recovering some of her outgoing personality, said, "Exactly! But as you know by now, fashion always goes to the extremes, until it can't go any farther." She looked up at Jillian, and made a face and a slight shrug of her shoulders and said, "Anyway, from my understanding, Sniphle played with her DNA and as her hair grew out, it really seemed to be redder than red. But I remember at the time one tech saying that Sniphle seemed to try for more. I understood that to mean the red-hair thing, but now I think there was something different. Something else he was playing with in his DNA chip-chopping."

At this point, Jillian asked the outstanding question that had her puzzled. "But where did all the money come from to do all this?"

Her eyes sparkled a little and Wendy smiled, responded to the new direction her story was taking, and said, "Okay, this is shadowy, and you can tell no one else." She looked at the junior nurse for a while, wondering if she should continue. But the convincing innocence of the girl allowed her to continue. "Eventually, Sniphle achieved what he was angling for: a subservient, invisible spy. Sniphle's Director Organisation began with an industry he understood, with tentative forays to DNA and biochemical organisations becoming the first on the growing list of victims. They sent Triton in his spectral form with his photographic memory to steal information. They sent him to legal departments of companies about to submit product patents for new goods and formulas. Once Triton had returned with the new data, Sniphle's team hurriedly submitted the newly stolen ideas to patent offices worldwide, then waited. In time, the biochemical companies' legal teams gave their original packages to the patent offices, only to have their work rejected as already extant. Subsequently, Sniphle's legal teams would negotiate and come to lucrative royalty pacts with the victims—and the money rolled in."

Over the next hour, Wendy told her tale of the events that followed, starting with other undercover services offered. But unlike many secretive and information agencies, they never caught Sniphle's agents or kept their data safe, no matter how well concealed.

Triton, though, was now comfortable with his night traumas, having at last understood the who and why he was being pursued during his dreams. He was now aware why he and others with similar abilities were the only outlet for these afterlife souls. He knew it drew them to people like him, meaning no harm, merely trying to hang on to their own existence, albeit in spirit form. To him, his time with the sinister Sniphle was over, but the new reliance on Sniphle's latest concoctions and, on a separate plane, Salena's bed had him reluctant to move on.

Salena, however, was intensely in love with her charge, and helped Triton fight to overcome the devastating effects of withdrawal from Sniphle's pills and potions. Between them, they eased him away from his reliance. It was here where she saw his strength, and her unconscious inner self felt an irrepressible need to be the mother to his child.

All could see the intimate closeness of Salena and, unluckily, her lover. They reported it to Sniphle. They also reported Triton's reluctance to take all his allotted medications, which resulted in him becoming more alert to what they were pushing Triton to do. Sniphle acted swiftly and set out in a new direction, harnessing another aspect of Triton's abilities. He had earlier noted how the spectral presences Triton had encountered had congregated around the boy and his grandfather. He questioned whether this could be another aspect of how they could use the boy going further; could they also use the spectral manifestations? He set out to test this by slowing down the speed of the transition stage to allow the phantasms to gather around the boy prior to his travels.

His first task was to unbind the lovers and regenerate the boy's reliance on his team's concoctions. His first move was to quash Triton's sexual desires without suspicion aimed at his team. This proved to be much harder than dropping a simple extra pill into the daily mix, as the couple's passion overcame most of the chemical mixes.

Next up was to overcome Salena's suspicions and influence; but this also proved harder than expected. Sniphle's plan of dousing Triton's desires and enthusiasm for Salena with strengthening chemical mixes eventually did its job. Left on her own with only a shadow of her lover to counter Sniphle's carefully laid plans proved too much for her. She became overwhelmed, overcome, and frustrated with what was happening. Ultimately, her frustrations resulted in an explosive outburst, giving Sniphle his opportunity to ban her from the clinic, which Triton could barely understand. They escorted her off the premises, and no matter how hard she tried, she could not contact her chemically reduced, incoherent lover. Sniphle had earlier reported to Triton's parents that Salena had made clinical errors when administering his medications. Then, no matter how hard she tried, she could not convince them she was anything other than a manipulating schemer who had stricken their only son.

It was at this point that Triton's concerned parents began steps to take their son away from Sniphle's care. However, Sniphle moved further down his path of ruthlessness and into one of psychopathological paranoia. He lost all reason at the fear of losing all he had worked, as it uncontrollably slipped away. His need to separate the boy from his worried parents took, for him, a logical psychopathic path: eliminate the parents.

It was a simple task to persuade an addict reliant on one of his concoctions to kill the innocent couple, and then give him something special as a reward. Sniphle found it easy to arrange the horrendous act, knowing he had the tools and person to conduct the task. His antisocial traits did not allow him to question himself. He rapidly put the means, the person, and the victims in the same place. Once Sniphle gave the word, the deed was done. The media reported a senseless robbery and killing of a middle-aged couple by a homeless junkie found dead in an alleyway, whose own cause of death was by an unidentified drug cocktail.

At this point, Triton became an orphan, alone without support, outside of the Sniphle's Director Organisation. Sniphle's team could now direct their victim to do as they bid without constraint, while money from the stolen patents rolled in. They perfected a series of concoctions to put their special victim into a state where they could direct him to wherever and whenever they wanted. They questioned him after his travels and became intrigued by the gathering of spirits as he made his way from place to place. Next on their list of questions was to find out if Triton could persuade the spirit entities to gather and stay in the same location. Triton did in fact achieve this task without too much bother, with the help of his grandfather, who seemed to grow stronger now that Triton had recognised him. As Sniphle commented, "They have quite a community now; perhaps we can use them. They have wants, we have needs."

The directors of Triton's escapades were becoming worried by his gradual withdrawal from reality when not being sent on travels. He just lay on his bed, unmoving. However, while day-by-day he withdrew into a foetal position, his minders ensured he kept up an AI regimented and driven physical routine.

Sniphle had backup plans if his first "Special" experiment should fail, and he made increasing follow-up contacts with the families of his other twelve implanted foetuses. One by one, he contacted the unsuspecting parents of the six females and six males, discovering that only ten of his altered embryos had been viable. Of the six males, four had survived; and of those, two had serious mental aberrations, while the other two had extreme social problems. This confirmed to him his long-term view that the female of the species was stronger than the male.

First, he approached the parents of the two boys with serious social withdrawal problems, Ariel and Arche. He could help them, he claimed, with a regime of drugs his team had developed. The two disruptive thirteen-year-olds responded to Sniphle's directives very well at first, and their tired parents signed over the care of their boys to him after his team's reassurances.

As suspected by the team, both had abilities similar to Triton's. The team then gave the pair the same concoctions as given to the firstborn, and they were soon "running errands" to spy for differing clients, some industrial, some governmental.

And so, the Director Organisation grew.

Salena left heartbroken; her lover gone. Triton's reliance on the drugs was pitiful. Sniphle's team of Directors, as they became known, had brought him to a point where he was just as wilful as the wallpaper in a room. His unfocussed eyes observed, but she knew he could do nothing else.

Salena discovered she was pregnant by Triton. Although not a surprise, her pregnancy didn't go well. She didn't have the background support of her lover. The messy divorce of her parents and her own recent decisions had alienated her immediate family. Her estranged father, travelling worldwide as work directed, and her mother, reduced by a terminally threatening illness, had broken the family ties. A few friends and her sister helped her, while she made do the best she could on the limited support.

When the baby was born, Salena knew she was different. Luna seemed to be aware from the start, her eyes sharp, as if she understood what was going on around her even though her bodily development seemed in line with other babies of the same age. Teething, crawling, walking, potty training all seemed typical for her age, but there was a problem. She needed more; she had a full-time reliance on her mother. Her speech development was slow, only being able to say "Mummy" by age two, and she apparently could not grasp the concept of interaction. Salena heard whispers in her head and became convinced that Luna was trying to talk to her mentally, not vocally. As a result, doctors and specialists investigated as much as they were able, but could find nothing out of the normal, suggesting that Luna was a little slow in developing and would catch up later. All this was expensive and time-consuming for the unemployed Salena, who struggled to support herself and the toddler.

Sniphle had heard of Salena's plight, and had problems of his own—the other two teenage boys, Ferdinand and

Pan. They were both very unstable and fragile, tending toward seizures, going into spasm whenever Sniphle's group got anywhere near them. They were of no use to Sniphle; however, he had prized them away from their parents, hoping to use them as he had done with the other Specials. Such was Sniphle's nature. He would not let them out of his reach, and set about a plan.

He sent out emissaries to play on Salena's plight, and they began working on her financial and emotional problems. First, they offered her a house of her own on the understanding that she would take care of the two fragile boys. As part of the deal, the house would be hers, and she would get paid a nominal amount to take care of the boys and for her own welfare.

There was a second prong to their plan: to get the newborn, Luna. Here they offered advanced medical aid and funding for the uncommunicative girl. Salena knew it was a risky deal, but hoped the extra funding might help her daughter. There was the added plus and relief of having a stable, guaranteed home while looking after the needs of the two boys. She moved into the large, detached house on the outskirts of town and settled into a life of duty to Luna, Pan, and Ferdinand. It was during this time that Sniphle's agents gave a snippet of news to Salena that Triton had died. This was another blow to her emotional state. But the D.O. had planned this untrue piece of news to coincide with the other decisions she was having to make.

Occasionally, she took her young daughter to the Director Organisation, as they now called it, to conduct a testing program on the child. As the months wore on, her condition did not improve; indeed, when judged against a child of the same age, she seemed less advanced. Although she seemed very responsive to her surroundings, it was when asked to do anything physical that she let them down. She would not, could not, respond to speech or actions asked of her, nor could feed or dress herself, even though she was now into her eighth year. Eventually, the Directors offered to take her in as a resident in their facility. Against her instincts, Salena allowed Luna to go, but held out the hope that her ex-employer would help the growing child respond to life around her.

Almost a year passed before she heard the grim news that doctors had found a fast-growing tumour in Luna's brain. They showed the evidence of the inoperable tumour to Salena in a series of scans spanning only four weeks, with the prognosis that she would die within a fortnight. The trusting mother reluctantly accepted the findings, hoping her daughter wouldn't feel any pain during her last days. Sniphle, though, had a wealth of experience of delusion, and was able, with the help of chemical concoctions, to fool her. Cruelly and with great pleasure, he took to watching as she grieved for her daughter, wasting away. Finally, Salena's mother-guilt, intensified by Luna's staged death, said to have occurred while she slept in a cot beside the child. Sniphle fooled all with both the death certificates and a staged funeral. Here at last he had what he wanted: a child of nature born from his own incompetent DNA mixes hidden in not one, but in both parents, Triton and Salena.

He did not realise that you can't toy with Mother Nature without consequence.

Sniphle had faith in this concocted child. He knew Luna was intellectually aware inside her child's body. He suspected she was on a fresh path of human development, one of an intelligence far greater than normal. Also, he hoped and suspected she might follow her father's talents by travelling into the spectral world. Sniphle pondered; just maybe, adolescence, instead of the instinct to just walk, would trigger Luna's abilities and talk. He tested this by introducing her to hormonal drugs that would bring on her puberty early.

At first, the now-nine-year-old responded to others. She conversed and did whatever was asked, although there was hesitation, as if she were thinking, contemplating to herself, "Should I, or shouldn't I?"

The inherited physical attributes of her parents made her appear older than she was. With the addition of Sniphle's hormonal drugs, she took on the form of someone in her early teens. Sniphle wondered, was she ready to assume the duties he had in mind for her? His malevolent mind didn't consider the child's needs; she was only another victim under his control. Without further thought, he moved her into the D.O. with the other Specials. His plan was to introduce her progressively to the program he was using with the others. Unrestrained, he said to himself. "A program of training runs first, I think."

13
Aussie Colin

Fresh from a good night's sleep, she awoke with a desire to investigate the possibility of escape, but knowing she needed to consider the pitfalls. *First, I must convince them I need fresh air.*

When Ngoosi arrived that morning, Luna was up, showered, and dressed. "Ngoosi, do you think we can go for a walk outside today?" Then, using her child-like wide-eyed expression to emphasise her plea, she asked, "I think it would be good for me to get out prior to my next directed travels. What do you think?"

Ngoosi's eyes brightened as she began mentally planning what they could do before saying, "Yes, fresh air! The sun is shining, and you seem in good spirits. I'll ask someone nicely and say it would be good for you. Meanwhile, here's your breakfast. Eat up—you may need it."

By the time the smiling nurse got back, Luna was spying out her window and ready for a walk in the sunshine. As they wandered down the corridor, she tried to recall another time when she walked with a purpose. *I don't remember ever walking anywhere, knowing I wanted to go somewhere.*

With intent, the pair walked down the corridor before coming to a door. Ngoosi pressed a button and doors opened. She stepped forward into a box-like room, encouraging the curious girl to do likewise. Once inside, Ngoosi pressed another button.

"Whah... what's happening?" Luna cried. "The box feels like it's falling; it's as if my breakfast is staying in the same place, and I'm falling through it."

A few moments later, the doors opened. Luna shot out of the little room, looking back at it in shock as Ngoosi calmly stepped out of the lift as if nothing had happened. On looking round, Luna saw an enormous glass-fronted wall with a double door leading to the outside. Leaning forward, Ngoosi opened it and invited the shocked girl to step outside.

Once outside, Ngoosi directed them towards a children's play park and said, "I thought you might like this. There are rides, grass, trees, and running paths for you to play on, if you like. But! They've warned me not to allow you to play with or be in contact with others."

Luna took the words in silently, looking unperturbed but resenting being controlled. *I'm a prisoner, but what was my crime?* Looking up and seeing the vast green area of grass, she ran. *What's that smell? It's unlike anything I've smelt before!* She slowed, and the noise of a man sitting on a machine racing across the grass drew her to wonder what he was doing. She asked Ngoosi just that.

Ngoosi glanced at the man and back to the expectant girl with a smile of understanding. "Oh, he's cutting the grass. Can you smell it?"

Luna wondered at the smell but was interrupted by the shrill cries of children waiting to launch themselves down a slide and wondered how it would feel. She wandered onto the grass and made for a tall tree that was shedding the odd leaf, a victim of the approaching autumn. Unlike passing through the trees from her jungle travels, this tree was solid to the touch. The smell of the cut grass, the rustle of the leaves, the chill of the wind, the effort to walk; it was all so different. Her body froze momentarily as tears welled with the realisation and profound shock. *I've never been outside before. WHY?*

Ngoosi saw the change of mood as the normally vocal Luna became quiet, and knew something within the girl was different. "Come on, Luna, let me treat you; let's take a bus ride to the mall and I'll get you an ice cream. What flavour do you like?"

"I don't know." Luna was in shock. There was so much she didn't know about the world.

Unlike the ride she had taken with Ngoosi's mom, the ride on the bus was another revelation. Feeling a tenseness in her stomach and a vague sense of wanting to be sick, she ran through what was occurring. *It's so noisy—the roar of the engine, the tyres on the road, the chattering of women and children, the honking of horns from other vehicles. It's all happening at once.* There came a physical shock at the unexpected forces of acceleration, then stopping, throwing her forward a little. *There are so many people on the pavement, some walking fast, others stopping at shop windows, others looking into their communicators... there are so many of them, but few are interacting with each other.*

The bus stopped and Ngoosi gestured for them to go, and out they went into the metallic air of choking fumes and city dust. Once on the pavement, Ngoosi spoke up. "Come, let's get something nice." Taking Luna by the hand, the knowledgeable nurse led the dazed girl through the doors to a vast arena of shops, restaurants, popcorn booths, and play areas at ground level with moving staircases to other floors. Although aware of it all, Luna was in shock at the number of people and shops, and the video screens and holograms all firing information at them. Ngoosi coaxed the reluctant girl onto the moving stairway. As they rose to the next floor, she saw an accessible area with quick-food outlets. On their balcony with its glass walls, she could overlook the floors below and, on the other side, the outside street. Here she had a better view of the rush of people dodging past each other without appearing to look.

Ngoosi directed Luna. "Look, there's a table by the window. You sit there, and I'll get the ice creams." In a daze, the wide-eyed girl obeyed and sat facing the outside world beyond the glass. She began taking in the multitude of rushing people and the lines of vehicles making marginally less progress. Ngoosi shouted something to her, but she did not respond, still too much in wonder at the overload of information thrown at her. A few minutes later, the laden, grinning nurse bustled into the seat beside Luna. "Now, what flavour do you want? I have options. There was a two-scoop promotion, so I got two scoops for each of us. You can have a scoop of Salted Caramel with a daub of vanilla on top, or a scoop of coffee with a helping of crunchy pistachio."

Luna, worried about salted caramel, selected the pistachio option.

The pair settled into their portions of ice creams, which helped the darting-eyed girl to calm down. Eventually, her tense shoulder muscles softened, and she relaxed, looking around the balcony and into the Saturday rush of shoppers below. Ngoosi also calmed as her charge's nervousness eased, noting how the girl began taking in more of her surroundings. As she calmed further, the nurse settled into catching up on her social media prompts.

Luna used the head-downed preoccupation of the nurse as an opportunity to further investigate her surroundings. Gently easing back her seat, quietly whispering, she said, "I'll be back in a mo. I won't be long. See you in a jiffy." Only receiving a nod in return, she was off to investigate, wandering around the balcony gallery, taking in sights and conversations in wonder: boys gathered chatting about preening girls at adjacent tables, grandparents taking in the sights in wonder at recent social changes, children being coaxed into taking another bite of unhealthy food while being promised an equally unhealthy treat if they finished. There were also busy working staff, secretly wondering why they had spent years studying higher mathematics, political science, and European history, only to find employment supporting an acceptable level of cleanliness in a shopping mall while bored out of their minds.

Luna found herself at a rail overlooking the busy scene below, and just stood scanning the area, occasionally homing in on whatever caught her eye. But silently, her supernatural awareness was gaining purchase into her conscious mind. Spectral images appeared and became clearer as they flittered into her awareness. She concentrated and saw glimpses of colourless, translucent figures. Knowingly, she allowed her inner self to become more aware. She unhurriedly eliminated the noisy world around her, focussing her efforts on the flitting forms. Just as the butterfly flaps its wings around a field of flowers, she saw in depth a colourless figure hovering around a busy shopper. There, another, and another, as her senses became more accustomed to the apparitions, the odd shopper having several hovering figures floating in attendance.

Luna was in awe of the scene, noticing some butterflies slipping from flower to flower, searching for nectar of some sort. *But what is this? They've noticed me. There's one beside me now. A man!* Luna could see him clearly as he smiled, knowing that she could see him. Surprised with herself at her acceptance of this new situation, her heart beat a little faster. *What now?... Is he trying to talk to me?*

In her mind she heard him reply, "Don't worry, I'm not here to harm you."

In her bristly frame of mind, the fire within Luna answered, "Yes, I know you can't. How could you?" As she waved her hand through his translucent image, she said. "You're like smoke; you can't do anything to me." She studied his gaping smile and kind eyes. "What is your name, old man?"

He smiled wider, revealing more of his kindness, and said, "Colin, but most call me Aussie Colin." Then in a calm tone: "But to address your concern—you have it already. I'm not here to harm you, merely to gain recognition that you can see me. Few of the living can. But there is one thing you may not know. We *can* do damage to the living. Know this: when we understand where we are after our physical deaths, we also understand the good... and the bad. To the good, we observe them and hope they can help us run down our spirit life in peace. But to those who have dark, uncontrolled thoughts... we can get inside and confuse their minds. Sometimes they don't recover from what we can do. Be sure we're not here to harm; we're here for other reasons."

The shock of a hand on her shoulder brought her back instantly. "Luna, are you all right?" From her inner state, and from talking in her mind to the man's spirit, the question catapulted her back to the physical world, flooding out her spectral senses.

"Oh, Ngoosi, you gave me a shock! I was just taking in the amount of people here. If we can, can we come back here another day? I just love to watch the people and the families. Maybe I can be like them one day. What do you think?"

The somewhat shocked carer could see the open-eyed enthusiasm of the girl, but knew not to encourage her too much. "Well, dear, let's see how you feel when we get back, and let's also see how the Directors feel about it. Why don't you tell them how much you loved to be out here? Perhaps they will arrange it again for you. I'll give them a report of how good you've been." She saw the slight downward glance of the girl's eyes and continued, hoping to give the girl a lift, "I'll tell you what. As soon as we get back, I'll recommend regular outings for you. How about that?"

Her eyes cast down to her overtight trainers, Luna nodded a thank you and gave Ngoosi her hand and said, "What's next?" with a smile on her face. But inside, she knew the kind nurse couldn't do much, given the nature of the Directors she had met.

The journey back was subdued, although Ngoosi did her best to keep her growing friendship with her charge as positive as she could. Luna now had many more reasons to escape the clutches of the Directors. She knew she was a slave and wondered why the other Specials like Elara had done nothing about it.

Luna finished the day by having supper with Nurse Margret, chatting about the other Specials, and found to her astonishment that all had joined the group at roughly the same time, 19 years previously. Puzzled by this, Luna asked, "How old am I?"

Margret, who had always been a little wary of the girl and not sure why she asked, hesitantly said. "I'm not sure," then, giving herself a little time, added, "You came here six or seven months ago in February, but I think Director Sniphle had you housed in his private clinic for several years before that."

Luna could see the reluctance in the nurse and softened the next question. "It's just that I saw lots of girls and boys at the mall today having fun, and I wondered, if I weren't in here, could I join in with them?"

The innocent nature of the question was enough to coax a reply: "They tell me it will be your birthday just before Christmas, I think."

At that, Luna thought, *enough for now*, and dropped her sensitive questions, trying to put the nurse at ease. They talked about the mall, people, ice cream, and noisy busses with smelly passengers wrapped up against the cold. After watching some vetted media programs prepared for the girl, it was time for Margret to bid good night, and Luna tucked herself into bed.

Around midnight, she was awake. *Now I need to follow up on what else is here. First, I make myself comfortable, eliminate outside noise, make sure my pillow is comfortable. Next, slowing my heartbeat, I know I am getting close now.*

My eyes are closed; I see the lightening centre of where I'm to go. Then, almost without delay, There I am, below me now on the bed, eyes closed and peaceful!

Now I can travel through the door, a right turn along the corridor, passing Sheila, the duty nurse, who's filling in some details on her screen. Further now, on towards Sniphle's office; and there, another corridor branching off to the right. What's down here, I wonder? Ah! There at the end of the short passageway, outside the door, on a small nameplate, the name... Triton.

With no other way available, Luna entered the room through the closed door and found a sleeping man curled up on the bed. In a heightened awareness of something new, she wondered, *Is he another one like the women in my corridor?*

But before she could contemplate it further, a voice entered her head.

What is your name, girl?

14
Two of the Boys

At the outset, the two new boys, Ariel and Arche, were medicated with drugs similar to those helping Triton overcome his night-time trauma. Sniphle's team then individualised the dosages to suit each boy. Under instruction, Triton was told the boys were there to be helped, as the team had done for him. As the Directors changed the concoctions to suit each individual, they gave him the arduous task of introducing them to his spirit friends. At first, the boys were in awe of the visions of the ephemeral bodies. But as they tried to latch onto the boys, the spirits understood the fragile nature of the situation, and gave the boys space. Aided and guided by both Triton and his grandfather, each boy accepted the nature of his new situation. They appreciated the spirits were not there to harm them, but in fact, to help. The severely autistic boys, with a reluctance for touch, relished being guided to novel places without the dread of physical contact.

Grandfather showed how he could touch nothing by showing how his hand and arm could pass through a door. He then bent his arm at the elbow and drew laughter from the boys as only his hand reappeared and waved at them. Both boys' excitement threw off their extreme social anxiety inhibitions. Together they proved it to each other repeatedly, as their nature directed, both understanding their world was now different. Between them, they began investigating the world around them. For a time, the boys became fixed on investigating all the places they had heard about that sounded special. At first, it was Grandfather who went with them and helped them to select the locations. The Taj Mahal was Arche's first choice, as he had heard about it from one of his aunts after she had visited some time ago. Together, he and grandfather made the journey. Out through the window, across the fields, the mountains, the seas and green jungle lands, deserts, and finally down the river plain to the magnificent marble building. Calmly, the pair made their way through the closed door and unhurriedly took in an almost empty interior while intrigued by the flocks of tourists gawping from outside. For Arche, it helped calm him, and inwardly he began to throw off his lifelong anxiety while in other people's company. He was outside that world.

Ariel, on hearing of the adventure from Arche, wanted to be more adventurous. He decided on Mount Everest. "I want to go to the highest place in the world." He followed this and the excitement of trying to explain what he had been doing with the lowest point on land. At the outset, Grandfather tried to think through where was all this leading, but remembered the minds of the boys and their delicate psychological nature.

While they became more confident and more adventurous, not only did they tick off places and sites to see, but they also excitedly took groups of ephemeral spirits with them. They visited pyramids in Egypt and Mexico, the underground river in Palawan, the Grand

Canyon, Angel Falls, and many other localities, ticking off natural must-see sites. Then came the North and South poles within moments of each other. Arche was not to be bested. He suggested he wanted to go to the International Space Station, which put many into a minor panic until one spirit told them he already had done so. He relayed this and the other unexpected journeys to Sniphle, who became interested when told of their off-earth flights. The days, weeks, and months passed while Sniphle and his team perfected the potions to achieve the 'go-retrieve' directive strengths for each boy, all the while pacifying their natures.

The boys' parents visited Sniphle's new purpose-built complex on regular occasions to assess their troubled offspring, each time finding their boys becoming more socially accepting. However, whenever they tried to take the boys home with them, the boys became almost unmanageable. Sniphle's team had trained to deal with both boy's disruptive natures and to accommodate upset parents. Eventually, the families could see the boys were clearly happy where they were, and after all, Sniphle's team was paying the bills. They were told they had received medical grants to perfect medication suitable for other children with similar conditions. The boys seemed happy, and it satisfied the parents that their troubled offspring were in expert hands.

15
A Chat with Triton

Luna hovered over the bed of the man lying in a foetal position, but the shock of the question in her mind assaulted her senses. Instinctively she backed away and, almost as if ordered, said, "Luna... My name is Luna."

Within her thoughts came a response to her answer, "I remember a Luna a long time ago, but it's hazy. It may come back to me soon."

There was a void, as if both were trying to look farther into each other, and an internal silence settled between them. Eventually, the unstirring figure on the bed adjusted his head. "My name is Triton ...." Again, there followed a pause. "Do you know who I am?"

"No, but I know you must be one of us Specials, because I can talk to you as I've done with Elara on two occasions. But why are you separated from us?"

He responded, but didn't move any further, instead remaining in his near-foetal position, turned away from her. "Luna, I was the first. The term for us, Special, is because of me. Sniphle's various drugs to control the way they send the rest of you on missions, and then command you to return, were all because of experiments conducted on me. At first, I could come and go as I liked, but they've developed concoctions that take away our choices of when, where, and why we travel. Now they have all of us doing as they bid." He fell into a silence, as if pondering his own thoughts, then continued. "But you're new, and so young."

Luna moved to a more helpful position and studied his face, somehow familiar, like the others. His shaven head sprouting red hair, as did Elara and her own. *Are they all brothers and sisters? Maybe I am too! He's a good-looking man, from what I can see, but a little arrogant.*

A feeling of pointed amusement filled her mind before she heard his words, *Luna. Whatever you're thinking, I know what it is. Unlike speech, we can't hide our thoughts. So, girl... you think I'm arrogant, do you?*

She wished she hadn't let her feelings leak out, and quickly replied, *Oh! I didn't think... I'm sorry.*

The feeling of amusement continued. *Don't worry... you're so young, and I'm just having a little fun with you.* He paused a moment, as if something had triggered a minor panic in his thoughts, and asked, *Luna, why are you here? Has someone sent you?*

No, no one sent me. I came on my own. I was just searching for what else and who else was here in the building.

At once Triton replied, as if shocked at what she revealed. *Are you telling me you came* unaided? *With none of their concoctions?*

Yes! She was a little frustrated by his questioning. *On my own!*

Triton acted as if stunned, and turning on his bed, asked, *How? I haven't been able to travel on my own for years. Not since the directors helped me to overcome my night terrors that made me so reliant on their other potions.*

With that, Luna began her tale of her first remembered travel across the sea. She told him of what followed, and that some kind of hiccup with the AI monitoring her dosages of drugs had allowed her to have a break from the Directors' control. She revealed she could now travel as she liked, without their concoctions, telling him of what she had done, to where she had travelled, and upon returning how she could watch what the Directors were planning for her. This was a revelation to Triton, who stirred further, and with a little difficulty, repositioned himself on the bed and, with eyes now open, said, *You mean you could listen in on what they were saying?*

Putting an emphasis on her reply, she answered, *Yes, and I don't like it. I can direct myself any time I want, just as I am now. You see me here talking to you, can't you?*

Triton felt he should take a little of the confrontation out of their talk and mischievously said, *Now who's arrogant?* Pausing a moment to let it sink in, he continued. *No, I'm joking with you. Seriously, I used to do it, but the drugs they've given me over the years have taken that talent away. Now I can only do it when they direct, and unfortunately, wherever they direct.*

As his words entered her mind, she could feel a sadness along with them. She understood what he was saying and vowed to herself that she would train her mind to never forget her own routine. She liked the freedom of going when and where she wanted, and not being directed by others. Curious to see if Triton could do as she was able, Luna then asked, *"Have you been outside of here?"* Pausing, *"Recently?"*

She waited a few moments as he shaped his response. *"That's what I do most days, to wherever they direct. But in the flesh, no."*

Luna waited for more. He didn't expand, but she felt a sadness radiating from him. She then relayed what she had been doing during the day. *"I went out with one nurse today; I mean out of the building, and we got on a bus and went to a mall."* She remembered the excitement, the feeling building once more into her memory. In her adolescent mind, she remembered the ice cream, then drifted to her discovery of the spirit people wandering from one unaware shopper to another, always searching. *I saw other people there, spirits. I spoke to one of them, the same as I am doing with you now.*

At this, Triton jerked round, turned in his bed. *"What... you can do this now? How come?"* He remembered it had taken Sniphle's concoctions to help him achieve this and help put paid to his night traumas with the help of his grandfather. *"Be careful. Don't allow the Directors, or anyone else, to know you can do this, or they will have you and you will never have your freedom."* He paused, and Luna could see his face change from a relaxed pose to one of eye-sharpening concern. *"Don't let them know anything of what you've told me."* Pausing, then emphasising, *"EVER! Let me think through our conversation."* He then restated what she had told him and got her positive replies before telling her it was time to leave his room, but to come back tomorrow if she was able.

She realised this was the end of their meeting and, remembering his interest, said, *"Triton, I intend to go to the* outside again. Is there anything on the outside you want me to find out or check on?"

He glanced round at her ephemeral image, taking in her youth and vague features, giving him hints of something in the past. It triggered forgotten memories, and he began reaching for answers. *"Yes, there are two things you can check out for me. But wait a minute... are you spiritually travelling or actually going out?"*

"I was thinking first of travelling, and then with a bit of luck going on the bus with Ngoosi if she will help me."

"Good. In that case, please check on my Aunt Amy and her husband Brian to see if they're okay. They used to come here after my parents died. However, Sniphle somehow persuaded them I was in a vegetative state, and through his kindness, he would ensure the Director Organisation would look after me for the rest of my life."

"The other thing I would like you to check on are two boys, Pan and Ferdinand, sent out to a private address on the edge of town. Apparently, they were part of the ten surviving Specials, but Director Sniphle and his team couldn't control them. So, he had them housed away from here, but within easy reach should they improve."

With that, he relayed the addresses he remembered, then abruptly curled once more into his foetal position and bade her goodnight.

As Triton tried to put the day to rest and relax into a sleep, he tried to think of other things, not of Luna. He remembered back to Salena and those joyous days. He sadly remembered Director Sniphle and the directors showing him news clippings of her death. His attempt to disappear into sleep became interrupted by the continuing thought of her. He thought, too, of his failed attempts at searching the spirits of the dead for her. He remembered the last time he had seen his mother, and her somewhat faraway look when being spoken to by Sniphle. But keeping him from sleep was the knowledge of Luna and her tales of travel without Sniphle's chemicals.

Although it was late in the day, Luna's head was buzzing, and she knew sleep would be impossible. After her overwhelming visit to Triton and his request to find his loved ones and the two troubled boys. She resolved she would visit his aunt first. Then, after settling her reflections, she readied herself for escape from the building to the address he had given her.

I'm free again, out of this building, across the country to the town, then the road, now the house set back with a well-manicured lawn, painstakingly kept flowers and fruit trees near the end of the garden. Let me merge inside. Oh, it's like the garden; everything in its place, the quaint furniture, paintings on the wall, photos dotted on tables and ledges. I can see these people are like Ngoosi's mum; they like old photos. Over there I see an old photo of a newly married couple, then Triton as a baby, then as an adolescent boy, and others with what looked like his mum and dad. There in the corner, another with an older set of people, perhaps Triton's grandparents. Let me travel around the house to get more insight about them.

She drifted her way round the house, then up into the bedrooms. *I feel this is a lonely house... this room with an empty bed with pictures and banners from Triton's school scattered round the walls. Maybe his aunt didn't have children, and she used Triton as a substitute. Let me try this room with the door a tad ajar. Ah, two people sleeping in bed. Let me move closer to have a respectful look at them.* She hovered above the sleeping couple for a few minutes. *I can take in their features and try to pick out Triton's brow, nose, chin and mouth, but I only see glimpses of them.*

His aunt turned in her bed, seeming to wake and disturbing the sleeping man, who said. "You OK, love?" She pulled back the covers a little and said, "Oh, I was just having a dream, and Triton popped into my head." Then, rising from the bed, she called back to her partner, reshuffling his position, as she made her way to the en suite bathroom, "I need a pee."

Luna smiled and sensed, *These are gracious people, with everything in place. But they seem to have more time on their hands than things to do. They're missing Triton and seem lost in a time where he was their obsession, way back in his teen years. This makes me sad and angry about why this has happened.*

Aunt Amy returned to bed and snuggled into her husband's back, thinking of Triton and her own still-born children while Luna watched on for a few moments before turning once more and headed away.

Sadly, she crossed the edge of town, noting the odd late-night car trigger a traffic light to turn a different colour. She travelled on without thinking too much, then allowed her positive feelings to catch up and remembered the other address Triton had asked her to visit. "Ah yes, the two boys."

16
Denzel Dou

The all-seeing presence continued to look down.

There comes a time when considering the merits of Keno′ T Sniphle becomes crucial. Whether it be his undoubted accomplishments in the development of human advances, or his manic drive for his own benefits at the expense of others.

But. It was my coaxing that drove him to do as he unconsciously has.

When he messed around with complex systems he did not understand, he would always get unintended consequences.

Although I coaxed him to do as he has, if humanity is to survive into the future, others like him need to better understand how complex properties sometimes, somehow, emerge from simple rules.

The success of Ariel and Arche, the two autistic boys, was an enormous surprise. How could they accommodate the spirit souls and encourage them to go with them on their journeys when, if a spying project was too complex for the boy, he would ask an accompanying spirit to aid and fill in the finer details? The spirits would happily supply the data in payment for the company of the boys.

Eventually, an experimental project uncovered a sequence whereby the newly produced human DNA-shells now manufactured for parts could accept limited memories. The memory bubbles in question comprised odd, unrelated events lasting only a few seconds, extracted from the memories of brave scientists. Another limitation to the experiments was the memory bubbles, these becoming no longer part of the donor scientist's own memory.

When made aware of this development, Sniphle directed his team to revisit his earlier work to find a method of charging the manufactured DNA-shells' empty hippocampi with memories. Armed with the new memory bubble knowledge, he used the considerable talent of Triton to get a ghost-spirit to enter a fresh DNA-shell.

For Triton, the choice of ghost figure was hard to make. His first instinct was to offer his grandfather the opportunity, but caution interrupted his choice, him having had the ghost gang around for several years and mostly ignoring their presence. There were a few candidates who came ready to mind. There were, as he imagined them, a great deal of options. Nimble spirits, angry, passive, conniving, sporty, potentially domineering, timid. There were many human types and traits, plus male, female, and all in between. He also considered those of the spirits new to being in their unfamiliar state, and there were others who were fading towards the dark and into nonexistence. Who to choose weighed heavily on him, but even so, he did not take heed of the unsubtle coaxing of Sniphle and the Directors.

Eventually, he invited an artist who had committed suicide when he contracted motor neuron disease and could no longer express himself in the way he wanted. Denzel had been a gregarious extrovert who brought an intenseness to most aspects of life. His art was striking, as was his political argument, his love of women and life. But once struck with the illness, it diminished him. Being unable to express himself and his love of life eventually brought him to extinguish his life with his own hand.

The adventure of a fresh life overruled all caution, and Denzel signed up to an agreement that tied him to the Directors for the rest of his DNA-shelled life, should the experiment prove successful.

The D.O. team set a routine, calculated potions, checked and rechecked. As Sniphle explained to a closed Directors meeting, "We do not want this DNA-shell to go AWOL once he's resurrected. We need this one, especially tied and secured. Oh! And don't let Triton or anyone else know what we're discussing here, or someone may lay a huge legal liability on us down the line."

At last, after the selection of a suitable male DNA-shell given the title Denzel Dou, the directors gathered around windows of the sealed room with the suitably pacified Denzel lying on the bed. Some wondered why they had secured him with restraints around his body, arms and legs, but Sniphle explained, "We do not know this man; nor do we know his mood; we do not know how he will react to being brought back to life."

He awoke.

The smell of over-used disinfectant was the first to assail his senses, even before opening his eyes. The penetrating hard flash of surgical lighting closed them at once, followed by another attempt with them half-closed, allowing his irises to compensate. He focused first on a callow young man in a white lab coat looking back at him intently. Then, noting movement to one side, another figure. He turned his head farther to note a tall woman, also white-coated. But while turning, he felt restricted in his movements and discovered he had straps confining his arms and legs with another across his chest.

Dr Lucy Pearson stepped forward, somewhat apprehensive of what the directors had instructed. They had used a DNA-shell assigned to the spirit based on an almost ideal physical specimen. The perceived physical threat he posed was unknown, made worse by her innate fear of physical men. To this extent, she resolved to keep a tight control of how the first interview was conducted. Perspiration droplets formed on her top lip, that and her wide eyes betraying her nervousness. At last, she said, "Are you with us?" Then, upon seeing his eyes react, she said. "What is your name?"

Calmly, he responded in a tone that seemed to rise. "Denzel. Why do you ask?" Smiling upon seeing her reaction, he continued, "What's yours, and who's the pretty guy at the end of my bed?"

Lucy ignored his question, and after first glancing at a checklist held in front of her, asked, "How do you feel?"

Denzel answered as he always had in his earlier life. "You have warm eyes, and do I detect just a crease of blushed cheeks behind those painted lips?" He raised his bottom lip, nodded, and said, "I think I would like to paint you... have you ever posed nude?" The rush of words almost put her off her stroke, but it locked into her, a memory she would revisit. Then, recovering, she fumbled back to her notes and said, "Can you describe how you feel?"

"Physically or emotionally? But I suppose you would want it all." He continued without waiting and mused, "So, where do I start?" Again, he didn't await an answer. "I will tell you, but first remove these restraints, then we can begin. While we're on the subject, can I ask why I'm strapped up like this?" He looked into her eyes once more and persisted, "What is your name, if I may ask?" He reverted to his previous manner of introducing himself to attractive women by dropping his face a little and raising his eyes and giving her a light smile.

Denzel's kind eyes and his manner, completely without physical menace, allowed her to relax her mind about any threat. She said. "Thomas, without totally removing the restraints, can we make Denzel a bit more comfortable before we start? He seems to be very vocal but not violent." The man at the end of the bed loosened the restraints and played with a hand-held device, instructing the bed to reposition into a sitting mode.

At last, she relented, easing her officious tone and said, "Lucy. My name is Lucy, but people call me Ma'am."

Denzel smiled, as if remembering other conversations with attractive women. "I like Lucy. So Lucy, where do we start?" Pausing a bit, in a smiling tone, he again added, "Lucy."

There followed half an hour of questions about his past, checked out against documented knowledge of his life, his work, and his loves. His relaxed attitude prompted Lucy to ask if he wanted to stretch his legs and whether he wanted anything to eat or drink. His request for a cup of green tea brought a slight surprise, as did his actions once allowed out of bed. He stood and began a short routine of bending and stretching, as if assessing his own physical prowess. While still awaiting the tea, and before settling into a chair positioned at the table, he looked first at his hands. He turned them back and forth before reaching down inside his pyjamas, feeling his genitals, then said, "Why have I a light olive colouring? I used to be black." Then, looking down at his groin once more, he said, "However, you seemed to have done me proud down here."

Thomas grinned, and Lucy, suppressing a smile, looked away for a moment before replying. "I'm sorry, we must have mixed up; I'll note that and ensure any future recipient on this program gets their original skin hue and texture." Then, talking to Thomas as if Denzel were not present, she continued, "It will help them acclimatise into their original personality without the need to realign themselves." Then, directing her eyes toward the first of the program and trying to gain a dominance over him, she said. "But for you, Denzel—get used to it."

She collected a folder from a slim case. "Right, let us get started. Before we let you roam around the complex, there are several formalities to be ironed out and a series of legally binding documents we must sign. I must also inform you, if not explained before, that you will not be leaving this facility unless we go with you. Legally, you do not exist." Then, confronting him in an eye-to-eye, serious manner, she asked, "Do you understand this?"

Denzel saw now she was being extremely business-minded, and he wasn't with a gang of free-minded artists, as in his prior life. His mood subsequently changed, and he returned her look. "Yes, Triton informed me. Let me also say thank you, but it's in my nature to look for alternatives to serious people and their serious talk." He smiled to himself, glanced at Thomas and back to her, fixed a playful look on his face, and said, "Lucy! What colour panties are you wearing today?"

17
The House on the Hill

Soaring high above the moonlit, blueish-tinged countryside, Luna gathered her ideas of what next. *Okay, now I must find the two other specials, Pan and Ferdinand.*

She recalled the address Triton had given her, and instinctively sped from his aunt's home to the city where she had started her journey. On the edge of the city, up on a hill, the large house stood. Confident now with her abilities, she entered without restraint, passed through a window, and found herself in a spacious, busily furnished room. There on a wall was a sizeable screen with several suitably positioned seats nearby. In a corner, surrounded by three chairs, a table with two crumb-covered plates beside empty coffee cups. The floor was covered with a worn carpet with unsuccessfully washed stains spoiling its traditional pattern. Luna passed through a door into a wide corridor leading to a stairway.

"Okay, as it's late, they've surely all gone to bed. Let me try the stairs." In surprise, she drew back. "What was that? A translucent face of a man at the top looking down at me?"

In open-mouthed amazement, she stopped. Staying still, it was obvious he was in the same shocked state as she. He took a backward step and merged into the wall, backing his way through, with his surprised face the last to leave. The alarm wore off Luna with a realisation that he seemed to be like those she had met in the mall, but there was something else to this one that intrigued her. Deliberately, she drifted her way up to the head of the stair and paused before continuing through a half-open door. There, in a large room, were two beds. On one was a heavy breathing man, sleeping; while on the other was another, violently shaking as if in spasm. Luna had never witnessed such uncontrolled behaviour in anyone before. His mouth was open, shouting aloud, his eyes staring in terror.

From behind Luna, bursting through the door and passing straight through her spiritual form, a woman rushed to the convulsing man on his bed. At once she began trying to calm him with words, her hands soothing him. "Pan, Pan, calm. It's okay, I'm here. There is no one here to harm you. You're just having a terrible nightmare. Look around, there's only Ferdinand in the other bed, and he's asleep as normal."

Pan's darting eyes calmed. Then, over the woman's shoulder, he saw the spirit girl. At once he became agitated again, eyes fixed in fright. With his words coming in a disjointed burst, he said, "There... is a g... girl in... here! She's... just b... behind you!" Instinctively, the woman half turned and stared momentarily into the dark, unlit room. Seeing nothing, she turned back to the distraught man. "Pan. There's nothing, there's no one here."

Alarm at what had occurred, Luna read the situation. *I can't see the woman with her back to me in the moonlight, but I must reassure the poor man I'm not here to harm them.*

Luna tried as best she could with a calm, youthful voice. "Pan, she can't see me. Only you can see me. She can't hear me either. Please relax. I will go, because I have upset you so much."

Thinking beyond the situation that had occurred, Luna spoke to Pan once more to calm him while drifting back towards the door. "Pan, I'm not here to do you any harm, and I'm upset myself because you're afraid of me. Please, please calm down, I'm so sorry to have upset you."

Pan settled, responding both to her words and to those of the woman, still visibly trembling because of his outburst.

She spoke to him in her mind once more, saying, *Pan, I'm going now, but can you tell the lady I'll come back another day? I will not be as I am now, but I will be like you. I will be in my physical form. I'm only a young girl, and I'm not here to hurt anyone. Please tell her.* She hesitated a moment. *Pan, I'm so sorry I upset you.*

Comforted by Luna's reassurances, he hesitantly told the sceptical woman trying to calm him what had occurred, while keeping his eye on Luna. He began speaking in his hesitant manner, his words in staccato. "Th... There is a g-g-girl in the room, and sh-she has told me sh-she is not here to h-h-harm us. She will also be b-b-b-back soon to meet us all."

Once again, the woman looked round briefly, trying in vain to see the transparent girl, but to no avail. Then back to Pan, then hugged him in reassurance. With him settled, Luna looked at the now-stable man, with the woman tucking in his blanket before she began exiting out through the window and away across the rooftops. *Tomorrow I will return with Ngoosi and talk to them about Triton and how he asked after them.*

Ngoosi's presence with a rattling breakfast tray awoke her, and she duly went through her morning routine, munching through a plate of cereal, washing it down with a mixed fruit juice. "Can we go out again today? I promise to behave myself." Luna looked forlornly at the nurse and said, "It's my last day before the Directors start my program again."

Ngoosi made a non-committed reply. "We'll see, but I will have to get permission. But let's try." The nurse cleared the tray away and bid her farewell.

Twenty minutes later, the beaming nurse returned. "Right! Let's get dressed and go. I'll be back in ten minutes, so don't hang about. I have to get some paperwork signed, then we're off." She looked at her watch and said, "Will 10 o'clock suit you?" Luna nodded enthusiastically and dug out her only pair of jeans and a top.

The two exited the principal building of the complex after a minor interruption, while the officious gateman checked Ngoosi's papers. He reminded Ngoosi they had to be back by 4pm that afternoon. She looked at Luna briefly and nodded back at him.

"So, what do you want to do today, a walk in the park and lunch at the mall again?"

Luna's face became serious. Looking directly into Ngoosi's smiling eyes, she said, "No... would you take me to Eastcourt Road on the outskirts of town? There's someone there I want to meet." Luna could see the potential of conflict passing across Ngoosi's expression and added, "Then back to the mall. Let's have some of that ice cream again. I loved it," adding enthusiasm to her bright green eyes.

The nurse contemplated the change to her plan, and seeing the outward innocence of her charge, nodded. Then, looking at the bus timetable, she said, "Okay, let's do that, but don't tell anyone or my arse will be in a sling."

The ride out to the outskirts took only 15 minutes before the driver told them this was their stop. Luna recognised the street at once and made her way towards Number 232 which, just as she remembered, was set back from the road. Confidently she rang the bell and stepped back, looking up at Ngoosi, beaming. A few moments later, a man in his thirties answered the door. He gazed at the pair with a look of *What do you want?* Luna stepped forward and confidently said, "Can we see the lady of the house, please?"

The man swung round and shouted, "There's someone at the door for you, they don't look to be anyone official!" He turned back, taking in the odd couple in front of him: a young teenager dressed in unfashionable out-of-date clothes, and a mid-forties black lady dressed in the contemporary trends.

Moments later, a woman drying her hands with a kitchen towel looked at the pair, and her face fell in eye-staring shock.

A surprised Ngoosi was first to react. She said, "Salena, how are you? It's me, Ngoosi. I haven't seen you for, what is it," pausing, "10 or 12 years?" Before she could start again, she could see the reactions taking place as she saw her long-time friend visibly shaken, her colour drained. Ashen faced with tears flowing beyond the creases on each side of her gaping mouth, Salena, fixated on an equally dumbstruck girl, said. "Luna!"

"Mummy...?"

18
Welcome to New Bismarck

Denzel's adjustment to his new body took longer than he had expected. Whilst he knew he was no longer dead and no longer a spirit, the joys of being alive required necessities he had forgotten. The daily routines of life were tedious following the freedom of his spiritual activities. The needs of sleeping, rising, bathing, eating, and the accompanying need to deposit bodily waste in a WC proved tiresome. To him, these activities took up valuable time, as did the constant monitoring of his progress by the directors. But their one preeminent question, voiced by Senior Director Sniphle frequently, was, "Can you travel outside your new body?"

Denzel took the question in and mulled over it several times before answering in his joking way, "No! But I will try if it helps." It was the last thing Sniphle and his team wanted. In readiness, they had a cocktail of potions to ensure that when he went to bed, he stayed there. But to Denzel's disappointment and to the Director's relief, no matter how hard he tried to escape his new body, he could not.

However, the social life within the complex eased his frustrations, and he remembered that life has its compensations. He became a focus of great personal interest within the realm of the social club. His DNA-shell body was based on an ideal model. Despite some rejections of his overt masculinity, it enthralled many of the female and trans staff. This added to his breezy manner; his lifelong range of stories and his inherent love of women made him a popular figure.

The directors filled his days with a series of never-ending tests covering a range of physical and psychological matters. Repeated tests followed to assess any degradation of his bodily and brain functions, but apart from normal wear-and-tear, as the doctors reported, all seemed well.

His artistic mind wanted something and needed a channel. In an outlet of frustration, he burst out to his listening admirers at the social club, "My head is filling, and I need to empty it." He requested canvas and paints to offload what had been building in the months since his rebirth and began a series of paintings following the style of his later work when alive almost seven years before... but with hints of an afterlife.

They coaxed Triton to meet Denzel Dou, a meeting which was, as they suspected, monitored. Denzel Dou walked into the social club sweaty-palmed, expecting a clambering group. Seeing only Triton and a few off-duty parties acknowledging his presence, he wondered to Triton at the bar and said, "What are you drinking, mate?"

Although the two exchanged stories in the presence of wide-eyed nurses, both he and Triton felt the evening forced, both knowing there was no longer the camaraderie they had enjoyed in the spirit world. Sadly, for both, although Triton enjoyed Denzel's company, there was no longer any spark of being in a place of complete freedom.

The result for all concerned—Triton, Denzel and the Directors' team—was disappointment. So Triton returned to his bed and Denzel to his painting, the directors having no chance of further study of Triton's abilities.

With the success of the Denzel Dou program, Sniphle's mind wandered, and he allowed himself to dream of a fresh vision for the human species, albeit under his direction. In his mind, he pieced together the several aspects of a master plan.

First on his list was the outright purchase of a laboratory producing the DNA-shells and setting about gleaning techniques and expertise of the processes needed to manufacture the shells. During this time, he looked for and eventually found a sovereign island, New Bismarck, that might be amenable to his persuasive proposals. Here, he planned to conduct another necessary step to achieve his greater aim. But to do this required face-to-face meetings with the dominant hierarchy on the island.

The company yacht arrived at the only bay suitable for taking a vessel of its size on the island. Sniphle and his medical team disembarked onto the rickety walkway, ushering them from the late 21st century to another age where physical wealth, although desirable, was not a priority. Sceptical advisers of the island's prime minister, some of whom it had educated in other countries, greeted them. Without exception, all wondered why the Bio-Wonder Boy had chosen their recently recognised independent island state to visit. Although their seas enjoyed good fishing, unlike many other South Sea islands, they did not have the lush beaches enjoyed by similar islands. Their Antarctic-fed seas were not overly warm or inviting to the scuba-diving community unless guided by an expert. Only the very hardy ventured to view its fish life, apart from a new cage-diving outfit.

But the Bio-Wonder Team was here, and the puzzlement as to why buzzed around the island community. The Prime Minister's son, Tupaia, headed up the six-member team to greet the soft-skinned foreigners as they arrived at the end of the shaky pier. His large, hard hand engulfed Sniphle's, as did his smile, but Sniphle was never one to be pulled in by a grin. He saw behind the generous face a pair of bright, wary eyes looking for anything threatening to parry.

The open nature of the islanders' welcome was there to put the strangers at ease while they tried to fathom what was behind the visit. They ushered Sniphle and his team to a large, yet open building made from local materials, but having a concrete floor. On one side there appeared to be a complete wall of secondary areas housing security offices, comfort rooms, and padlocked offices. To the other side was a large open kitchen area where inquisitive staff craned their necks to glimpse the new arrivals. But it was the open-style roofing that amazed the visitors, with its thatch-like Tad-Tad covering, which he later learned was pared down bamboo. The western guests were seated overlooking the bay and offered Buko the local coconut milk drink.

Tupaia came forward once again said, "Sirs, welcome to our island." And without waiting for an answer, asked, "How can we help you?"

Sniphle opened, "You are Tupaia, are you not?" and in his blunt manner continued, "Can we see your father? I have an important proposal which may benefit all your islanders."

Tupaia eyes narrowed in suspicion, but he gave a reserved smile, replying, "Of course! Your team informed us of this before your arrival, and we have planned to take you to his residence. I'm afraid he is not as mobile as he used to be." Then, lightening his eyes a little, he said, "I think his days of captaining the island's rugby 7evens team are catching up on him."

The PM greeted the multibillionaire visitor with grace and, like any expert hunter, waited for his guest's first move. Sniphle too waited, but was first to break the diplomatic silence. "Prime Minister, we're here to offer you and your islanders an opportunity. We know your wonderful island of New Bismarck is new to the list of independent countries, and to help, we are offering your people free education and a new medical facility."

The old man looked into Sniphle's eyes, and with an almost-Australian accent, asked, "But what will it cost us, and what do you expect in return?"

Sniphle, ignoring the questions, went on as if following a written script. "We also propose building a bio-laboratory that will have, as an additional feature, a state-of-the-art hospital. The Director Organisation will furnish the facility with the latest equipment, and to begin with, man it with our own medical staff. However, as time goes on, we would expect your people to take over as their training levels rise." He stopped a few moments, waiting for the PM's response, only for the PM to reply again, "And what do you expect from us in return?" At this, the PM continued his pointed stare into Sniphle's watery eyes.

Tupaia could feel the silence growing, and put forward the views of his own people at the gathering and, siding with his father, said, "So, you think of us as uneducated!"

The worried, agitated Sniphle rubbed his damp hands on his over-long shorts. Realising he may have trodden on a few toes, he cleared his throat and hurriedly said. "No! No, it's just that most local areas, countries, continents, they all tailor the education of their peoples to suit what is necessary for the local economy to survive, be it fishing, farming, fabrication, financial or office work. We at no time inferred that your people are unintelligent."

The PM saw the possibility of an opportunity, and thought to himself, *These foreigners are desperate.* Countering, he said, "So, what's in it for you?"

Sniphle ignored the question again. "We will build new schools, and will provide specialist teachers more aligned with the new requirement for bioengineering."

The PM exuded a sense of annoyance, then glanced at his son in a pretence of boredom. He then eyed the others in the gangly foreigner's entourage, then back to the speaker himself, pointing a finger at him. "What's in it for *you?*"

Sniphle continued, ignoring the question. "You have such a beautiful country; you have truly wonderful people. It would be a shame for them not to have an opportunity to improve their standard of living."

The PM stood. "But. What's. In. It. For. *You?*" the PM boomed, towering over Sniphle. Polynesians tend to be large people. "You and your friends here could do this anywhere in the world, and at a far lower cost. Why! Why! *Why* do you want to spend all this money and time doing this for *us*? Think about it... by the time you have built the facility, educated my people to your standards, you!" firmly prodding a large finger into Sniphle's chest, "You will be older than me by the time it's finished to the standards you're outlining. So, little man, *why?*"

In a concerned move, Tupaia stepped forward, knowing his father's powerful personality, and said. "Let's take a few minutes; we have some nibbles and refreshments." This allowed the heat to deflate from the situation, and all settled down as the staff mingled with loaded trays of local delicacies.

Sniphle had never been in a situation of verbal and physical confrontation before on such a level. But although his heart pounded, he rose to the task, knowing the goal he was aiming for was more important than the anxiety hit he was experiencing. Following a second round of light-bites served with more drinks, a worried Sniphle once more approached the PM. "Prime Minister, may I introduce you to someone who you may find interesting? He is an artist who paints in the style of Denzel Covington, the well-known British artist who died seven years ago."

The PM, not known to be a classic diplomat, rankled a little, tilted his head to one side in a show of scepticism, and said, "You are not telling me you came all this way to introduce me to an artist? Or are you here for something a little more important? I have peoples to help guide through their lives. I must ensure their physical health, their educational needs; I must also ensure we take their security seriously. You cannot tell me you will get us all to paint pictures, can you?"

Sniphle, not put off his stride, stepped back a little and with a pointing limp hand said, "What do you think of him? Is he not an excellent figure of a man?"

The PM, who had a life's history of gauging men on a rugby field, could see how well-built Denzel was. "Yes, and so what?"

Sniphle, finding a small chink of an opening, said, "With his style of painting, is it no coincidence that his name is Denzel? In fact, it's Denzel Dou." He waited a little for the PM to react.

The PM, somewhat put off by the question, filled in the answer almost without thinking, "Denzel TWO!"

Sniphle smirked and nodded. "Please keep what I will tell you quiet. This is for your ears only. Let's go somewhere less public." At this, the PM could see there was something important coming, and gauged whether to allow the sneering foreigner to guide him. But there was something about the tie-up with the Denzel character...

The PM showed them into his private quarters. As he settled back into a soft seat, Sniphle started, "How old are you, Prime Minister? Let me guess—seventy-eight, isn't it?" Once more revealing his smirking smile, he said, "Forgive me, but I have done a great deal of research on you. In your youth, you were a world-renowned rugby player. You had a few injuries, yes, but overall, you played through them. They have given me to understand you have had an adventurous life. You've had your loves; you have had a few hits. Your mother and your youngest son drowned; all played a part in building you." He paused, allowing the old man to understand he had done his research thoroughly. "All this will soon end." Sniphle paused again, looked coldly into the PM's eyes before saying, "And not too far along, you will die!," letting a silence to build. "How would you like to live your wonderful life again?"

The old man smiled as he remembered several incidents said, "Oh yes, wouldn't that be good? Although there are a few embarrassing mistakes I would try to omit."

Sniphle took his opportunity and said, "PM, I offer you a fresh life in a new body. I am offering you an opportunity to be..." He stopped, as if rethinking his words. "I and my team can bring people back to life. Not in their own old bodies, but in new, flawless, ready-made ones."

The old man was sceptical, and Sniphle could see him shutting his mind to the unbelievable proposal. Sniphle felt a tightness in his chest and fought to subdue it. In desperation, he knew it was vital to convince the old man. "Wait. Before you throw me out, let me reintroduce you to Denzel Dou. It's especially important you just talk to him."

The desperation in his voice persuaded the old man to allow Sniphle to continue.

They showed Denzel in; he approached the two seated, silent men. Sniphle greeted him by asking a question. "Denzel... how old are you?"

"Good question," he said, the imp in the artist bringing him to smile. "This is a loaded question, and I will answer it in several ways. This body I now call mine took 600 days to grow in a laboratory and finished almost a year ago. They designed it to be twenty-five years old when completed. Now it gets interesting. This mind of mine, including all my memories, was fifty-three years old when it died." His eyes smiled. "So, where does this leave us?" He stopped once again. He looked to Sniphle, then to the PM. "PM, to answer this man's question is difficult," he said, pausing once more for effect. "It is now seven months and three days since they invited me to gain access to this body, which took 600 days to grow. So! Am I 53 years old? Am I just over 25 years and seven months old? Am I seven months and three days? Or am I 600 days plus the seven months and three days? I just don't know."

There was a silence while all tried to take in what he had said and put in place the different and conjoined ages of the artist.

The wary PM raised his hands, focussed on Sniphle's worried persona and said, "If I believed your story, as I get the implication, you are offering me a new body to replace this weary old body of mine... I must ask you once again, and for the last time. WHY?" The PM could see this was a bribe of the most extraordinary extent, and repeated, "So, why are you offering all this for the use of our small island? You can get purpose-built facilities in several countries with well-educated populations at a fraction of what it will cost to build and run it here." The PM looked closely at the Bio-Wonder Boy. He saw the gaunt Sniphle dressed in freshly starched beige shorts with a pair of thin, hairless legs falling out to long black socks and sandals below. The PM then looked to the well-portioned Denzel in marked contrast to his damp-faced companion and wondered why they were here.

He waited a little longer before he rang a bell. Moments later, his son arrived. "Tupaia, these people are wasting my time. Can you thank them for their visit and show them to their boat?" His face was immobile, with only the eyes hinting at movement, while his eyelids lazily blinked from time to time in a show of boredom.

This threw Sniphle's left eye into an uncontrolled nervous spasm before he blurted, "Okay, wait!" After pausing a second, he went on, "There *is* something we would want in exchange." The PM's eyes continued to blink, with no other facial expression. Sniphle had been in many negotiations in the past with aggressive people, but there was a physical menace from the PM he hadn't encountered before. The PM waited for the move without a word. "As I showed before, Denzel is not an original-born person. We generated him from DNA. What we have managed is to get the spirit of the original Denzel to settle into this new body. What Denzel does not have is a passport! A place to call home! What we would like to happen is for your country to provide international recognition that he is a person."

The PM got it at once. "So, you want us to recognise Denzel as a person, and therefore give any other manufactured person the same status."

With shoulders back, chest out, and in dominant form, the PM said. "Stop me if I'm wrong! You want to use our island to manufacture DNA-shells, then when someone dies, and a spirit comes along to inhabit the shell, you want us to provide them with a passport."

Sniphle looked down in a show of subservience, his cards fully on the table. "I wouldn't have been so blunt, but yes, you have it, precisely."

Still in full robust control, the PM said. "Is there anything else you want to tell us?"

Blustering, Sniphle said in a series of hesitant, unconnected words, "No, not really... We will, of course, supply full training... and any out-of-pocket expenses... Eh, we have drawn up an outline agreement for us to discuss."

The PM still didn't change his expression. "Do not take us for fools. What you will do is auction off new bodies to extraordinarily rich old people nearing their demise. If I understand you correctly, to make everything legal, you want us to give them a passport to prove they have legal citizenship here. The only reason you want us to do this is because of the time, years, even decades it would take to put it through the parliaments of any..." pausing, giving emphasis, "*developed* country. So you wanted to take advantage of us."

Denzel pulled himself to his full height and robustly stepped forward. First, he looked to Sniphle, then to the PM. With a stony face, he unflinchingly exerted his physique and bravado, looked the PM in the eye, and said. "Yes, Prime Minister, you got it."

Despite knowing Denzel to be a DNA-shell, the PM liked the openness of the likeable artist, broke into a smile, and said. "I like someone who talks straight! You stay in the meeting while this one," pointing at the bald Sniphle, "and I talk this through. I didn't get my corpulent frame by taking crumbs from the table." He walked a few meters to a window and sat in an armchair with a gleaming coffee table in front of him. "Right, Mr Sniphle... Sit! Now, do you like rum?" Without waiting for an answer, he said. "Good!" and called his son over. "Tupaia, my son, get four glasses and a bottle of my favourite rum. We have some discussions to go through. Pull up chairs for you and the others and come join us.

"Now, Mr Sniphle, do you like scuba diving? If so, I have a proposal!" The old man, glancing at Tupaia, as usual, began his negotiations with a curveball. After taking a sip of the rum, he looked at the shocked, damp faced, puzzled Sniphle. "So, do you?"

19
Let's Play a Little Trick

For the two boys, Arche, and Ariel, their lives were a mixture of play and getting to know different ephemeral souls. Although each boy's own persona was one of wariness to others, they happily accepted their spiritual entourage, eager to extend their own lives.

Within the growing team of Directors were those who recorded all that the boys were doing while under the influence of their potions. They logged on to where, when, duration, and state of the boy's minds when travelling, and, importantly, on returning. They also had the AI recording all aspects of the dosages, mixtures, and the physical condition of the boys prior to and after their bouts of out-of-body travels. This allowed the Directors to repeat any aspects of the boys' travel should they need to do so.

The boys reported having travelled to the greatest depths of the oceans. They investigated the deepest caverns on Earth. They entered volcanos to report the range of colours, amazing them as they passed through the larva's different layers and depths. Of all their adventures, only travelling to the greatest depths of the oceans seemed to throw them. Here, they reported how their orientation became lost and confusing. While in their spiritual form, having zero gravity awareness, they reported not being able to know up, down, or sideways; the dark was beyond dark. It was only the presence of each other and the accompanying souls who helped them to remain calm that they could push in a direction. While in the deep, they, together with the accompanying spirits, combined to remind each other to where they had come from and the way back to the surface. But two miles down and beyond was a place they never wanted to go alone.

The two autistic boys were becoming true pioneers of all they could imagine. With the medications, they travelled wherever they wanted. However, there was always medication to recall them if required. With a loyalty to Triton, they spent much of their down-time relating the latest adventures to him. They had stories of accompanying sharks through passages of underwater cliff edges while in heavy currents, and stories of flying with an albatross while skimming the ocean waves. Together, they passed through termite mounds, beehives, and became a part of butterfly swarms. Their unique ways of thinking brought new insights to the outwardly inactive senior member of Sniphle's DNA altered clutch.

Although seemingly lethargic, during his missions, Triton searched, mindful of all that Arche and Ariel were escaping to and aware of where they travelled... but he travelled farther. He searched for Salena, cruelly snatched away while he was in the clutches of the Director's potions. As time moved on, he convinced the Directors he was content. He convinced them by staying silent, without wanting to leave. With his act of subservient behaviour, they relented with the heavier dosages. But he waited, knowing the Directors were in control of his mental and physical health, knowing that if he valued his sanity or his life, he should remain quiet. But he searched on, always looking for his long-lost love. However, he was unaware of the tangled web of lies and deceit fed to him about Salena. They had told him she had run off and later died, many years ago, during his initial days at Sniphle's first clinic. They informed him she had died in a house fire and even supplied him with a fictitious article from a newspaper as proof of her death.

This focussed Triton's search among the dead for her. He was relentless in trying to track her down, but such was the spirit's world's reluctance to talk about anything other than themselves that it limited information. From the time of her reported death, he searched and eventually concluded, sadly, that her spirit might have faded from people's memory and into the dark energy. At this point he lost hope and further retreated into himself, causing the Directors to treat him with a little more delicacy.

Triton's thoughts turned to Luna, and why she had triggered the feeling that he had met her before. How had she been able to travel and come into his mind? How had she travelled without the support of the director's prompting... or had she! Was she on a mission for them to pounce on one of his unguarded moments and trick him? His mind wandered into paranoia, and he grew suspicious of this new Special. He asked himself—did Sniphle repeat his DNA manipulation, and produce another like him and the batch of twelve? Only this time, with no chemical stimulations? Triton's paranoia convinced him that must be it. Luna must be an alternative version of the DNA modification. He thought further about the logical outcome of this: *all of us first generation are no longer needed!*

We will need to deal with this new one, Luna. I have strengths the others don't have; I have strengths they do not understand. I will deal with her before the Directors spread their mind games through her. But she has some strengths I no longer have, and she can travel with no need of potions.

Curled in his foetal position, his mind explored further. *Why didn't anyone tell me about her? It was she who contacted me without prompting from anyone. Or did she? Was this the director's plan all along?*

His growing paranoia convinced him; Luna was an agent of the Directors and was a threat. With this in mind, he planned to eliminate her as a hazard to himself and the other survivors of the first batch of twelve. He remembered being told that apart from himself, only ten of the twelve had made it to being born. Of them, eight were housed in the facility like himself, while the other two were said to be badly disturbed and taken care of by a volunteer who had rejected any help from the Directors. He did not trust Sniphle, and this was just the thing the nasty man would cook up. First, to get an innocent girl to befriend him and the other eight, to gain their knowledge and ability, then finally to drop them when not needed. Sniphle had protection. Therefore, getting to him would be exceedingly difficult. The simple way to avoid his threats would be to side-line his agents, Luna being the first.

Margret came into his room as usual an hour later on Sunday morning, bringing with her his preferred breakfast of a fruit and muesli mix accompanied by a fruit juice.

"Margret, how long have you been looking after me now?" he asked tiredly.

"Oh, it must be fifteen or sixteen years." She paused a little, remembering. "Ever since you first arrived. Why do you ask?"

"We have seen changes, haven't we... remember when we were in the old clinic? Those were enjoyable days, weren't they? I used to have a lot of fun with you girls, didn't I, or should I say, didn't *we*?" She blushed a little, remembering the encouraged lax ways they had in those days. "Then we moved into this place, where everyone seems to be in a regimented rush to do things." She smiled, nodding, wondering where this was going. He changed the subject. "What do you think of the young girl, Luna? I've heard some people don't like her."

"Yes, overall, she's okay, but sometimes she's a bit of a stuck-up little madam. It's only Ngoosi who seems to get on with her. She seems to think she knows what's going on here, even though she's only been in our wing and travelling a couple of months." Margret approached the bed and involuntary looked from side to side as if looking for eavesdroppers. "I think Luna seems to think she's above us carers, and in ways acts superior."

Triton broke in, "Let's play a trick on her and take her down a peg or two."

Margret smiled. "As much as I would like to, how are we going to do that? You Specials can't socialise too well without being monitored by the Director's team."

Triton's eyes narrowed a little in intrigue. "It would be easy to give her the jitters. Do you remember you told me about the night she went through the heebie-jeebies and was doing the rapid eye movement thing? Well, we could do it again. All you have to do is to switch her AI monitor off and on when she's hooked up. It should take her down a peg or two. It won't do her any harm overall, but it will teach her a lesson if she knows we can do it any time we want."

With a growing excitement, the nurse smiled. Remembering the reported REM incident involving Luna, she said, "I know! Let's teach the girl a lesson."

Triton caught up in the moment, his face beaming, said, "Yes, let's do it. She's due back from her holiday break tomorrow morning after the last episode."

Margret smirked a little, patted Triton on his inner thigh, "Yes, leave it to me, I'll give her a little fright, just to take her down a little peg or two."

Triton settled back into his foetal position and planned the next stage, going through the scenarios, the dangers, the resultant consequences, and the pitfalls if found out.

Around lunch time, he asked to be wheeled into the social room where he could catch up with Arche and Ariel if they were not travelling. He liked to hear their stories, though they repeated many of them, mostly without embellishment from the last telling.

He noticed many of the senior members missing, along with his favourite, Denzel. But despite his many pointed questions, none of the members of staff were forthcoming about their absence. He enquired of the boys if they knew anything, to which they told him they knew nothing, although there was chatter from some of their congregating ephemeral friends who frequented Denzel from time to time. They said that he was on a holiday in the South Seas with Sniphle.

He returned to his room and settled once more into his foetal position and tried to retrieve his earlier skills of travelling without the need of the Director's drugs.

20
Why is Triton So Special?

Inside the large rambling house, Salena began going through the motions of telling her two residents, Pan and Ferdinand, to set out drinks for the visitors. The visitors themselves settled into chairs around a communal table with the earlier breakfast plates still in place, smeared with the remnants of the last meal.

The mother and daughter hadn't let go of each other since entering the house, but, interrupted by one boy. Pan had recognised Luna at once, and his eyes began a repetition of movements from Luna to Salena and back again, over and over. "It's her, the girl from last night!" he declared in his interrupted speech. Salena took notice and settled him down in her motherly way, as she had done the night before, interpreting Pan's garbled speech, realising now why he was in such a state; he had recognised the girl. It was she who had been the invisible apparition that had upset him... but why, she wondered? After the shock of seeing her daughter on the doorstep, her mind raced, catching up with what was developing in front of her—Pan and her lost daughter seeming to know each other, and the appearance of her long-time friend Ngoosi turning up on her doorstep.

The carer in her took over from the shock. All were silenced by what had occurred, with only Ferdinand hovering in the background, having first opened the door. In his damaged mind, guiltily suspecting it was he who had caused Pan to melt down. Salena broke out of the surprise first, unwillingly releasing Luna's hand, and on seeing Ferdinand's growing distress, asked him to hurry with the drinks while still settling Pan.

The silent Ngoosi knew Luna had taken her in, but was not resentful, having only a little admiration for how the girl had tricked her. However, there was a large potential problem growing in her mind that, if not dealt with, would seriously endanger her position within the Director Organisation.

Luna refused to believe what was before her, blank eyes wide open while her body could not move. She felt dizzy with a growing tightness in her chest. She was unable to find words to express her rushing feelings, her mind tumbling. In front of her was her supposedly dead mother. But was it her mother? She shook her head in mouth-trembling shock. *No, it can't be. They told me she was dead... They told me they had found me wandering in a woodland area and they had found a dead woman close by and it was my mother.* With a shaking hand, she first reached to Ngoosi for an instinctive support while thinking through the events. *They had also claimed the shock of her death had probably caused my memory loss of the event. But if she is my mother, what now?*

Salena, who had broken out of the shock after seeing her lost daughter, took the immobile girl from Ngoosi. She pulled her to herself while in unblinking disbelief.

Eventually finding Pan in her eyesight, showing signs of agitated stress, she drew him to her. Without letting go of Luna, she settled Pan into the comforting arms of Ngoosi who, although in shock herself, found the reassuring presence of someone close comforting, even if it was the fragile Pan. Salena took her lost daughter's hand once more and instinctively pulled her close, where Luna felt surrounded by her lost mother's scent. Their eyes once again filled as they clung to each other. Salena's mind was scrambling with how Sniphle had duped her into believing her daughter dead; yet now seeing her, feeling her youthful body sitting beside her, feeling her touch... How could this be Luna, after she'd died? *I went to her funeral. She died of a brain tumour; I saw the scans.* But within her was the growing realisation this *was* Luna, and Sniphle had laid an elaborate, unforgivable evil hoax upon them both.

It was Luna who recovered her voice first. "Mummy, they told me I lost you in a forest and they found some of your clothes near a waterfall." In her continuing shocked state, Luna's words came out in a jumble. "Mummy, they told me they found me and have been taking care of me ever since. Director Sniphle suggested that the reason I have no memory of it was because of the shock of losing you. The nurses told me I couldn't speak until about a year ago, and before that, Director Sniphle had me housed in a private ward for several years." Luna fell into a silence before recovering, placing the events of her past. But words came tumbling out. "Mummy, how long is it since you last saw me? *How long is it?*"

Salena began putting the pieces together, and answered, "I lost you just before your fourth birthday. It was after that the Directors started to re-engage with me and tried to help me through your loss. They helped me buy this house and asked me to look after Pan and Ferdinand as a housemother to them. I was told their own parents were drug addicts and couldn't look after them themselves, saying the boys were incredibly special but fragile. The boys needed a place to call home and protected from outsiders. The Directors told me both were... damaged. They also told me both Pan and Ferdinand didn't like to go outside, that they feared crowded places." Salena looked away for a few seconds, as if recalling something important revealed during this time. "They also told me the Specials had limited lifespans, and that they wouldn't live much past their late thirties."

Ngoosi looked up, nodded, and filled in a few more details, saying some were in early decline already. "However, I'm not sure of Luna. She was in a special room and was the sole patient of Director Sniphle for years until six or seven months ago, when they assigned her to a room in our wing. That was when I first met with her." She smiled in Luna's direction and caught the eye of the girl nestling into her mother. "Since then, the Directors have been undertaking several programs with her, and from what I've gleaned so far, she hardly needs any of their concoctions to travel. The AI that reports it only needs minimal dosages to push her on, and these seem for direction only. However, I'm not sure of all the details. They keep us nurses at arm's length most of the time, but we pick up on some of their conversations."

Ferdinand arrived with a pitcher of chilled water and glasses, which Salena acknowledged, and shuffled her seat forward to the table. "I need more than water, but this isn't a time for anything stronger. So, as it's almost time for lunch, let us all settle down and talk." She then turned back to the retreating Ferdinand. "Ferdi, be a love and put the kettle on." He smiled and nodded, soaking in the calm Salena had created.

As a result, the boys relaxed; Pan's speech proved to be more understandable, and despite the women trying to get to their own prime topic, he forced his story to be told. He looked directly at Salena without deviation; he told of his meeting with Luna the night before. He told of his fitting seizure episode, and that when that happened, he could travel around the house in his mind as if flying while his physical body was in contortion. He relayed how last night he saw Luna and tried to hide, but after glancing round to Luna nervously, he told how she could follow him.

Luna brightened a little. "You mean you've done this before, travelling outside your body?"

Salena answered for him, "Yes, they can both travel and have done for a long time. I think that's why Sniphle got his people to fund me." She sighed. "He knows about their talents, but as they're both very fragile, he hasn't bothered us. However, knowing him as I do, this could change."

Luna remained quiet, staying close to her mother as Ngoosi brought Salena up to date with the latest news from old friends, the Specials, the Directors, and the new facility. To Luna, almost all they discussed and revealed was new. Warily, Salena asked of all the Specials by name, but skirting away from Triton, asked to what extent the girls and boys had developed their differing roles within the director's regime of divergent drug concoctions. After an hour, there came a natural break brought on by Ferdinand with a spoon in his hand requesting what time would their lunch be today.

Luna followed Salena into the kitchen, never allowing her out of her sight. "Mummy, why did you leave the Directors and the Specials?"

A tingle ran through Salena before she said, "Oh, it's a long story, but Mr Sniphle and I didn't get on too well, and we had a few differences about how to treat the first of the Specials."

Luna remembered her conversation with Triton, and that he claimed to be the first Special. "Mummy, do you know Triton? How was he in the beginning? He seems to act superior."

Salena broke in immediately, her voice sharp and searching. "How do you know Triton? He's dead!" For the second time in the day, she had an almost heart-stopping moment. Her mouth dropped open, which she attempted to cover with her palm. Shocked, she began shaking her head from side to side in denial, while in her mind she recollected the events she had been told and believed. With her colour drained, she looked at Luna, unbelieving what she was hearing; she searched her memory for an understanding of what was being said to her. Unsteadily, she rose to her feet and shouted, "Ngoosi!"

The nurse made her way along the passage to the kitchen, looked through the door, cocked her head to one side, asked, "What's the problem?"

"You didn't tell me about Triton!"

Almost calmly, the nurse replied, "You didn't ask. Besides, from what I heard, he and you left on acrimonious terms. So, I thought I had better skip talking about him unless you brought it up."

A glimmer of suspicion began in Salena's mind as an adrenaline rush had her heart thumping, but forcing calmness, she said, "Tell me about him." But without waiting for a response, she started again. "I was told he had slipped away and died after he had overdosed." Salena stopped, remembering the events, and knew it was important to choose her words thoughtfully. "Ngoosi, the Directors told me Triton had stolen a stash of drugs they had been giving to him to ease his night-time traumas. They said he had fled Sniphle's clinic and run off. It was later reported they found him dead of an overdose somewhere in Eastern Europe. They even showed me a newspaper clipping reporting his death."

Ngoosi, whose face had become ashen and had lost her normal smile, responded, "They told us you had a row with him, and that he had instructed Sniphle and the team never to allow you to see him. They ordered us never to talk about him to you or anyone else. As it was over ten years ago, I thought everything had settled down."

In shock, Salena remained silent, as new tears welled up while taking in what the Directors had done. Luna, fidgeting round to see her mother's face, said, "Mummy, why is Triton so important?"

Salena could feel goosebumps as she connected the train of events that had been playing out. She smiled a little, took Luna and tugged her to her breast, and revealed, "Darling... He's your father."

A moment later, eyes sharp and astute, she looked up to Ngoosi. "Whatever you do, don't tell a soul."

Luna and Ngoosi began their journey back to the Directors' facility in near silence, seeming to believe others in the bus were there to listen in on their conversations. Heads together, they agreed. They should say nothing about these discoveries. Triton wasn't to be talked about under any circumstances, and Luna should sleep on her revelation before contacting him. They agreed time wasn't as important as making the right decision on how and when to talk, if talking to him was a possibility.

Late that night, a senior member of the Directors' team arrived at Triton's door. He approached the sure-sighted, calm-faced incumbent. "Triton, we have a special job for you."

Without changing his expression, Triton said, "Ah! Dr Vernon, if my nasal passages are correct. What is a Senior Director doing in my room so late on a Sunday night? Mischief, no doubt."

The sneering Dr Vernon, doing his best to impersonate his boss, replied, "You were always almost too clever, Triton. It's a pity you never made it out of here. Instead, you run errands for those of us who are not reliant on our concocted compounds. But let us get back to the point of why I'm here." He approached the bed. Then, leaning closer to Triton's face, he said, "We have an important errand for you. Director Sniphle is in the Southern Ocean at the moment, putting the last touches to negotiations to ensure all," pausing before emphasising, "inhabited DNA-shells get life recognition. Shall we say... a passport?"

Triton's ears pricked up, remembering his friend Denzel while trying to ignore Vernon's foul-smelling breath on his face.

"We need to eavesdrop on the conversations the PM and his cabinet are having within the hour. If you can be there and report back, it will give us a heads-up on anything extra they may ask for during negotiations tomorrow. We all want this to happen without hiccups, even you, so let's get you prepped up and off to the island sunshine, shall we... Oh! I forgot," Vernon sneered, "you don't get a tan laying in this bed, do you?" With that, he opened the door and a prep-team swarmed in.

21
Off-to-On

The day exhausted Luna; she had never in her memory walked so far, albeit just under two kilometres, or encountered such traumatic revelations. As promised by Ngoosi, the pair arrived back at the facility before the 4 pm curfew, the growing friendship between them ensuring that nothing of their momentous day revealed. Without thinking, both accepted the girl's fatigue, and relieving her tired limbs from her clothing, got her into a shower, then into her scant nightwear. Natural sleep overcame her, even though Luna had at first set out to take her mind elsewhere.

Her holiday over, morning came, and daily routines made their way back into her life, although Luna was more sluggish than normal. Margret entered the room and gently woke her for breakfast. As usual on days like these, when the Special was assigned to travel, breakfast was light: a bowl of cut fruit, a piece of toast, and juice. During her slow progress through the fruit bowl, the Prep-Team arrived and set up the parameters assigned to her. Continuing, they made sure they loaded the AI monitor with the correct stimulants calibrated for each phase of her travel plan. All done, checked and rechecked, they exited Luna's room, leaving Margret to tidy up the breakfast debris.

But with Triton still in her mind, Margret had an agenda. Unobtrusively, without fuss, she flipped the AI module's power switch Off then On again, hardly making the machine tremble or blink; but it reset its dosing stimulants to the considerably higher normal settings.

The Director team assembled as scheduled at 9 am and instructed the AI to start the preliminary dosage to place Luna into the Dormant stage. As was the norm, they assigned a junior member to remain with their charge until the Twitch stage began.

Luna lay on the bed, her muscles complaining whenever she made any meaningful movement, but mentally alert, thinking, *They have me on the bed again; the Prep-Team have done their duties and have left me to the Director team for my latest escapade. I wonder where they'll send me this time. But I'll play their game, remain calm, and wait until they press the AI to give me the instructions on where to.*

Although physically exhausted from the previous day's outing, her mind was active, with her thoughts abuzz about yesterday's meeting with her mother and the news that Triton was her father. After deep thought, she knew her route, but needed to wait a little longer. Luna remained outwardly lethargic, laying on the bed with the first of her programmed new chemicals coursing through her system, vowing to herself that no matter where the AI instructed her to go, she would travel as she wanted. *While I await the Director team's arrival, I think I'll travel down the corridor and see if my father is available.* With just a little mischief in her young mind, she thought, *I wonder what he'll say when he finds out about Mummy and me. Now, all I have to do is just relax and find my own trigger point.*

Meanwhile, the returned Triton, fresh from his astral excursion to New Bismarck, laid on his back in the position the Directors preferred him to be in when travelling. The last of the wake-up dosages administered and, although he was still in his induced relaxed state, Dr Vernon entered his room. With the remains of a hurried breakfast still in the corners of his mouth, the Director said, "What have you to tell us, Triton? Give us the lowdown on the PM's meeting and what they have up their sleeves."

Triton had no second thoughts, and using his renowned photographic memory, he relayed the outline of the meeting. In detail, he told of its active participants, subjects covered, legal hot spots, and the extra requirements the cabinet required prior to signing any agreement. Open-eyed in wonder at the complete report, Vernon asked, "So, in principle, they agree with our proposal, do they?"

Without embellishment, Triton had relayed what he had heard and gave his opinion. "This is something I can't comment on, but in principle, they seem very keen to go ahead with getting the legal aspects ironed out. At first sight, their legal team said there are no colossal problems."

Triton blinked a few times, as if clearing his eyes; and, frowning, looked away to the side of Vernon. There he saw the translucent figure of Luna appear before him.

The excited Luna, ignoring Director Vernon, concentrated on Triton, and spoke to him in his mind: "I found your aunt; she and her partner are fine!" She waited a little longer to ensure he caught all she was telling him before seeing him completely concentrating on her. "I also visited the address you gave me for the two boys on the outskirts of town." Without allowing him to respond, she continued, "My mother, Salena, sends her love." Pausing further, with a beaming face, she add a little emphasis: "... Daddy."

His eyes lit up in shock, Triton ignored the insistent physical presence of Vernon, straightening up in the bed and addressing the spectral Luna in his mind: "What!... She's alive?"

Luna responded at once, "Daddy, she thought you were dead. That's what they told her."

Luna felt a bodily shock and knew her physical self, laying on the bed in another room, was being subjected to a new AI-injected stimulus. Unlike those before, this was stronger, almost like an unexpected punch in her back. *Whatever they've given me, it's unlike anything before, and I can't resist its drive.* "Daddy, I have to go," she cried. "they're sending me somewhere. I thought I could resist it, but this is stronger than anything before!"

"Wait, you..." he gasped, trying to form his thoughts as his mind raced with what he had heard from her and the added interrupting voice from Vernon in the background. Without focusing, Triton voiced, "Don't go!"

His eyes opened wide and mouth hesitating, the unaware Vernon replied, "I know you have just returned, so don't worry, we won't go, and will wait until I have the rest of your report." However, it wasn't Vernon Triton was talking to. Triton's alarm at what Luna was saying had confused him.

Before he could reform the words in his mind for Luna, she replied, "I can't resist any longer. This is so strong—far stronger than anything I've felt before."

At last, Triton remembered his conversation with Margret the night before, and the plot to turn the AI console Off, then back On to reset it. His heart gave a jolt. "Oh, no! Oh NO!"

The dosage drew Luna back to herself, lying on the bed among the sprouting tubes and cables. She saw, too, that she was twitching from time to time, which seemed to concern the monitoring team. The Senior Director present, Director Trokker, said, "We shall send her now; she seems to be in Twitch mode."

The younger Director, Ranghan, countered, "I don't like it: unlike the others, she's normally quite at this stage. Can we wait a little?"

Trokker had no tolerance for the junior man and snapped back, "No, we do it now! We promised Director Sniphle Luna would be away before lunch, and we want her back before he calls later this afternoon."

The subdued Ranghan quietly replied, shaking his head, "Okay, then, what's the mission this time?"

Trokker sneered at the half-heard question, and in her officious tone—aimed at being more male than the others in the room—said, "We are *not* waiting!" Then she looked around, selected her target. "You!" pointing at Director Ranghan, "Get a move on—that AI and I can't wait forever, otherwise Luna will throw off the effects of this stage's dosage."

Teeth clenched, the irked Ranghan moved over to the AI and pressed the green 'Travel-Stage' button.

Almost at once the twitching subsided, and the girl seemed to relax, as if waiting on a high board ready to dive into clear water. The chemical release triggered, and deliberately, in she dived. But as she reached the new phase of consciousness, her vision became opaque, her window to the outside like frosted glass.

It relieved Ranghan, watching the AI readings dance along their displays without spiking and showing issues. As if triggered by the sight of AI wave form, he called out, "By the by, what is her mission this time?"

Trokker rounded on him, "You should know. Didn't you go through it with her when you prepped her?"

Ranghan, for once, found his balls. "That's your responsibility. You're the Senior Director present."

Trokker instantly looked down at her checklist and saw the girl's destination, a collection station in Brazil, but she hadn't read through the assignment, nor given directions about what to do. Instantly she said, "Quick, we have to get her back. Give her the antidote... now!"

Ranghan did as bid and duly pressed the mushroom-shaped red AI button.

Agitated with worry, the sweaty-palmed Trokker waited a few moments before muttering, "Are we getting her back yet?"

Ranghan, asserting himself, gazed back at her in a challenging manner and said, "There doesn't appear to be much change to her readings. Let's wait a little longer and hope she's not too far in."

They waited. Time moved on, but the girl gave no sign of returning to her body, apart from a series of sharp spikes marching their way across the AI screens.

Luna was lost. The frosted vision in front of her changed, becoming clearer, but still without presenting a form she could understand. There was a constant drumming all around her, but unable to pinpoint the source, she tried to put it to one side... yet it remained.

Where is this? Where am I? What is this place? If I go forward a little, I may find a familiar place. With the drumming pulsing into her, Luna found she could move ahead, and found a great cavern where to one side she detected a trickling sound. Then, remembering her past flights, she knew that although she seemed to be in a cavern, she could pass through the walls. Without knowing to where, she cautiously moved through and found a vast space with other walls, thinking they could be other caverns. She passed through another wall into a rushing corridor of objects running in one direction towards her and through her. She followed the direction they were going, not at their speed, but slower, trying to understand what was going on. Onward she passed, wondering, *Am I deep, deep under the ocean, in the mush below the water level?*

Time passed as she tried to remain calm. *I'm getting lonely here. I need help. What do they want me to do... is this a test? Where am I? Why am I here?*

She deliberately moved on, trying to understand.

Late in the evening, Sniphle arrived back at the facility gushing with the success of his work in New Bismarck.

He had taken up the PM's invitation and had a scuba dive while inside an enormous cage three meters square, a full four meters long. It being towed at a depth of 3 metres underwater by the support vessel through shoals of fish absolutely mesmerised him. Only the small juvenile barracudas could chase their prey inside. On the outside, he and Denzel could see the other predators—sharks, and the occasional pod of dolphin eyeing both the divers and the shoaling smaller fish pulsing in and out of the cage.

The PM had sold Sniphle the large cage-diving idea, while Sniphle had his primary mission accomplished.

With Denzel beside him, the pair had enjoyed the transfer flight back, taking in what they had achieved: an agreement from the PM that any of the DNA-shells taking on an "ephemeral spirit" were granted a naturalised certificate of New Bismarck citizenship.

When they returned, Sniphle held a late-night informal meeting of the Board of Directors. Denzel, in a good-natured semi-drunken state, showed his freshly stamped New Bismarck passport. The pair recounted their journey to and from the South Seas Island with a laughable rendition of Denzel's hiding in the company yacht on the way to the destination, then his flourishing display of his new passport on arrival at the British Passport Control on the way back.

In a side-group of the meeting, Director Trokker remained silent, trying to evade any chit-chat that required releasing information about her day's events. For once, Sniphle was in a jovial mood. He travelled from group to group. He highlighted the momentous achievement both he and Denzel had made, and how their success would affect each of the Director Organisation departments.

As the Directors mingled, Sniphle caught sight of the travel director and, calling him forward, said, "Bennon, how is that research program I left you with? You said you would send Arche and Ariel on a program to unique places to see if they had any difficulties or, as we suspected, plain sailing."

Director Bennon, for once, was in a comfort zone because of his successful achievement. Modestly, he told Director Sniphle a little of what the two had carried out. Knowing Sniphle's exacting nature, he would save the excellent stuff until there was a board meeting. But he gave a teaser of what had happened. "Yes, they both reported the journeys were easier than expected, and the visit to the Moon Base brought back an impressive number of details we were not expecting. I'll fill you in later regarding that as part of my full report."

"What about their visits to other places?"

"We're in mid-stage with this one. Arche claimed he travelled to Mars but did not home in on the Mars Base. He claimed he found the planet easier than he thought, and that the travel time was better than the speed of light. But he grew a little worried about finding Earth for the trip back. However, he reported it was much easier than he thought, so next time it should be a breeze."

Sniphle grinned from ear to ear. All seemed to go according to plan. He looked around the room and spied the back view of the elusive Trokker talking to Denzel.

"Trokker, how about you and that little Special I left you with?"

With an untimely heaviness to her bowels, she felt a need to visit the comfort room, but knew she could not escape. Director Trokker knew it was time to either come clean or use her best evasive lawyer-politician-speak, then talk without telling. "Director Sniphle, you're talking about Luna. Well, we did as per the program, starting early this morning. I won't go into all the details, but we followed the regular program stages. Dormant, Twitch, Transition, Travel, etc." Then seeing, an opportunity to gain time, she broke off from her tale, her eyes catching sight of Marketing Director Cunningham. "Hi, Harry!" She turned back to Sniphle and apologised. "I'm sorry, sir, where was I?"

Luckily for Trokker, Cunningham's report was more important than Trokker's assignment at this point. Sniphle called him over. "Cunningham, how did the survey go? Did you get any nibbles at our proposals?"

The slightly overweight Harry, wearing a jacket with stress marks across its back, said, "Oh, yes! I've been waiting for the opportunity to talk to you about it. I suggest...."

Director Trokker saw her opportunity. "Excuse me, gentlemen, I need to go to the ladies' room. Do you mind a moment?"

They made room for her and continued their discussion. The officious Sniphle, forgetting Cunningham's earlier words, said, "So, Harry, what have you come up with?"

"Well, of the ten proposals on our agreed list of rich punters, we have seven very interested and of those, two are definite." He grinned. "However, trying to sell new bodies to old people is an incredible leap of faith on behalf of the buyer. Old people can be very stubborn about handing over cash."

A sneering smile crept across Sniphle's face. "Come see me in the morning. I want you to set up meetings with the other seven. We'll offer the two positives a ninety-point discount for their faith in our offer. Then we'll give a fifty percent discount to the rest if they take it up. After that, no other discounts to anyone else when the word gets out about what we're offering."

Cunningham, smiling, said, "They're not always old with money; one of the two has a terminal illness and wants a replacement body."

Sniphle raised his glass to Cunningham. "To the terminal ill; may they never get cured." Sniphle laughed out loud while eyeing the others in the room, watching most of them do as he had without knowing the reason for laughter. He knew his dominance, and in a good mood for once, called for an extra glass of champagne, ending any other work-related conversations. But it was Denzel's increasing rowdiness that brought the meeting to a close when he suggested an inappropriate meeting with Trokker.

But in Sniphle's head was an unanswered question...

22
Coffee for Trokker

Luna's unending journey continued, as she tried to take in and understand where she was in this rushing world. Things were becoming a little darker, and the surrounding objects were slowing; things were changing. She stopped. *I have to find a way out of here, but not back the way I came.* She noticed a small channel and entered. As she followed it, there seemed no end until it met with a fresh path. This then joined another larger path. The larger path picked up speed, then went into another passage, and the speed increased further. *I don't know why, but I feel I'm going somewhere now.* She became increasingly angry. *Why didn't they explain to me where I was to go?*

The increase in speed was no longer smooth. It came in surges, as if she were being drawn instead of being pushed, until she came to a wall. But was it a wall? She thought, but on a closer look, she could see it was a door. The door opened, and she passed through in a rush before it closed again. Then all stopped. After she waited a moment, another door opened. This time, instead of being drawn along the passage, she was being pushed until she came to an enormous cavern where the surrounding walls became lighter.

The pushing and pulling were now at a level that had barely any effect on her, and she slowed to a stop. *Can I contact someone and ask? I have no voice, but I can reach out and see if I can connect to someone.* With all her power, she did her best to shout out in her mind. Over and over, she tried, but no response came.

If I had a body, I would just sit in a corner and cry, but my spirit-self has no way of expressing itself. She felt a depression coming over her as the realisation of her situation hit home: alone, lost, with no sign of what she could try next.

Luna's lonely mood quietened her, and she wanted to rest before renewing her search for a way out.

The next morning Sniphle, still full of goodwill resulting from his successful South Seas trip, began his tour of the facility, head up and smiling for once. His characteristic strut took him from department to department, spouting a message of how the company would soon conquer the pain of losing someone because of bereavement.

Eventually he made his way to the Specials' wing and stopped in on each room. He chatted to them about the recent developments involving their roles, gathering and transporting the ephemeral spirits as part of his overall plan. Ultimately, he arrived at Luna's room to find a traveller team in attendance, with Trokker hovering in the background. Under his lazy-lidded gaze, he made eye contact and smiled at each member of the team. "Hi, folks, how are you getting on? Please don't let me interrupt what you're doing; just pretend I'm not here." He spied Trokker at the far side of the bed, apparently engrossed, her head down into her tablet. "Trokker, what's going on? I thought you did the tests yesterday."

Others in the room went quiet, which the astute Sniphle picked up at once. He turned to Dr Ranghan and just looked at him, inviting him to speak.

"Good morning, sir, we are continuing Luna's program, sir."

Sniphle, disregarding Trokker completely, stared at Ranghan. "I was told you had done this yesterday." He held the gaze and Ranghan knew it was not a statement, but a question; the silence invited an answer. Ranghan, whimpering within, said at last, in a worried voice, "Err, yes sir, we started the program yesterday... sir." Then, nervously, he looked to Director Trokker and back to Sniphle, "Ah, but we didn't complete it."

Deliberately ignoring Trokker, Sniphle continued to question Ranghan. "What does that mean?"

Defensively, eyes wandering, searching for words, at last Ranghan said, "Erm, we set the program and followed the standard procedures. There seemed to be a minor hiccup when Luna began the Twitch mode... We forgot to brief her about the mission. When we tried to bring her out it didn't seem to work, so we left her to come out of it by herself as the chemicals wore off."

There was a tense silence while Sniphle turned to Trokker and back to Ranghan. Sniphle, with his jaw set under heavy eyebrows, set a grim expression on his face while his eyes grew colder. Ranghan could see that Director Trokker was in trouble, but continued his report. "This morning when we returned, expecting Luna to be out of it... she wasn't. This is where you find us now. Sir."

Stony faced, the cold-eyed Director turned to Trokker. "Remind me of her mission."

"Sir, we inadvertently directed her to go into her own body as part of the medical program we are running, instead of Brazil."

At once Sniphle rounding on her said, "And is she still in there... did she actually go in there?"

"We don't know, sir."

"WHAT!"

Sniphle vented his fury at the nervous Director Trokker, shouting, "Luna is the most valuable Special here!" Then, turning up the volume of his voice further, he sarcastically burst out, **"And... you... lost her!"** He spun round to one nurse, pointing a steady finger at him. "You go get a security team now. Trokker: I relieve you of your duties but stay here; security will escort you out until I deal with you." He turned back to the others, focusing on Ranghan. "I want a report of all you've done, including the AI settings. Everything—I want everything." His eyes roved around the room with malice, looking for someone else to vent his rage on. "Who handles her vitals?"

"I do, sir."

"Staff Nurse Roberts, isn't it?" Then, remembering their past, he continued without an answer, "Pick your most reliable colleague, and the pair of you had better keep her alive for your own sakes. You two are responsible, got it?" She nodded while her eyes nervously flicked up to his face, away and back again. He changed his demeanour a little and ordered, "Don't forget to give me a complete record of her REM patterns." With that, he turned and headed for the door and waited for someone to open it for him. As he left, he shouted back at Trokker, "I'll see you in my office. Don't go anywhere until security arrives."

Luna awoke from her fitful sleep, trying to work out the enormous cavern, and watched as the sides and roof seemed to expand and contract. *Where is this place?* She knew she needed to get out of the cavern, which, apart from small alcoves to rest, gave her no sign of a way out of her plight, if there was one. There was another opening through what looked like the way she'd entered, but instead of pushing her in, it was drawing her out. *I have nothing to lose; let's go for it.* Through and up through a large passage, up and up through a gate and into a forest of curves. *What is this, an electrical storm? There are charges everywhere; I must get out. But there is something here... I feel it drawing me, almost magnetically.* She followed a path of convoluted patterns, sometimes tightening, other times long and curving, but leading nowhere, never appearing to end. She noted the dead ends of some paths, like coming to the end of a tree branch with small electrical charges flickering from time to time.

Trokker waited in Sniphle's reception area with the security detail hovering around her. She tried to engage in polite conversation with his ever-present personal assistant, Janice; but her manner was like a sponge, taking in conversation, but never reciprocating. The wait was a deliberate act to put her on edge. Janice offered drinks.

As a relief, Trokker accepted. "Coffee, black, a little sugar please," she requested, almost humbly. The coffee finished; Janice informed her she could go in now.

The confident Sniphle remained at his desk as he greeted her, saying, "Ah, Trokker, come in sit down over there on the seating area close to the window." She did as bid, noting that the security beast behind her remained at the door. Sniphle looked at his watch and back over at her. "Trokker, you're sacked. You're going! But thank you for your efforts. I think we should celebrate your contribution to the success of the organisation over the past years and give you a little something that you deserve." He pressed a button on his desk, and almost instantaneously his assistant, Janice, walked through the door carrying a bottle and two glasses. She placed them on the small table in front of the window, turned to Sniphle, and with eye contact and an emphasised slow nod to her boss, exited. Sniphle once again looked at his watch. "Now, let's go through yesterday's events, shall we?" He retrieved a paper from his desk, looked down on it for a few seconds, and began. "As I am given to understand, it was you that gave the orders to start the girls' travel program."

Trokker looked down and nodded.

"Is that a Yes, or No?"

Such was his tone that, head down, she said, "Yes!"

Sniphle, with a calm, expressionless face, continued, "Now, just so I get things right and not blame anyone else. It was you who should have double-checked the Prep-Team's set points on the AI, and you did not." Pausing, "Am I correct?"

She nodded again, then softly, "Yes."

"As the Senior Director in the room, it was you who was responsible for giving the girl her briefing prior to the commencement."

This time Trokker protested a little. "Sir! The last time I attended one of these, it was a junior that gave the briefing and you," glancing up at him, "you, sir, were the senior in the room."

He rounded on her with narrowed eyes. "That's because I gave him orders to do it, as part of his training. Before you start on me, I saw him giving the briefing and have footage to prove it. But let's not get away from the subject of you and Luna's loss. You didn't give her the briefing... did you?"

Beaten, Trokker looked down once again and nodded.

Again, his eyes narrowed at her response, and he spat, "Yes or No!"

"No, I didn't give her the briefing." With that, she looked to the window and the serene green trees leading to hills high on the horizon.

Sniphle returned the sheet to its folder, waited a moment, then nodded and said, "Okay, done! I just needed your confirmation of the events." He turned to the security guard. "Can you open the champagne and pour out two glasses?" Lying to the guard, he said, "I would offer you a glass, but you're on duty and we follow protocols here, don't we?"

Once the drinks poured, he nodded to the security officer to leave. With the door closed behind the guard, Sniphle went to his desk, picked out a recording device and switched it off. "This is evidence of our conversation... for the record."

He sauntered over to where Trokker was sitting, collected his glass, and toasted a token "Cheers." In return, she gave a low volume return, "Cheers."

He looked at his watch once more and sat down. "Now, we don't want you telling anyone else what we do here, do we? So, I have taken the precaution of ensuring you do not give any information about this facility to anyone." Without giving her a chance to speak, he continued, "I asked Janice to offer you a coffee prior to coming in here." Malicious in his tone, he smiled before sneering. "We poisoned it! Now, had you not confirmed any of yesterday's facts, I would have given you an antidote with the champagne, but poor you, you did not, so you are going to die." Once more he glanced down, looked at his watch, and noted, "In an extremely short time."

She looked at him, then through the glass, to which he mockingly commented, "No, not the champagne, but the coffee. Janice will have cleaned, disposed of, and replaced the coffee cup already, so there will be no evidence in case of an investigation. Now, do you want to jump out of the window before you go into a painful spasm, or shall I get the guard?"

A rising terror began within her psyche. She responded, "The autopsy will show poison in my system."

"No, it won't. You should know, part of our work here is chemical compounds, and we have scoured the earth for all kinds of substances. When mixed properly, we can do almost anything with them... as you know." His malevolent smile grew broader.

Trokker was not one to panic, but unstoppable terror held her speechless as she mentally waded through her options.

She grasped the situation, as he seemed to have thought of everything, knowing that without an antidote, she would soon be dead. But terror eroded her calm exterior. She rose, noticing how time seemed to have slowed, before looking Sniphle in the eye. As panic arose, her breath became shallow, and she felt the first of the numbing effects of the dose they had given her. In a desperate need to escape, she said, "Can I visit the loo? I desperately need to pee."

Within his dark, psychotic mind, pleased with his planning, he grinned at her and said, "It won't matter," shaking his head while leering ever more. Then, almost in light humour and in admiration of what he had planned, he reached for a button on his desk. "Now will you jump, or shall we help you?"

The terror had found its level. Her body, now in uncontrolled tremors, overcame any coherent thoughts. She launched herself in desperation at him with a glass in hand, at the same time putting all her efforts into eye-bulging fits of screaming for as loud and long as she could. The screaming lasted until the guard threw her out the window. Many silent witnesses remembered how she screamed all the way down until almost severing her head as it smashed into a small wall 20 floors below. The rest of her body splattered itself against the pavement milliseconds later, leaving her broken body with no recognisable form.

23
Never-Ending Pathways

The Directors gathered around Luna's bed, each with their own expertise, wondering what the next step should be. She had been in a semi-comatose state for 12 days and was showing extreme signs of an impending cerebral breakdown. Newly promoted, Ranghan stepped forward and, giving no opinion counted as positive or negative, began. He reported on her brainwave records, showing the worrying slide in her daily activity. He described that at first, in the first few days of her being locked in, her REM and brain activity were far greater than any of the other Specials. She was recording spells of eight- or nine-hour stints of REM, followed by four or five-hour quiet periods, which Ranghan called sleep mode. However, over the twelve days, this had diminished to just over an hour REM, with the rest of the 24-hour period as what seemed in sleep mode.

Sniphle looked up to Dr Abbott. "What do you have, Susie? How is her physical wellbeing?"

The doctor looked down at her records, then presented a series of physical parameters normal for Luna prior to her incident. Dr Abbott followed this by showing a set conducted only thirty minutes before the meeting. She cast her eyes up to the expectant Sniphle. "Unlike the other

Specials' conditions, overall, Luna was in an excellent physical state. However, we've noted a decline in her musculature that includes her heart showing the odd blip. I'm not happy about the way things are going. There is a significant decline." With her report complete, she closed her tablet page and looked to Sniphle, saying nothing else. But her face was stony and her eyes deadpan, giving him an emphasis on how critical things were.

Sniphle looked to the last member of the directors involved with Luna's ongoing situation, Dr Bennon. Without prompting, Bennon gave his assessment. "We've tried to recall her frequently, and as you know; we have had no response. We've tried an entire series of our known medications. We also tried them in differing dosages, and unfortunately nothing has worked." He looked up from his tablet. "We're at a complete loss as to what to do next."

A glum, stony-faced Sniphle took it in silence. "What about you, Nurse?" Looking at Senior Nurse Roberts, he asked, "Have you anything to add?"

She shook her head. "These people are far more qualified than me," nodding to the others and continued. "As much as the other nurses and I have grown to take Luna into our hearts, we have nothing more to offer. Like you, we're all genuinely concerned about the situation."

Sniphle nodded, as if taking each of their reports into his head, filing them, sorting them, and ticking off each of the reports, rechecking fact against fact. He began, "We don't entirely understand how these Specials operate, but they are essential to our business. As I understand it, when we engage them to go on a mission, they travel outside their own bodies by entering a realm we can only try to understand. The facts are the facts; they can bring back information when there is no other way. They have proved they can travel anywhere, and I mean *anywhere*. With Denzel, we have the irrefutable fact that he died, and his spirit has now entered the body of a man-made human generated from a selection of DNA. These Specials we use to gather data can talk to the spirits of the dead and understand their problems."

For once, Sniphle was without a thought of what to do next, but voiced his inner views. "They can gather the afterlife spirits together and get them to go with them on journeys, wherever that may be, be it down a mine shaft or to the moon. We can get them to do almost anything. But at the moment, they do not understand what they are capable of; if they did, they would be dangerous... to us. Therefore, we need to keep them under control and their physical bodies reliant on our medications."

Sniphle remembered who he was with, and glanced around at the others and waited, allowing them to understand what he had said. "The Specials have opened a door for humanity to continue life far beyond our normal spans." Raising two fingers on each hand, he said, "Three score years and ten, as they thought in the past."

The youngest, Dr Abbott, frowned, to which Dr Bennon breathed, "Seventy years."

"Director Sniphle, where are you going with this?" questioned Ranghan.

Sniphle slowly breathed in and looked round to the others, who noticed a telltale tic in his left eye, triggering an unpleasant grin that spread across his face. "These are our bread and butter. When they go, expire, die, we have no one to replace them."

With malice, his jaw set and venom colouring his face red, he said. "What Trokker did before she implanted herself on the pavement outside our building was that she incapacitated the best Special, namely Luna." He shifted his stance drawing them to pay attention, "Therefore, we need you to redouble your efforts and bring her out of the state she's in, doing no further harm to her. I want you all involved and any decisions you come to; I want them peer-reviewed before we implement anything. Got it?"

In unison, all nodded their heads and voiced a yes.

Meanwhile Luna, though embedded and lost within the never-ending passages, awoke from a sleep, no longer searching for a way out, knowing she had already covered many of the passages and caverns within this place. *Although I search, travelling through the passages, some splitting into many, becoming impossibly smaller, if I follow routes that lead to larger passages, I end up in the opening and closing chambers and sometimes into the area of electrical discharges. If I look closely at the opening and closing chambers, it's almost like the opening and closing of a goldfish's mouth, regular and rhythmical.*

Without understanding where she was, she found her despair deepening, clouding out any rational ideas. Her psyche reached into depressing corners of her mind. It turned her wanting to escape from this endless series of pulsating caverns, passages, and tight chambers into a spiralling hopelessness. More and more depressed, she felt drawn to go home and out of this area, while feeling this was the place to be, that it was her home, and she was here to stay.

Her increasing depression caused her to rest more often in a quiet place where she might sleep. *I feel too exhausted to go further. My head is full. I'm alone again.*

Sniphle took Janice with him to take notes on the contents of his next meeting and to remind himself of critical issues. He always had problems with his recent meetings with Triton. The number one Special had somehow gained an advantage over him, and yet, he didn't know how it had happened. Although having a physical advantage over him by controlling his medicinal dosages, Triton always seemed to come out of their meetings with the upper hand, no matter how bodily disadvantaged he was. This time, he would take Janice to help him keep his agenda pointed in the direction he wanted.

For once, Sniphle knocked at Triton's door before entering. From just inside the room, he said, "Triton, can I ask you to do us a great service?" Approaching closer, he sat on one of the two soft seats in Triton's room, gesturing to Janice to do the same. "I'm sorry. I didn't introduce you to my personal assistant, Janice Dove. She's here to take a few notes and to remind me of any issues I may have forgotten."

Triton turned onto his back and worked the bed controls to get himself into a sitting position. The duty nurse, Margret, rearranged his pillows, making him acceptably comfortable, and stood to one side. Irritated, Sniphle, never wanting too many witnesses to meetings, directed her to leave, saying, "Margret, we shouldn't be too long, maybe an hour." He then instructed Janice to make sure the door and its peep-window curtain secured.

With Janice to give him a little more confidence, Sniphle didn't exert his sneering stance and quietly said, "Triton, our friend Denzel has been a magnificent success. We want to take his example further. There are some extraordinarily rich people in the world, and we would like to help them... of course, they would recompense us for our services." Triton remained quiet, with a look he had developed for Sniphle's meetings, a smile not dissimilar to that of the Mona Lisa, maintaining it with only the occasional lazy blink of his heavy eyelids.

But Sniphle remained calm, trying to get to his point. "Since we got back from the South Seas and secured a legality to placing ephemeral spirits into DNA-shells, we now need paying customers to get the entire thing going." He looked into Triton's eyes to see if there was any response, but seeing none, continued. "The rich have money, but when they die, the recipients of their wills get the wealth. Therefore, unless we get them to tie over the money to the DNA-shell before they die, we and they will not benefit. It's a tough sell trying to convince them to sign their money over to an almost brain-dead assembled DNA-shell." He looked at the notes and to Janice, who nodded. "We can take another path first. I believe we can first target any obnoxiously wealthy families with a terminally ill child, husband, wife, or relative whom they may want to keep alive but can't. We can offer these unfortunate people a new body once they die. In that way, the rich can keep their ill-got gains once the spirit transfer takes place." He smiled at the irresistible nature of the idea of proposing to a traumatised mother the hope that her child would live instead of dying before her.

Triton responded in a bored way, apparently having no genuine interest in what Sniphle was saying. "So why are you telling me?"

This pleased Sniphle. He had a response ready and said, "I would like you and the two other boys, Ariel and Arche, to search out these wealthy people and report back who has a... a terminal... problem."

"And what's in it for us?"

The sneering aspect of Sniphle reasserted itself and disregarded Triton's response. "I'll come to that. But think of it—these wealthy families have children who have nothing to aspire to. When they finally get to an age when they think about what comes next, many are already down the slippery path of self-destruction. Smashed-up cars, drug addiction, the recipients of blackmail pressures, lack of intellect, you name it. These children rarely have what it takes to maintain their parents' long-laid plans, unless they get past those awful first years of adulthood."

At last, Janice spoke up. Moving forward, she said, "The parents want what is good for their children, but it's heartbreaking to see their kids lay their own paths to an early grave."

Sniphle, sour-faced, looked to her, his eyes telling her to remain quiet, then said, "We can help them. The children will have a fresh start with a new clean body, with the chance to learn from their earlier mistakes." He sat back in his chair and looked over at Janice, then nervously back to Triton. "Well, what do you think?"

Triton responded, showing Sniphle he was way ahead of him already. "I already understood this before you took Denzel to get his new passport. There are many other options available for this process, but you know you can only achieve it if we Specials introduce the spirit of the dead person to the DNA-shell." His eyes refused to blink, leaving only the enigmatic Mona Lisa expression.

Sniphle reacted to his irritating nervous tic, noticeably twitching his left eye. He thought, *Triton has me again*, but added a bit of humour to his view, pleased he wasn't playing poker against him. "Yes, I know you're the only people who can do this. But I would like to assure you all that we will offer you the same... of course, without payment."

Triton at once responded. "What else?"

Triton's reaction caused a nervousness in Sniphle, and he forgot what else. He looked to Janice, who offhandedly gave her boss the notes, who fumbled with them before saying, "Eh, what else. Oh, yes. I meant all the Specials. You three men, plus the six women and the girl, Luna."

Triton's eyes sharpened, fixing on Sniphle, as he said, "About Luna. She's new; I've heard she is younger than the rest of us Specials. Where did she come from?... She's not like the rest of us, is she?" There was a concerned reaction from both his visitors, prompting his Mona Lisa guise to become intense, frowning, inquisitive. Thrusting his head forward, Triton, raising his voice, demanded, "Tell me about Luna. You're hiding something."

Both looked at each other, pondering whether to tell, but Sniphle knew they couldn't deny Triton. Sniphle knew he had to explain part of the story of what had happened, and knew he couldn't lie, as Triton would see through any deception. Hesitantly, he relayed the complete story of how the girl came into her current reduced physical and mental condition, but left out her earlier history. Triton became more animated, with more fire in his words and a matching facial expression. "How is she now?"

Sniphle, although concerned, didn't want Triton to have the total story. He said, "As of an hour ago, there was no change; although, to be honest, we *are* a little worried about her situation."

Triton reverted to his expressionless self and said, "Director, I have understood your earlier presentation and will talk to the others about what you're proposing. I'm calling this meeting over; you may leave now." He readjusted his bed down to its reclined level, turned, and adopted his foetal position.

Janice and Sniphle remained in silence for a few moments, and eventually both grasped that the meeting was, in fact, over. She was first to rise and stood while the shocked Director haltingly made his way to his feet and followed her through the open door.

24
Daddy

Triton called for Margret, remembering their previous night's conversation. "Margret, we've done something terrible, really terrible. If Luna should die, it will haunt us for the rest of our lives." Triton looked up from his bed and into his nurse's troubled face said, "Yes, I know you switched the power off and on for a little fun. We planned it that way. But the consequences are out of this world, and I truly mean out of this world." He reached over to her hand and pulled it towards him. "I must reach her somehow, but getting to her may be beyond me now. I'm too reliant on the medication. In the past, I would have been able to travel without too much prompting." He gripped her hand a little more tightly and looked into her filling eyes. "I'll try to reach her without it, but if I can't, we'll have to get some meds from somewhere, somehow."

She nodded, saying nothing, only silently continuing her remaining duties until finished. As she closed his door, she turned back and heard him say, "Okay, let's try to get back to my teenage years and begin my free travels once more."

However, try as he might, he couldn't get to the place where he was free to travel without the medication. Although he made progress, Triton fell short, and inevitably he relaxed into sleep. When he awoke, Ngoosi was there with his evening snack. Puzzled, he said, "Ngoosi, how are you? Long time since you were here. Is Margret off duty?"

With a worried face, Ngoosi said, "No, I'm your new temporary carer. They've taken Margret off the Specials roster. They assigned her to the DNA-shells."

He sat up, his eyes darting while thinking through how this could be, and said, "What? Why is that?"

"I'm not sure. It happened suddenly, but there was talk of her being in the meds lock-up room. As you know, only the Directors are allowed there. I guess they have to follow rules until there's been an investigation... who knows?" Busying her way round him, making sure all was okay, she cautiously asked. "Do you know about Salena and Luna?"

Triton responded, realising it must have been Ngoosi who had gone with Luna to see Salena initially, "Luna came to me just as they were sending her to travel. She told me Salena was still alive, and that I was her father. Is that true?"

"Yes, it was me who took her to Salena's, at an address on the outskirts of town. I was there when Salena came to the door, and the pair of them just fell into each other's arms. Luna and I stayed most of the day, just catching up. I promised to take her back as soon as we could make it after she brought you up to date."

She waited for Triton's response, but only saw him taking in her words, as if logging them. She changed the subject more towards Luna. "I also understand Luna isn't doing too well, and we're all concerned about her." With tears filling her dark eyes, and in a tumble of words, she relayed as much of the gossip she had heard, telling him of Luna's locked-in syndrome and that the Directors were giving Sniphle hourly updates.

Triton, new to the locked-in syndrome, responded almost sternly, "Quick, you had better get Sniphle in here now. I don't want any of the others here until I talk to him. Ngoosi, please don't let on to any of the Directors about what you know. It's important for all of us."

She could see at once he had something urgent in mind, and with no further discussion, she turned and was out into the corridor and down the few steps to Sniphle's office.

Sniphle dropped what he was doing and was at Triton's bedside in moments. "Is something wrong?"

"Why didn't you tell me just how bad Luna's situation is?" He waited a few moments for a response, but Sniphle wasn't sure what to say. Triton put him out of his misery, angrily shouting, "She's locked in!" Triton waited a moment before he answered the question himself, shouting, "Yes?"

Sniphle felt a wave of embarrassment sweep over him as he felt a flush of sweat on the back of his neck, knowing now he should have told Triton earlier. On looking down, he answered. "Yes, she seems to be locked in."

For the first time since Sniphle had known Triton, he caught a blaze of anger directed at him. In fury, Triton fired at the Director, "You should have known what you were playing at. You've already done this with Denzel! We invited his spirit into a body, albeit a DNA-shell, and you asked him if he could exit. The answer was...?" He looked at Sniphle, inviting an answer.

The subdued Director answered, "No... Denzel wasn't able to get back out."

Triton began again. "She's locked in and can't get out. To make matters worse, I understand you didn't tell her where she was being sent! That means she can't get out, and to make matters worse yet, she doesn't even know where she is. She's absolutely lost! If she follows just the veins and arteries in her body, she will be on a one-hundred-thousand-kilometre journey without knowing to *where*." His eyes became hostile under his brow. "Someone ought to be shot for this fuck-up." He waited a moment, seeing Sniphle reflect the memory of Trokker. "What are you going to do about it?"

Sniphle remained silent for a long time before he summoned the courage, and at last said, "To be honest with you, we've run out of options."

Triton tried to sit up further in his bed. Swiftly aided by Ngoosi, he started, "I recommend you send me in there to get her out. As it's not my body, if I can reach her spirit, I should be able to guide her out, much like the other Specials when we guide ghost-spirits."

Sniphle at last found his voice and said, "Like you, Triton, I am anxious about her, but I'm also worried about losing you too. The risk is too great... I just can't let you go."

"In that case, I will instruct the Specials to withdraw our help in gathering and guiding the ghost-spirits. Your proposed DNA-shell business will die before its birth." Triton smiled and looked into the Director's face.

The psychotic devil in Sniphle sprang out as if at last finding Triton's weakness. "Remember, Triton, we have the power to force you to do as we direct!"

Instantly Triton replied sternly, "Yes, you can send us to wherever you want us to go, but when we get there, it's our call. We try to help those poor spirits; you just want to use them to gain power and money for yourselves. No, Director Sniphle, you *don't* have complete control over us."

Sniphle could see that Triton had once again outmanoeuvred him. Head down, he nodded, as if in consultation with himself. "Okay. She's the future. She's important, but let's all be exceptionally careful. I'll organise your Prep-Team to get everything set up ASAP."

Preparation, although hurried, was checked and double checked before Sniphle nodded his head towards Ranghan. Triton lay as he usually did when being readied for the journey. He felt the first of the injections, followed by the buzz of its chemicals beginning their journey. He waited. Next, he would feel his body twitch a little, a process he and the others hated. Then came the instruction to travel. This was the part he enjoyed; first the feeling as the chemicals rose through his body towards his brain, then the numb fuzz of not knowing. Finally, the release to travel. Now he was away, first looking down at his bed and at the white coats around him, seeming to question each other whether he was travelling at all. *No time for them. I must get to Luna.*

In her room, he found her with Dr Abbott, accompanied by Senior Nurse Roberts, both actively checking the AI and her physical self. From what Denzel had said, there were different methods of entering a body, depending on what you were trying to achieve. To become part of the body, you had to assimilate, not just expect it to accommodate you. He thought back, remembering. *We should become at one with each other, mind and body, but if I achieve this, it will be hard to find a route out.* Worried, Triton knew to enter tentatively.

Now where am I... where am I? he thought once he had. Despite the many years he had travelled, this differed vastly from anything before. There were many things going past in a rush... no, a flow. *This must be her bloodstream... but where is her spirit?* For a brief time, he allowed himself to get carried along, and instinctively knew it would be impossible to catch her among these flowing corridors and in the cavernous places they sometimes emptied into. *Think; there must be another way.* Then it came to him: just talk to her.

As he had done before, he remained quiet for a brief time while he gathered his mind together, cutting through the surrounding chaos. "Luna! Luna, can you hear me? I'm here; it's me, Triton."

He repeated his call a few more times before there came the unmistakable signature of her entering his mind. With a sad, slow voice, he heard Luna say, "Help... I'm so sick. I'm so lonely."

"Luna, it's Triton. Do you know where you are?"

At first, thinking it was a hallucination, Luna replied and said in a rush, "Oh! Daddy, where are you? I'm lonely. What is this place? Help me!" Feeling a need to protect her newfound father, she added. "But be careful. There are so many passages and openings. Don't get lost; remember where you are before you move."

He felt an unexpected release of tension and a sense of great relief. "Luna, you're caught in your own body. Relax and just keep talking to me, and I'll find you." With her voice filling his head, he relaxed himself and allowed his senses to absorb her words more and more. His senses gravitated towards her until he found her mind filling into his own.

"Hello, my wonderful daughter—you're no longer lost! I've found you." He allowed a little time for her to respond, but nothing came from her. He voiced in his head once more, "Shall we go? Let's get out of here and go somewhere!"

Suddenly his head overflowed with a loudness as she filled his senses, almost blinding him to other thoughts. "Yes, take me out of here. I want freedom from here—get me out! Stay with me, don't leave without me, I was so afraid! Oh, Daddy! I've been so lonely." Her almost overwhelming presence crowded out his own. He tried to concentrate on his first aim: getting them out of there. He remained calm, even though her personal pleas bombarded him. As coolly as he was able, he thrust aside her barrage and called out to her, 'Please try to relax; together we can make it, but stay with me. I first have to manage our way out of here. Some of your thoughts are trying to keep us here, so stay with me.'

She knew what he was telling her and found a quiet place to allow him to focus his efforts.

He concentrated as best he could, thinking only of escaping her body as it closed in on her spirit. He focused and allowing himself to assemble his spirit above her still body, noted the carers still busying themselves around her. Once settled, he asked, "Luna, are you still with me?"

At first, struggling to respond with her word-thoughts, Luna at last replied in a gush of relief. "Oh yes, thank you, thank you, thank you. I thought I was in that place forever."

Relieved, his inner tension quieted before finding a little humour, attempting to lighten her thoughts of dread and subsequent relief: "It's your own body, remember; it's just that they lost you in the plumbing."

Luna felt overheated, and in her agitated state, a clumsy jumble of words began tumbling out and into Triton's mind. "I want to get away from here with you. Let's travel out and away, across the land and sea, into the clouds. I want to show you the sunshine, the dawn, the sunset. Let's see it all. Stay with me; I don't want to be lonely anymore."

A little hesitant at first, Triton said, "Luna, I'm not sure I can. Their directive to me was to go into your body and bring you out if I could. Their medication gives me the drive to do this and go to that specific location. I can't do it on my own any longer. I don't have the willpower to escape their clutches."

With a new sharpness, Luna responded calmly, "Okay, let's try together. This time, you stay with me." Silent for a moment, a new idea came to her. "Let's go see Mummy together. I can show you where she is." Then, pausing with doubt, she asked, "Do you want to?"

For the first time in his memory, he relied on someone else to guide his way. "If I can, I will," he responded. "If I can lead you out of that place, then perhaps you can lead me to her. So, lead away, my wonderful daughter; let's at least try."

She waited for him to occupy her thoughts, then turned away from her still body and headed for the door, asking, 'Are you still with me?'

Unusually for Sniphle, he seemed on edge in front of the rest of the team. When entering Triton's room, he found Ranghan and the nursing staff monitoring both Triton's AI console and Luna's remote displays. "What are the signs?

How are they doing?" He looked to the AI console and up to Ranghan, watching it.

Ranghan's response was, for once, assertive as he explained that the heart rates for both were elevated, but not into their stress levels. Both had REM, but it seemed relaxed; their brain activity was also within the excited range, yet nothing was out of the normal levels, judging from their historical records. Sniphle reached for something else to take his thoughts away from the tension. "While we're here waiting, let's discuss their overall health. From the records, I see that Triton's decline is slowing a little; how are the other Specials doing?"

"One moment." Ranghan looked at his tablet and scanned through, bringing no answer for a time, aware that any slip of error did not go down well with his boss. At last, he found the right combinations of data he needed. He replied, "Here we are. As we suspected, they're all in decline at approximately the same rate, although the females are slipping into the decline faster than Arche and Ariel. If they continue to decline at the same rates, I think they'll only have another four to five years with us. The gather-and-transport routines they perform now will markedly decline in number and quantity. I think it probable that within three to four years, they will become unreliable." He remained silent over his tablet, waiting for Sniphle's response. But there was none, only his eyes moving without focusing on anything in particular.

"Just keep me up to date on their decline, no matter what mood I'm in," he said at last. "I want a weekly report posted and issued to all senior staff, is that clear?"

Ranghan both nodded and voiced his acknowledgement of the glum Sniphle's statement. Sniphle turned and left the room, calling back to the others, "As soon as either Triton or Luna comes out, I want to know at once!"

Luna called to Triton once more in her mind, "Daddy, are you still with me?"

She repeated her call a few times until he eventually responded. "Yes, I think I can do this on my own, but I need you as a guide. So just remain with me until I give you a confirmation." She waited a few moments before there came a call in her head. "I'm free and travelling with you now."

Luna followed her normal routine, down the shiny corridor and out through the window, out over the houses below. 'Are you still with me?'

For the first time in a decade, Triton felt an excitement that, had he a physical body, would have had him in a breathless sweat. "Yes, I'm following you now. So where to?"

"Mummy."

25
The Centurion Club

A chance remark from one of the staff in the accounting office of the D.O. facility sharpened the ears of the ever-avaricious Sniphle. When running through the figures for the proposed plan to extract funds from the wealthy to provide them with new life, the office junior complained that the signed-up wealthy individuals were only a small proportion of the worldwide populace. "Why not offer this possibility to as many as we can?" he asked. There were factions within the marketing department who argued for exclusivity. Sniphle mulled over the comments of the junior accountant and came across an idea to create a 100-club, ensuring he would always have a waiting market.

Sniphle gave his presentation to a group of 100 people whom he addressed as *the Centurions*. "I... that is, we at the Director Organisation can assure all of you will live far past your one-hundredth birthday." From the stage, he smiled at the attendees, "With your marbles all in place." He smiled again as he jokingly rotated his finger round his temple. "That is... If you sign up with us."

They took in his mirth, enjoying his informative performance, which hinted at eternal life for those on the scheme. He paraded Denzel as proof of the presentation, inviting them to quiz the famous artist. Many remembered

Denzel's earlier life, when he had rubbed shoulders with some of the attendees—and sometimes went beyond just rubbing shoulders.

After Denzel's presentation, there followed a cocktail hour where Directors, guests, and a few other invitees mingled, discussing in groups what they were being offered. It was during this time that the whole assembly grasped that what the team of Directors had claimed was true, with Denzel being proof. There followed side meetings with individuals, each shown an example contract, allowing some to examine the fine print. Although some items drew a negative response overall, they considered it fair. And while trying to keep the seminar as light-hearted as possible, Sniphle reminded guests that to be part of the Centurions Club, they would need to stump up an initial $100,000 as a non-refundable deposit. As they signed the documents and handed over their cheques, he gave each of them a bag of 100 marbles as mementos.

Of the hundred guests, only a handful declined the offer, some claiming God's will would be their fate. But to the Directors, their reluctance to sign was insignificant, as was their number. The event was a complete success and would allow them to fund the South Seas project without digging into company funds.

With the fruitful meeting concluded, the senior staff remained within the confines of the hired hotel conference room, doors closed. Those Directors who stayed behind casually sat around a large circular table cleared of the cocktail titbits and congratulated themselves, giving particular praise to both Sniphle and Denzel. The initial enthusiasm subsided, numbed by the naturally pessimistic members, reminding them all the days of the group of Specials. All knew of their built-in limited life expectancy, but again, the enthusiasm generated by the pot of gold blinded them to reality. Now, with the promise of money beyond their imagination generated by some of the richest people in the world looking towards eternal life, a certainty was dawning.

The Organisation had just taken deposits of nearly ten million dollars. Now they needed to fulfil their part of the contracts. Sniphle drew up a time frame to accommodate these deposits. First, they would need to generate sufficient DNA-shells, which would take almost two years to grow. However, DNA-shells from other sources were available in an emergency. Once their own manufactured DNA-shells were ready, it was just the waiting for their customer's demise. After a Centurion death, the Specials would meet and collect the spirit, then guide them and ready them for implanting into the DNA-shell. Without the Specials, it couldn't be done—and time was not on their side. Sniphle had known this from the outset. He was now trying to put together a contingency plan if timing did not go to schedule.

His first thought was to rush through the building of the DNA-shell facility on New Bismarck. If the timing of that was slower than required, he had seven DNA-shells available, but could purchase others from other laboratories. However, he wouldn't have control of their physical attributes if the customer wanted specific characteristics.

The next problem was the timing of the customer's death. If they had a terminal illness, he would have to ensure there was no attempt to keep them alive. Should they suffer from a severe mental breakdown? What then? Whether it was via a progressive illness or stroke, allowing the body to remain healthy, what then? His thoughts turned to euthanasia in any form that would satisfy his plan. There was so much to consider now. His head was in a spin.

Sniphle's principal problem, however, was the limited longevity of the Specials themselves.

"Could we clone them?" was his question, but the longevity problem stemming back to the 20th century and the famous Dolly the Sheep came up. He reminded himself that there had been problems with her being brought up in an enclosed facility. They euthanized poor Dolly to save her suffering when she reached only half her normal life expectancy.

Denzel reminded him of an unproven truth: "Nature is not an easy bedfellow, especially if it's her bed."

26
Daddy, this is Mummy

They travelled together much as the Specials travelled with the companion ghost spirits, both aware of each other, almost melding into one. This was Luna's second celestial trip to the house. She remembered the layout and guided Triton through the front door and into the room with the enormous TV screen and comfortable chairs gathered around. Ferdinand, lazily sitting in a soft chair, felt their presence, but continued his focus on the gaming screen, ignored them. Luna glided towards the kitchen, where they found the figure of Pan, now aware of them, but going into spasm at first sight. The noise he generated called Ferdinand away from his concentration to see the helpless man as he gyrated. "Salena," he shouted repeatedly until they heard movement from the staircase. But to her, only Pan's body appeared, writhing on the floor. His spirit was out, and aware of the father and daughter.

"Why are you here?" He paused, looking at Triton suspiciously. Then, catching Luna's eye, he pointed at Triton. "Who is this?"

"Pan, you remember me, I'm Luna. I came with Ngoosi in my physical form a week ago or so."

"Yes, I remember all that, but who is *this?*" His spiritual form again pointed to where Triton hovered.

In her understanding of Pan's limited social skills, Luna projected her thoughts to him in a calming tone, saying, "It's Triton. He's my father. Do you remember when Salena, Ngoosi, and I were talking about him when I was last here?"

At that point, Salena came into the room and did her best to calm Pan as he lay writhing. However, his spirit-self was mentally aware and spoke to Luna, "Yes, I remember." He remained quiet for a moment and continued, "Although my body is weak, I'm aware of most of what goes on while I'm in this state. You know, Salena can't see you, and I don't think she's aware of the spirit world except for what you told her last time." He was quiet a moment, as if thinking, and asked, "Do you want me to tell her about you both when I recover from this?" pointing to his own body writhing on the floor.

"Yes, thank you. Please tell her I was here with Triton to show him she's alive and well, contrary to what Sniphle and the Directors told him."

Salena, though, was aware of something going on. Although she was dealing with the consequences of Pan's fit, she felt something else was happening. "Luna, are you here? Is there any way you can give me a sign if you are?"

She waited, but both Luna and Triton found it beyond themselves to make anything happen in the physical world.

Triton stopped. He instinctively knew they weren't getting through to her, and instead took in the changes of his former love: her breasts a little fuller, her waist a little larger, her dyed blond hair showing its distinct tinge of red at the roots. He remembered her sharp eyes displaying her innate intelligence within her weary, creased face. Smiling to himself, he recalled an old uncle who had once told him about women, "It's not what they look like, it's what's between their ears." He gauged her anew. *Yes, she's the woman I fell in love with and probably still love. Luna's right: we need to get back to a life in the physical and not this spirit world, where we're at the beck and call of our puppet masters.*

The pair drew back from Pan, still in seizure, with Salena trying to minister to him. Hesitantly Luna began, "We should give them room. Maybe we should leave and come back in our physical forms," but at that moment, Triton broke into her thoughts.

"I'm getting a pull-back from the Directors; I can feel it. They've given my body the return injection. Maybe I've been away a long time, trying to hunt for you back at the facility. Perhaps the directors were getting worried!"

Luna responded, "Then we'd better go, and I had better show myself as being found."

As they retraced their steps, they followed Triton's return speed. She turned to him, becoming lost in her concern that she might not see him again, but knowing she would. Her whole being wanted to stay with him and was desperate to do so. While she knew she would rejoin him when they had recovered from the travel, she dearly wanted to hug him now. She needed the physical contact, despite knowing that in their present form, it was impossible.

Upon arriving back at the facility, they glanced at each other, agreeing it was time to return to their own rooms. At their beds, each looked down and began settling back into their quiet bodies.

At once, a commotion erupted around each of their rooms at the realisation that both were starting to re-emerge.

The Directors present went for their communicators to summon Sniphle, while the nursing staff looked to the AI to confirm that all bodily functions were working within their set parameters.

Sniphle rushed first to Triton's room, which was closest to his office, and pushed through the attending Directors. "Good afternoon, Triton. Congratulations: you did it, we got her back. I'm told she's still drowsy and has said nothing yet, but her eyes tell us she's back."

He forced himself to calm down. Triton, aware of the pressure for him to relay all he had achieved, held up his hand. Disregarding their questions, he asked, "Can I talk to her?"

Defensively and without thinking, Sniphle automatically said "No."

Triton, however, found a new resolve and vehemently insisted, "I want to talk to her. You take me to her bed, now! It's important."

Nodding, Sniphle, without understanding, instructed Ranghan to wheel Triton to Luna's bedside.

When they had come to a stop by her bed, Triton looked at Ranghan and insisted, "Leave us alone for a few moments. I want to reach out with her before you lot give her a complete physical and psychological run-through."

"Yes, of course." With that, Ranghan left, not thinking Triton might have an agenda.

"Hello, Luna. Are you back with us, okay?" Triton asked earnestly.

"Yes... Daddy."

"Shush, don't say that while the others are around. At the moment, I don't trust any of the Directors."

With the fear her loneliness would return once he had gone, she pleaded with him, "Please hug me. I've been so lonely... I just need you to be with me. Please don't go," she implored. Unsteadily, he stood out of his wheelchair and hugged her as she reached out with her arms wide and inviting. She whispered in his ear, "Let's get back to see Mummy as soon as we can."

While the thought of returning to Salena was paramount, he also knew it would bring dangers Luna couldn't conceive at present. "Yes, we need to get back to see her as soon as we can, but we'll have to plan it cautiously. You can't trust these people, and the last thing we need is to lose her now that we've found her. Let's stay in contact, and as we see the opportunities arise, we'll discuss it before we act. Two heads are better than one, especially when dealing with Sniphle and Co."

The pair filled each other's heads with questions and tried to give their answers as best they could, but there were large holes within their histories that no amount of talk could fill. Eventually, Ngoosi and Bong, accompanied by Ranghan, entered the room and broke up their talkfest. "Luna, we have to carry out some tests to see if we have all of you back," said the grinning nurse.

Ranghan spoke openly to Triton. "The Director says we should do a debrief to find out what happened, and to learn your approach toward finding her, and then the recovery."

Triton nodded while going through various scenarios of what to tell the man. He turned to Luna and said pointedly, "You remember nothing other than being lost, me finding you, and coming straight out to your bed... do you?"

She looked up into his eyes and without hesitation said, "No, I remember nothing else."

Meanwhile, Ranghan looked from one to the other, trying to gauge whether something covert was occurring, but couldn't tell.

27
An Invitation from NASA

Sniphle was having an excellent day. NASA had contacted him and invited him to their head offices for a meeting with their lead administrator. Also present would be his immediate deputy, plus the Human Exploration and Operations Head. He accepted their invitation, but never went to any meeting without being pre-armed. He stood up from his chair, glanced at the clock, sat down again, and excitedly jabbed the intercom and said, "Janice, hold all calls. I'm going to go see Triton—we need to find out what these people want before we enter the lion's den. I've heard stories about some of their methods of data gathering, and leaving small people broken in their wake."

For Triton, it was a welcome break to visit NASA, albeit as an uninvited and unknown visitor. Hovering through corridors, noting offices, conference rooms, and laboratories, he homed in on his task. While the task took a little time to arrange, he listened to a discussion with the three administrators following an innocent call from the D.O. earlier. Sniphle had phoned to ask the subject of the upcoming meeting, and whether he should come armed with any relevant materials. Following the call, the three NASA administrators met and discussed all aspects of the planned meeting, unaware that Triton was in their room taking his mental notes.

Once back in the director's facility, Sniphle asked Triton, "So, what do they want?"

"They've noticed your Centurions meeting with the hyper-rich and want to go a little farther with the concept." He described all aspects of the Administrator's internal meeting.

Sniphle wanted more. "Go on, what exactly do they have in mind?"

With more details, Triton spoke up a little more forcefully. "I know I've been lying in bed for the past decade, but I know the basics of what state this Earth of ours is in. We have an unsustainable way of life here now. Temperatures are rising out of control. Deserts are growing; the mistakes of Big Pharma and Big Farming are needing payback. Fisheries aren't making the comebacks predicted. Yet humans are still breeding uncontrolled. In short, all of us know we're running out of time, but nothing's happened about it so far." Triton looked to Sniphle and could see the Director had no genuine interest in anything he'd said. But Triton had enthusiasm for his report, and disregarding Sniphle's bluster, continued, "At last, we have a little hope. NASA, the ESA, the JSA, and the other space agencies are planning for the next step—going off world. But not just one or two of us; they mean for many, many of us to leave Earth."

Sniphle frowned a little, then, smirking, looked down on Triton laying in the bed. "I don't see any advantage in taking a couple of hundred people to the Moon."

Defiantly, Triton held eye contact and said, "When I said they want to go further, I meant a lot further. They want to use us to take astronauts to some extreme places." For once, Triton's normally enigmatic expression broke into a broad, uncontrollable smile, and he said, "They want us to send their volunteers to the moon and other planets."

Sniphle smirked without restraint, warmly taking in Triton's own smile. He sought to express his unreserved appreciation of all Triton had done. But his sneering, self-controlled, paranoid self kicked in. "But what will they reward me with?"

Triton responded with an uncharacteristic vigour, "The sky, no pun intended... the sky is unlimited." He started again in an unfamiliar tone, "They didn't put a figure on it, but NASA said they would save billions on rocket costs alone."

"So, what are they saying? Do they understand that to send someone anywhere by means of our ghost gatherers, they must be already dead? Basically, you can't have a ghost of a person who's still alive. Unless they want to kill off their astronauts and harvest their spirits." He began laughing to himself; then, frowning, looked to Triton for confirmation if this scenario might be true.

Triton took in what he had said, and nodded in agreement, but countered, "Go to the meeting and hammer it out with them." He let a silence grow while Sniphle thought through the options NASA would throw at him. "But there are a few more options you may not have thought of. Can I suggest you attend the meeting and keep an open mind, and however much pressure they load on you and your team, remember this: you have the aces, so don't sell yourself and the company down the river."

Sniphle knew he was sitting on a time bomb. He had built an empire already, and the options to come were ever expanding. He had possibilities of building DNA-shells in differing forms. The Centurion group had expressed a desire to have their new bodies closely resemble their current selves, regardless of cost. That would mean DNA manipulation, and while they could achieve this, it would take time. He knew that to grow a DNA-shell from start to readiness for spirit-implanting took 600 days. The Centurions would have to balance when to start the implementation of their new DNA-shells, whether it be prior to or after their deaths. If it were prior to, how long before? Could he then prepare them to commit suicide when the body was ready, or wait until after their death the necessary 600-plus days until they finished the body prior to their spirit insertion?

The building of the South Seas facility had sparked a few local problems. Delays in planning permission and the lack of ability in building practises were extending the expected completion date. The Directors raised in the Western world were in the majority, and although aware of the words "bribery" and "corruption," they had not entirely understood them. The project started leaking funds via bribes to circumvent local planning committees. They found out that to get key items delivered on time required easement monies to allow the items through customs. However, the local builders knew the various paths to tread, and while keeping some bounty for themselves, the bribes satisfied, and the project building went to plan, albeit with a six-month delay.

All aspects of the differing projects were facing delays, apart from that affecting the crucial part of them all: specifically, the life expectancies of the Specials. Their projected lifespan was keeping the Directors holding their heads in doubt about all the projects. Some were even contemplating daring to approach Sniphle with their concerns.

Senior Director Cunningham, along with Senior Director Bennon, upon hearing the growing concerns of most of the junior Directors, decided they would approach Sniphle. His explosive angry outburst was not because of their approach, but his own worries about what to do next. Though they had both entered his office with some trepidation after Trokker's reported "suicide," they were unaware of the extent to which his anger could manifest itself.

Still, deliberately unmoving, Sniphle's stony faced glowered behind his desk as they entered, "You, Cunningham, come here," he snapped, pointing at his desk. His nostrils flared; his head fixed above hunched shoulders. Flinty eyes stared out from under hooded lids. "You know nothing. Without me, you would be squirming in some rabbit-hole hospital for the insane. You dare to question me about anything?" He glanced across to Bennon, who was trying to remain still at the entrance of the door. "You're not going anywhere either. Get over here... NOW."

Without a word, the glowering Director had both men in a state of extreme fright as they waited near his desk. "Sit."

Both did as bid, and while Cunningham was still in a state where he couldn't even contemplate conversation, Bennon was bolder and said, "We were only trying to bring your attention to timing... that is, life expectancy and outstanding commitments, sir."

The irate director stood from his chair and looked down at the subdued pair in an overt show of dominance. Coldly he began, "Do you think I haven't thought of this already?"

Bennon had used up all his bravery and remained quiet, not even considering expressing a nod. Sniphle exerted his characteristic obsessive, vengeful, and paranoid traits. "Well, I *have* been thinking about it. It's been constantly on my mind since I found out about their fragility." He eased his physical menace a little, and as a result, the pair relaxed their thoughts away from mere self-preservation.

Still glowering behind his desk, Sniphle said, "There are a few options if we want to maintain what we're doing. First, we have the choice of doing as we have been doing. We wait for them to die and get their spirits to enter a DNA-shell. The only problem here is that we're not sure if the spirits will carry their skills and personality, although Denzel seems to have done so. The second choice is to clone each individual and grow the baby in a surrogate mother; then, with any luck, after they reach puberty in 10, 12, 14 years' time, they may still have their skills. A big problem here is the timing. There will be a delay between our current crop of Specials and the new babies reaching maturity that will not be good for us.

"The last possibility I've been thinking about is to build a DNA-shell using their own DNA set while they still live. In this way, we get to where we want quicker, but like all options, we can't be sure what we'll get until we get there."

Bennon raised his head. "Sir, have you thought about breeding them?"

Sniphle's temples almost turned a pulsing shade of purple in his explosive reply. "Christ, they're difficult enough as it is! The females have mood swings that only allow us to utilise them for a couple of days each week, anyway. The boys... well, they're something else. We have little control over them; it's only the medication that's holding them with us. Oh! and on that subject, if they didn't have the meds, we would lock them up in a home for the severely mentally insane."

Bennon, trying hard to put forward a persona of childlike innocence as a way of protection, asked, "So, sir, which way do you think is best... or shall we try them all? Is there any way we can help the situation?"

Sniphle remained silent, contemplating his own summary of what to do about the Specials, hardly hearing and disregarding what Bennon was saying.

Cunningham reasserted his bravado. Knowing he had grovelled enough, he waited for an opportune moment: "Sir, what about Luna?"

The mention of her name brought a scowl back to Sniphle's face, and his body language changed once more. Throwing his arms out in a gesture of rage, he growled at them, "Get out, the pair of you." As they scurried out, he stabbed the intercom key. "Janice, come in here. I have some options to put past you. Maybe your non-sciento-medical mind may help. We need help and fast. I have a dilemma here to sort out."

He moved to the chair by the window vacated by Dr Trokker only a couple of weeks before and sat down while Janice moved to join him. She remained standing until he indicated she could sit, and only then, hesitantly, she asked, "Yes, sir, how can I help?"

28
Are You Off Your Trolley?

Although father and daughter, the pair were strangers, torn from each other before her birth—each one with a hollow in their souls, not knowing there was a missing piece. But now that the absent part was there, they had completion. After having spent time together, the emptiness Luna had felt dissipated. Initially, she looked for any excuse to ask to see him, mainly on the pretext of gratitude for rescuing her. Triton felt the same, but could see questions being asked if the meetings became too frequent. Already one of the junior Directors had asked questions about why they were meeting, which was dismissed by the nurses as nonsense.

They both applied to go on outside trips—not unusual for Luna, but a first for Triton. Eventually, word got to Sniphle; he knew there was trouble brewing, and at once made their meetings difficult to achieve. Although Luna could still travel to Triton during her night-time mind sojourns, these couldn't deliver the physical comfort she needed for fulfilment. They resolved to meet, by chance, in the facility lounge area, using Denzel as a go-between to arrange their 'unplanned' meetings. Unreported to Sniphle, they grew closer, which to both was a relief after their time of being alone. The nurses noted to each other that Triton was smiling from time to time, leaving behind his old, evasive self. He was becoming a person to care for with a little more empathy.

Salena knew her quest to get realigned with her former patient and lover would prove difficult, to reconnect with her daughter almost impossible. She knew she would have to be both meticulous in her planning and precise in the way she carried out her plans. But on top of her thoughts now was the revelation revealed by Ngoosi during her visit with Luna. She knew now that her charges, Pan and Ferdinand, would probably have a minimal life and premature death similar to that of the other Specials living in Sniphle's facility. Although not her own offspring, she treated the fragile pair as though they were, and any life-threatening scenario brought an emptiness to her. It reminded her of the shock and loss she felt when told she had lost first Triton and then Luna those many years ago. Now that she knew they were both alive, the years of hurt were healing. But knowing Pan and Ferdinand would die within the next ten years dug deep within her. It also brought out a renewed feeling of vengeful hate against the deceitful Sniphle. The planning was to be her priority in the coming months, but without someone else to discuss the pros and cons of her plans, her misgivings were keeping her from taking action.

NASA, although normally a slow operator, treated the invitation of the team of Directors with urgency; and before the D.O. knew it, they had arranged special flights to their facilities. Normally Sniphle liked to set the pace of any interactions, but such was the NASA aura that they bulldozed him into an early meeting. However, Triton's heads-up information allowed the Directors team to plan and set out contingencies should the meeting go down with differing scenarios.

The NASA administrators welcomed Director Sniphle and his three other senior colleagues and came directly to how they thought a partnership between NASA and the D.O. team should work. Initially, they gave the team an overview of how the funding for the next phase of rocket-powered space travel was heading. They discussed how world leaders had charged all space agencies to plan for volunteers to inhabit the inner planets of the solar system, all brought about because Earth had arrived in a place where colonisation of other planets had become a priority if humanity were to survive. To conduct this phase of exploration would require people in substantial numbers and a cheap, reliable transportation system. When they heard of the Centurions Project, the Director Organisation had launched for the hyper-rich, the space agencies investigated its operation as far as they could. However, apart from the manufacture of DNA-shells, they didn't understand how the D.O. claimed to implant the spirit of a person into a DNA-shell. NASA explained that if their claims about spirit implantation were true, they wanted to use the Directors' skills to achieve the same thing, but on a grand scale.

Without hesitation, Sniphle called the security member at the door and instructed him to fetch a colleague in from the reception area. Within minutes, the jovial Denzel strode into the room, and without acknowledging Sniphle and the D.O. Directors, he met with the NASA administrators. In a searching way, he shook hands with each one, studying their faces and how they held themselves. Sniphle smiled to himself and thought, *The old devil is eyeing for a punter for his next canvas.* Aloud, he said, "Denzel, please tell these gentlefolk the reason you're here. Then I'm sure they'll ask you a few questions, so be ready for some searching insights." With a dramatic wave of both hands, Sniphle signalled the animated artist to begin his story.

When finished, Denzel remained quiet, as if inviting a response. Although they had heard parts of the story before, the incredulous NASA administrators were in shock, each trying to think of a question but falling short of anything appropriate. Sniphle broke the silence. "Denzel, tell them what it was like being a ghost, and how you observed the ephemeral world around you." Again, Denzel conveyed the way the other world he had come from fitted in with the world he was in now.

"How do they react to us living people?" was the first question asked, followed by a bombardment of questions Denzel had received before in one form or another. To each he had learned to be as exact as he could, keeping the answers short to field their many questions.

Although still incredulous at this once-ghost in an idealised DNA-shelled body, the administrators fully acknowledged what he was saying was undeniably the real thing.

The sneering, superior aspect of Sniphle's personality shifted forward, asking, "Now, what does NASA need from us?"

"We don't just represent NASA, but most of the national and international bodies involved with space travel." The senior Administrator, Alex Gordon, looked to his colleagues and said to the Director team, "You must understand that we humans need to expand to other planetary territories if the species is to survive. To do this will require us to build a series of exceptionally large spaceships to transport the volunteers to our chosen destinations. However, this exercise will take many, many years, with unforeseen dangers, if our calculations are true; and the failure rate is correct, craft and human fatalities will be substantial." The administrator's normally jovial face drooped, allowing the D O attendees to understand the seriousness and scale of the operation. "With these astronomical costs, the Earth's governments can't afford or counter the public backlash.

"Now, when we heard about what you are proposing to do for the Centurions..." Alex stopped a moment, trying to search for an acceptable phrase, but finding none, continued. "Allowing them to die, then transposing their life spirits into DNA-shells... that may solve the problem."

Sniphle and the other Directors thought they saw where this was going but were not entirely sure, so Sniphle said, "I'm uncertain what you're proposing, but we'd like to help if we can." Sniphle feigned innocence and took a route expressing an interest in anything other than the financial. "However, if you're asking for a large donation, I'm not sure we can be of much help—but we'll do our duty."

On the Administrator's side of the enormous conference table, Alex Gordon at once jumped up out of his seat. "No, no, that's not what we're looking for. What we want is for you to take the spirits of the volunteers and transport them to the DNA-shells we prepare at a particular rendezvous."

This time, it was Denzel who jumped in. "How are you going to get the DNA-shells to their destinations?"

After nodding to his senior staff members, Alex said, "That will be the simple part, as far as we can tell. We just build the DNA assembly plant at the destination." He stopped for a few moments to watch the faces of the Directors before continuing. "We build a DNA-shell manufacturing plant on-site, be it Mars, Europa, or any other destination. We then ask for volunteers to be..." pausing, his eyes searching for inspiration, "how can I put it... killed off." Alex smiled, with a glint in his eyes, then said, "Sorry, that's harsh... maybe euthanized is better." Looking sideways to his colleagues, he grinned a little more, then turned back to the Directors. "This is where you come into it. We then get you and your team to collect and transport the spirit volunteers to wherever we site the DNA-shells. Mars, one of Jupiter's moons, or in the long, long term to Earth-like planets orbiting distant suns."

Again, he looked at the shocked, serious faces on the Directors, and once again, Denzel spoke up. "Are you off your trolley? Who the hell would volunteer?"

The team of administrators seemed to smile in unison. "You don't understand the things some people will do. We'll have so many volunteers coming to us that we'll have to vet them to get the best for the first generation of pioneers."

There then followed a full presentation by both NASA and other international agencies via video links of how they would conduct and achieve their objectives. The Directors felt nothing but admiration at the depth and scope of thought put in by the space agencies. Their approach and thoroughness to the tasks necessary to conduct such scopes of engineering on distant planets made most of them feel their own achievements were insignificant. However, they agreed in principle to do as the space agencies proposed, albeit with a hefty chunk of funding and legal liabilities written into any contract involving the deaths of the "volunteers."

On the flight back to their facility in the UK, in the recently bought company jet, there were unrestrained celebrations of their wonderful achievement of snagging such a huge contract. However, Sniphle said only one thing to remind the others of what was to come: "Our Specials have a limited lifespan, and NASA projects take years— decades, in fact."

29
Centurions Die

Before the month had passed, the Directors had their first Centurion death, an over-the-top mid-fifties billionaire named Terrance Tolley. Reports emerged that he'd died while having an affair with his personnel director. An extremely disgruntled husband caught him in the act. Witnesses agreed that the only way to confirm who the blood-spattered face belonged to was the unmistakable tattoo of a cobra on the inside of his right thigh, alongside two flat testicles. The angry husband had used a baseball bat and repeatedly smashed it against the victim's head until his face looked more like an overloaded plate of fruit trifle than anything human.

The subsequent meeting of panicky Directors all concluded that whatever his method of death, the Centurion was undoubtedly dead.

The Directors moved on and negotiated with the victim's family the step-by-step payments, totalling $10 million, to bring their unfortunate father back to life. They invited them to select one of the many available DNA-shells most suited to the way they wanted to see their new father. His name was to be Terrance Tolley-Dou.

The next task was to search out the spirit of the original Terrance Tolley, which took time but eventually achieved by the group of other spirits who had taken an interest in what Triton, Ariel, and Arche were doing. The spirit of the dead man was still in a state of shock and convinced he was dreaming, but progressively the spirit world helped him to understand. He saw his family in mourning, his wife of 15 years angry at his affair but comforted by an eager admirer eyeing the vast fortune he thought was coming to her. Terrance's spirit saw many things and saw the advantage of a premature death. He began looking forward to a new life, hoping to omit many of his earlier faults.

He watched the procedure of his battered body being readied for burial. The negotiations with his family and the Director Organisation for his new body. He followed himself, being corralled by Arche and Arial, to a place where the wisps of his ephemeral spirit coalesced. The boys guided him to two women, Rhea and Elara, who coaxed his spirit to the South Pacific, where he joined up with his new body.

On a bed lay the inert figure of a calm-featured man in his early twenties, without expression. It was then that a serene, intelligent-looking spirit who introduced himself as Triton began calming him, assuring him of his fresh life. Hesitantly at first, the spirit of Terrence relaxed and entered the inert body.

Terrance Tolley was at first frightened once inside his new frame. In the weeks since his death, he had grown used to the freedom of having no restrictions to movement. But now he had the constraint of only being able to move by employing his own muscles. He tired at the end of each day, requiring sleep. However, food for his belly, beautiful women passing his eyes, and the sights of the island surrounded by tranquil seas were undeniable compensation.

The Directors had proved the process worked; and as part of the negotiated contract with Terrance-Dou, they presented him to other Centurions. Although there were press restrictions to the event, word got out, and the clamour for "eternal life," as the press put it, was irrepressible.

The Directors became inundated with offers. Although there were many demands for places on the list of Centurions, the D.O. explained to all in dire terms that this was an extended experiment that might be available to the public at some future time; but, was not available currently. Over time, the press died down in favour of another high-profile story.

Another of the Centurions died after a brief illness three weeks after the Terrance Tolley-Dou announcement. Minky Graham had been the front man in a rock group in his earlier life, and looked upon as a Wild Man of Rock. Underneath though, he was a sensitive soul whose inner persona was opposite to his public image, and it wore down his mental health. The result of years of acting under his false image resulted in a major mental breakdown. His public appearances ceased completely, but although still fragile, he recovered his mental health. This released his talent as a songwriter, allowing his output of songs and musical scores for other artists and film themes to flourish. His earlier lifestyle though, had fatally eaten into his vital organs, despite many medical interventions. After joining the Centurion Program, he resolved not to take any more medical treatments, and his ailing body rapidly gave up.

Once again, the team of Specials did their work of finding his lost spirit, persuading him to join them and travel to the South Pacific facility and join his new, pristine body. They renamed Michael Graham, Minky Graham-Dou, and he took his place in his earlier home, continuing his musical output.

Over the next eight months, six more of the Centurions died, and all followed the same routines once the Specials had found them. However, an incident occurred upon the death of one individual, Peter Bloom, who had questionable sources of wealth. Once his death occurred, the Specials started their normal routines of finding and guiding the spirit to its new body. All went well, and the spirit settled into its designated DNA-shell. However, not long after, nurses realised that Peter Bloom-Dou was having problems. At first, he complained he was hearing voices in his head, and that he couldn't sleep without being disturbed by dream-like visions. The Directors subjected him to several tests, starting with his DNA-shell; but apart from his elevated heart rate, probably caused by stress, they could find no fault. Next, they did a complete scan of his brain; again, nothing but standard readings. Finally, they monitored his brain synapses and found them abnormally active. They sent Peter-Dou away for a few days to allow them time to analyse the results.

During this time, Peter's symptoms became worse, and he had conversations with others inside his head. When asked if he knew who these people were, he claimed he did; they were people from his past. But what he didn't say was that these people were old adversaries of his.

One morning he awoke, and while still contemplating whether to get up and shower before or after his breakfast, he heard a voice in his head: "Hello, Peter, how do you like being in this new body?"

"Who are you?" the shocked Peter-Dou snapped back.

"Surely you know me! Let me see if I can remind you somehow. Remember when you and I started our first business together? You devised a method of extracting retired people's pensions on the pretence of investing the money for them. Then you persuaded me to falsify the process legally, such that these poor old people unfamiliar with financial dealings lost everything they owned. Then you fled. They lost their houses, kicked out on the streets. They couldn't pay for their medical needs, and as they grew older, their care. You did one more thing when you left... you forgot to tell me about your plans. That left me to carry the can once you disappeared. I, poor fool of a company executive, ended up carrying all the blame for those poor souls' financial losses. They sent me to prison, and while serving a four-year sentence, someone stabbed me in the neck. It was one of the pensioner's sons who was serving time for GBH. I bled to death on a prison toilet floor!" There was a pause before the voice turned venomous. "Unfortunately for you *and* me, we now get to live together in this new body."

Peter-Dou had heard of his old partner's demise years before, and had had no thoughts about it, but now explained to him, he had a little regret. "So, is that it? Now that you've told me, can you leave?"

"Oh no!... You and I have a new home together, so let's get used to it. Besides, I tried to see if I could escape from here, but there's no way out."

Peter-Dou, in a show of boredom reflecting his past-life characteristics, asked, "What's your name again?"

There was rage in the response, "Norman, you uncaring lump!"

Peter-Dou was getting frustrated at being lectured to by his former business associate and feeling a little guilty about needing time away. "Oh yes, I forgot, Norman! Listen, I've had enough for today. You're boring me. I need to rest."

"Okay, you rest. I'll just hang around and maybe rest too."

Director Ranghan attended the emergency call. "What the hell is going on here?"

The slightly overweight nurse stepped forward, perspiration forming under her lower lip. Hesitantly, she said, "Doctor, sir... Peter-Dou isn't acting normally. He said his name was Norman."

"Sedate him. We need to find out what's going on before we allow him to raise his head again. There's something strange happening here. I need to talk to Director Sniphle before I recommend any treatment."

The robust DNA-shell now designated as Peter-Dou took time to succumb to the shots given, but the new body now insisting on being called Norman drifted into the induced sleep. Three hours later, his eyes reopened. The carers recalled Ranghan, who addressed the agitated, restrained figure laying on the bed. "So, how are you feeling... what do you remember, Peter? Or is it Norman now?"

"Peter? Norman? No... my name is Annette Hartley!"

Ranghan looked to the duty nurse, and she nodded, knowing an extreme action was needed. Ranghan ordered new, heavier dosages, then waited until the body drifted back into the induced sleep. Another three plus hours later, and the restless new body appeared to be waking, but was again in an agitated state. Again, they called Ranghan.

The ever more-flummoxed junior director, not sure of what he was dealing with, asked, "Who are you?"

Many voices entered and answered in the body's crowded head, all victims of Peter's past schemes. Some had committed suicide; some had died after being unable to afford necessary medical care; others simply could not adjust to their new life status. Whatever their reasons for their premature demise, all blamed the original Peter... and now they would make him pay.

Even though he couldn't respond as his former physical self would, Peter's pulsing anger rose. "Fine. I'll just kill myself if you don't leave me alone."

Their responses were similarly simple. "Do so, by all means, please. We will follow you to the next body; and if you don't want to take that route, we'll give your spirit hell. Peter, there's no hiding place here, and you *will* pay the price for your past actions."

In the following days and weeks, they pushed and goaded him from the time he woke until the medical staff at the D.O. gave him calming medication. When they eased his medications to assess whether he was any better, the angry spirits took it in turns to babble into his head. They jumped in when the Directors or nurses spoke to him, answering questions and responding as they wanted. Occasionally, he could insert his own words into the replies, which only confused the doctors more.

The nurses and directors reported to Sniphle that he was showing multiple personalities in an ever-greater intensity. Eventually, Sniphle took advice from outside sources, who declared him untreatable and prescribed him heavy medication that kept him in a vegetative state. From time to time, they eased his treatment, but the conflicting personalities did not diminish, and the D.O. returned him to the medications.

For the vast majority of the living Centurions, the snippets of stories leaking out about Peter-Dou were unimportant compared to the success of the others who had died and re-emerged as their Dou selves. The beaming Dou's, as they became known, brought the director's fame and fortune. However, the Directors remained aloof to the clamour of the media and anonymous to the public at large. But they kept a rolling number of one-hundred Centurions as their original members moved on. In this way, they maintained the exclusivity of the membership while increasing their coffers. Now, to Sniphle's gleeful satisfaction, the deposit became $1 million to join the exclusive club. Then, on completion of the transformation, another $20 million...

30
There is a Problem

The years sped by, the Directors' coffers getting larger and the Specials' life expectancies getting smaller. For all Sniphle's faults, with his overwhelming drive for power, money and recognition, he knew who his ultimate breadwinners were. As time was against his original plan to implant prepared DNA from each of the Specials into surrogate mothers, he decided to wait until the Specials exhibited signs of terminal decline. He would then euthanize them as their time came and use a standard DNA-shell to house the resultant spirit.

For some reason, the Doctors found that the female Specials had the shortest life expectancies. Apart from Triton, who was the oldest, all the other ten original Specials, four males and six females, were showing advanced symptoms of decline. Only Triton seemed to be at the start of its progress. Rhea, the oldest female, now approaching her thirty-ninth birthday, had become unreliable when conducting tasks. She was taking on the characteristics of an unhelpful teenager, with increasing truculent mood swings and the occasional tantrum. She was reluctant to conduct ferrying assignments without argument, and when she did, she would sulk back into her foetal position, unresponsive to the doctors. Eventually, they removed her from the duty list and left her to do as she pleased. Meanwhile, the Directors made plans for her future.

As they now allowed her to roam the building, her first thoughts were to get out of bed and visit the facility's social club. There she met up with the ever-hopeful Denzel and relaxed for the first time in her life.

When the second oldest, Mimas, showed similar declining traits, Sniphle knew it was time to bring forward and implement his planned program for the Specials' entry into the Dou clan. At first, he tried to explain to the reluctant thirty-nine-year-old "teenager," Rhea, the plan he had for her. She resisted at once. But others had informed Sniphle of her friendship with Denzel, so he played with her mind by bringing out her vanity. He played with the truth, claiming that in the past, Denzel had preferred younger women. If she wanted to please him, why not select one of the DNA-shells she thought best? "At the moment you are thirty-nine; in a week you can be back to twenty-five." Rhea's face froze, and her pelvic floor twitched in spasm as she became lost in only one thought.

The euthanasia procedure required no further discussion.

When the time came, Rhea told her goodbyes to all the other Specials, orchestrated by the Directors, ensuring them the concept of younger selves was soon to be theirs.

Although the Specials had been part of the Centurion program for many years now, euthanasia was frightening to them, and they were reluctant to carry out the procedure. Sniphle was his forceful self, and bamboozled the sub-middle aged, teenage, spirited woman with the promise of a specially chosen younger body to live her life in. He then gave the order to the reluctant young duty Doctor to instigate the process, but true to Sniphle's character, he declined to countersign the order. Rhea died, betraying a slight tear of regret for her past life, despite looking forward to her new self.

Ariel and Arche waited for the expected call to find Rhea, and from experience knew there would be approximately a three-day interval before the spirit appeared. Once the three-day period was up, Ariel and Arche set out early to the agreed-upon location, where they found her spirit relieved to see them. Between them, they took her to a point where she met Ananke and Elara. They then went with her to the South Seas Island of New Bismarck, where Triton calmed her enough to enter her new self.

Rhea-Dou awoke and gazed round the room, seeing the smiling faces of the islanders, who were relieved she had awoken. They could see she was an especially important person - and not because of wealth, but because Sniphle himself greeted her. "Rhea." He smiled as she blinked her eyes in recognition of her name. "Rhea, how do you feel? Are you well? Do you notice any difference between this and your old self?"

Rhea heard the sneering tones sliding out of Sniphle and reacted as her suspicious temperament guided. She pulled back in the bed, drawing away from the Director, and with a raised voice she answered, "Hang on a minute, I'm not sure of all my bodily functions as yet - so back off, old man!" her tone a little spiteful. Sniphle, for his part, tried to understand, but lacked the empathy to recognise what had happened. He put her abrupt manner down to her, settling back into life in a strange place and a strange new body. In the week that followed, they subjected her to a myriad of tests mirroring those prior to her euthanasia. The same director doctors, overseeing the tests, discovered an uncomfortable truth: Rhea's personality was the same! She had carried over all aspects of her earlier personality, including her troublesome teen rebel streak. Denzel, who had convinced Sniphle that he should go with the Director team, worded the thoughts of them all.

"Houston, we have a problem!"

Mimas was easier to convince once Rhea had returned safely. The Directors then pressed ahead with her joining the Dou clan as soon as possible, hoping to maintain her placid nature. The Directors realised that all the other Specials should also go through the process as soon as sufficient DNA-shells were available, no matter their suitability to the subject Special. Subsequently, they repeated the process on all the females, helping to preserve their current social temperaments. But until now, Triton and the two resident males, Ariel and Arche, had not shown the extreme declines of the females. Their vital role in helping the others into their new bodies was paramount.

Sniphle noticed and became suspicious of the bond between Triton and Luna, and asked his staff to report back to him should they meet. While Luna had been on an extended rest following her misadventure, he was eyeing her as a second to Triton. It would be she who would take on the role of helping Triton into his new body when his time came.

To this end, Sniphle and the Directors unwittingly enabled the pair to spend more time together.

31
A Plan

In the months following Luna's traumatic experience of trying to escape her own body, she vividly remembered its long corridors, enormous caverns, pulsating valves, and her brain's electrical fields. Luna healed, and knowing the Directors' reluctance to push her while she was recovering, she took advantage.

Luna endeavoured to roam outside but often accompanied by a member of the staff, whom she knew not to trust. This led to her visits to see Salena while only in Ngoosi's company. At other times, she preferred going to the mall to observe people going through their normal routines of life and afterlife.

While in the mall, she felt a level of wonder as she wandered down each aisle of the food stores. She marvelled at shoppers selecting their desires. Apart from her brief visit to the mall to sample ice cream with Ngoosi, she had never in her memory ever been shopping before. It filled her eyes with wonder to see people buying food, drinks, clothes, shoes, electrical gadgets. All were new to her, as was the number of stores selling the same articles, be it a distinct colour, size, or cost. She studied the shoppers; sometimes alone, as couples, and occasionally as a family. She thought the shoppers amazing in the way they shopped and how specific their choices were. The carers eventually wearied of following her, and left for the coffee shops to catch up with their personal devices, leaving the girl who, in their eyes, was just window shopping. When Luna eventually tired, she would join them to share a coffee; then, relaxing, allowed her mind to wonder. Here she saw the occasional spirit as she had done before, keenly watching as they searched through the living, hoping for recognition.

But it was the physical visits to her mother that gave her the greatest joy. The pair talked and talked; they did the household chores together, which was again all new to the girl. She found out how old she was, how Triton and her mother had met, and the trauma of their breakup. With this came a realisation of Sniphle's true nature. Slowly, between the pair, mother and daughter became of the same mind: Sniphle was an evil person.

The other temporary escape from the facility was in her mind's travels. From time to time, she met with her father while housed in the facility. She also went with him on journeys the D.O. had targeted. Frequently, it was to help the Centurions to their new Dou bodies. She marvelled at his caring, persuasive manner as he helped the vulnerable dead.

On other occasions, he showed her the exciting new ventures being built by the space agencies on Mars and Jupiter's moon, Europa. She saw the near-completion of the intricate 3D printed facility on Mars, directed and constructed by a complex AI assembly plant. Triton showed her the preparations of the rockets being sent to both Mars and Europa, housing the DNA-shell manufacturing plants.

For her, this was a time of hope for humanity, and it caught her up in the whole exciting idea of new worlds.

While she wondered at all that they had shown her, she felt an emptiness. Her mother and father had inadvertently opened doors she had not been aware of. They gave her experiences and revealed to her the ways of life and death, and the ways people spent the time in between. She could see the deep emotion and passion that underlay her parents' resolve to join each other again, marvelling at their patience. She knew also that whoever had kept her medicated and imprisoned in her bed had also kept her from her natural form of life. Luna saw the need in others as they wondered around with partners. She had also seen the hollowness of people without them. Throughout her mall visits, she had also seen the loneliness of those in the spirit world. Her growing body and developing mind realised the need for something more. She knew who was responsible for her barren life, and in her mind there was very little restraint about what to do next... to eliminate Sniphle, to kill him.

First, she thought of how her father had been subdued as a young man in the medicated service of her proclaimed enemy. But no matter how good a man he was, her father did not have the capacity or physical attributes in his current state to overcome Sniphle and the Directors. This didn't rule him out completely. He had deep knowledge of Sniphle's operations and weaknesses, which would be of use. Next, she thought of her mother, Salena. She seemed to have the physical health, and she had the brightness of mind to help form a plan. Important, too, was that she had a reason.

Luna began discussions with her father and, aided by Denzel, she came to understand Sniphle's strengths and weaknesses. She then investigated whether there was a point at which Sniphle was at his most vulnerable, and if so, when and where. Usually, this was when he was out of the facility and without his most trusted acolytes, who held him in false esteem and corrected any of his in-house errors. When he was away from the support, he was less forthright to some, more vulnerable, yet somehow more dangerous.

Together, mother and daughter formed a plan to end him in a way in which he would find it difficult—or as reported by Triton, Arche, and Arial, almost impossible—to be revived into a new DNA-shell. Steadily, the plan came together. They identified his weakness, a method of killing him, and another of disposing of the body. Also, they found accomplices to carry certain parts of the plan without too much knowledge of what was to happen. Then they set about planning their own alibis, planning what was to happen to the other Directors once the deed done.

Luna voiced it first. "Drowning sounds good to me—a long, long way down." She remembered the stories from Arial and Arche of when they were investigating two miles down, and how lost they were at depth. "So, it will be while on one of his scuba-cage outings. What do you think, Mummy?"

Although there was a resolve to end him, there grew in Luna's mind a concern that it might not be the best way to achieve uniting her family.

32
We Are Weak

Time was the enemy.

The space agencies were almost ready to go farther after having built the engineering village on the moon. But its primary goal of sending hardware to both Mars and Europa was now over. Simultaneously the degradation of Triton's physical body and nervous system were tiring his guiding skills. The Directors knew that if this wasn't dealt with soon, they could lose him. Of all the Specials, his path to a natural age was becoming a reality. He was now approaching his forty-third year, while the ten others had already been replaced by DNA-shelled versions of themselves long before. Unlike the others, he had kept his independent spirit. He held at the back of his mind the fact that there would be a time when he could escape.

Luna, the only other remaining original Special, had grown and had become, like Triton, more independent in thought. Like him, the imprisonment of her bodily self by those who governed the regular doses of chemical concoctions tying her to her bed bit into her. Her understanding of self was too far out of range for the Directors to understand, and so her tolerance of them diminished. Her internal growth was soaring beyond her human form. She was slowly becoming aware of things only hinted at by an internal consciousness, many of which humans were oblivious to. She now began understanding nature's intended direction for her. This new, instinctive understanding sailed far beyond the limited comprehension of any dedicated human scientist, and with it, tolerance with her keepers.

The Director Organisation was unsure how, but they knew she was different. Her actions seemed quicker, more responsive to their chemical instruction. But she knew that no matter how much they tried to subdue her, she had a defence they couldn't penetrate. In the early days, they had given her increasing amounts of addictive drugs—but she had found a way of retreating into herself, whereby her mind had become independent of her drug-reliant, subdued physical body. No matter the concoction, she became apparently comatose and out of reach of them. They hadn't understood that she was on another level, simply looking down, listening in on their conversations, before speeding off to other places. Sometimes she joined up with others on their directed travels; sometimes she went on her own, observing other people. She fell in love with lovers, joining them in their exploration of each other. She investigated the processes of artists as they expressed their visions, be it with paint, clay, dance, or spoken word on a stage. With her emotions tumbling, she allowed herself to go with climbers on sheer cliffs, skiers, and sports competitors, each exerting themselves to accomplish a higher goal.

Luna moved higher still, becoming less human and enjoying another path.

But there was still the unresolved subject of Director Sniphle, who had become a tyrant. People of high wealth and influence had put him on a pedestal, treating him like a fabled god of old. No matter how many people wanted to be rid of him, the promise of never-ending life to those who desired his demise extinguished their ambitions. They feared their own lives being shortened to a mere lifetime instead of for however long they wanted. The powerful knew this, and no matter how inventive their resolve to get rid of him, all knew he had the tools and resolve to counter them... in this life or his next.

Triton was escorting a spirit of one of the just-deceased Centurions to New Bismarck when he noticed Sniphle in the reception room. "Why is he here, I wonder?" he asked himself. After the spirit had entered its Dou body shell, Triton's job was done; but he remained interested in what the Director was doing. He followed a group of islanders and Sniphle, and saw he was there to commission one of the new DNA-shell manufacturing facilities. It intrigued Triton. "Why him, in this almost insignificant job?" He followed them for a brief time until he saw the PM's son arrive and quietly chat with Sniphle.

Tupaia, in his calm, diplomatic way, said, "The tide is on the way out; we need to get a move on if we're going to catch those hammerheads."

With that, Sniphle did his usual and abruptly thanked the engineers, construction crews, and commissioning team for their efforts before he withdrew. Triton continued to follow as the team of Directors made their way to the vessel carrying Sniphle's dive-cage. Once on board, he saw the principal reason Sniphle was on the island: to go scuba diving.

Curious about the concept of cage diving, Triton hung around, taking in the impressive operation, and followed the operators as they went through their maintenance schedules. One thing that struck him was the amount of oil and grease the operators were using. They pointed out to one director, who had trodden in a small puddle of it, that the sea is the most corrosive substance around. It eats steel, even stainless steel, unless in the correct grade. Therefore, painting it with special epoxies or covering it with grease and oils helped ease the problems.

Triton also noticed the mechanism for raising and lowering the cage itself. They used a huge crane-like machine operated by a man receiving instructions from those below, telling him to raise or lower it depending on where the fish were shoaling. Triton, though, was further intrigued about the drive mechanism... where was its weak point?

When he got back home, he waited until the next time Luna came by in her ephemeral form, saying, "Luna, I think I have a way to get rid of Sniphle." Without waiting, he explained. "... while the dive cage is large," he told her, "The bars holding it all together are spaced only wide enough apart to allow smaller fish through, but nothing so large as a predator of humans. Once the diver is inside the cage on the boat decking, the cage, with its divers inside, it's lowered or raised to wherever the diver wants. The mechanical stuff behind this is simple - an engine and gearbox. Importantly, it has a clutch between them to allow the engine to change the gearbox drive for the cage to go up or down. The clutches are the weak link; they're a temporary break between the two. They're prone to slipping if the springs are weak, if there's a maladjustment of clearances, or if there's oil on the plates. Any of these would allow the cage to just slip deeper and deeper…"

By the time he had finished his explanation, it lost Luna in the mechanics of it all, but understood that if something went wrong with the crane, the cable could break, and the cage would go to the bottom. "How deep is it there?" she asked.

"At some points, two miles and beyond," he told her, and she felt a little of his pleasure at what he was telling her.

"How can we sabotage the crane without bodies? That's always been our problem. When we inhabit our bodies, we're weaklings, laying on a hospital bed. But when we're travelling, we have no physical form."

Triton answered. "Don't worry, we have an ally." He waited a moment for her to pick the pieces together.

"Yes," she drawled. "Denzel hates him too."

33
A Spare Shell

Once back at the facility, Sniphle reminded himself of Triton's replacement program. The 600-day gestation period was nearing its last stages. He had enjoyed the traditional good looks of the boy when he was younger and resolved to keep them. In Triton's case, he had used the man's original DNA to build the shell instead of giving him a choice of shells to choose from. In Sniphle's thoughts, Triton deserved a little extra. Though it took almost two years to grow the shell, Triton's condition could wait that long.

Meanwhile, Sniphle got word from an old semi-adversary of his: Salena. She had requested a meeting. Though he had kept a distant eye on her movements, they hadn't met since he'd sacked her those many years ago. What could she want? He asked both himself and his security staff, but nothing came to mind. But as she had kept excellent care of the two damaged Specials, Pan and Ferdinand, over the years, he thought maybe he should allow the meeting.

When she arrived, he rose from behind his desk, emphasising his gangly frame. "Salena, how are you after all these years?" he gushed. She was quiet for a moment as she looked at him, clearly remembering all that had happened. He displayed a fake smile and asked, "First, I must thank

you for all your efforts over the years. How are the boys..."
He frowned, trying to remember, "Pan and Ferdinand, isn't
it?"

"I'm sure your informants have kept you up to date,"
she said crisply, "but just in case they haven't, know that
Ferdinand is well. But even with his new body he is, as he's
always been, unreliable and monitored most of the time.
Pan is recovering from a chest infection. He's never been
the strongest of the two, even with his new body. But he has
a determination about him and seems to be growing out
of his extended juvenile mind." She stopped for a moment.
"And you?"

"Oh, I've been better, but we're not getting any younger,
are we?"

Salena maintained her pleasant manner, but changed
the subject. "You seem to have a good tan. Have you been
anywhere nice lately?"

She knows something, he thought. *Where is she going with
this?* He answered anyway: "Oh, I scuba dive, you know. It's
wonderful. We have an understanding with an island in the
South Pacific." He shifted his stance, projecting a superior
attitude, then pointing to the soft chairs near the large
window. "How about coffee?"

"No, thank you." There was something in his question
that bothered her, but she couldn't place it. "Listen, I won't
take too much of your time, but I need a little help."

"Oh!" He was almost surprised, having expected a verbal
pounding from her about some of the things he'd done.
"Go on, how can I help?"

Salena's face drooped; a glow of sweat appearing on her
forehead. She glanced out the window, sighing dejectedly,

then looked back and hesitantly relayed her current plight. "I'm dying. I am not sure if your goons have uncovered it yet, but I have stage 4 cancer. It's metastasised to my lymph nodes and has spread to almost all my internal organs. I'm told I'll die within a few weeks, possibly a month at most."

He looked into her eyes more deeply. Seeing the dark bags under them, he knew she was telling him the truth. Out of words for once, he remained silent.

Nervous, with a concerned look on her face, she blurted, "I'm the only one who knows Pan and Ferdinand and can look after them! Just so they don't spill any beans after I'm gone, I'm asking you to grant me the opportunity for a DNA-shell. That way, I can care for them for the rest of their lives and ensure any secrets they have in their heads don't go any farther."

Sniphle was in an excellent mood. Everything was falling into place, with an assurance his life would never be in the same state as hers. He'd just overseen the New Bismarck facility after commissioning. The NASA project was advancing, and he also saw the progress his own improved DNA snippet had made so far, with its completion only a few weeks away. He thought of all she had done for the boys, never having made too much fuss. Nor had she said much about what he'd inflicted upon her regarding Triton and her subsequent dismissal those many years past.

He strolled over to his desk and pressed a button. Moments later, Janice appeared. "Coffee, sir?" she asked, smiling.

He shook his head. Recognising what she was asking, he replied. "No, Janice. We won't be needing the coffee today. How about three sparkling glasses and an equally inviting bottle of Fizz? Salena and I have some discussions and planning to do. It's better done with an adventurous mind." He sat behind his desk and called Salena to join him, then called out to his confidante, "Janice, can you bring in my diary as well?" He turned to his visitor. "Salena, my dear, how would you like to go on an enjoyable trip to a tropical island?"

Staring at him for a moment with a frown creeping into her tightening eyes, she nodded to invite him to go further. Although recognising her uncertainty, he continued. "Remember, I've just returned from the South Seas. I've built a new facility to manufacture built-to-order DNA-shells for my Centurion customers." He paused, and with an overconfident look, said, "You know about the Centurions, don't you?" She remained silent, expressionless. "As part of the training of the local staff there, the staff had to grow trial units. It just so happens that there's a spare female unit. At the moment, it has no spirit assigned to it. Instead of just letting it out for spare parts, can I offer it to you?" At that moment, Janice arrived with the bottle, glasses, and his diary. "Shall we let Janice pour?"

While she poured, Sniphle settled behind his diary; then, talking to himself, murmured, "Now when can we make it? Let me see... I have NASA at the start of next week. That will be an all-week affair." He turned the page and looked up. "How about the following Monday?"

Salena waited in the house as she had done many times in the past, expecting a visit from Luna. The heads-up had come from Pan, during a spirit visit from Luna the previous evening. Right on time, the doorbell rang, and the dutiful Pan rushed to open it, then guided both Luna and Ngoosi through the large kitchen.

Without preamble, Salena said, "I have news for you. The D.O. is giving me a new body. I fly out with them next Saturday, and I believe they've arranged the procedure for the Tuesday following Sniphle's arrival on Monday."

"That explains it," said Luna, nodding with a sigh of acknowledgement. "The Directors are sending Daddy and I, plus Denzel and two carers, to a festival in the south of France, on the pretence that we deserve a break and a reward for helping with their new projects. He doesn't want Daddy to escort your spirit to the new DNA shell, for obvious reasons. Plus, he won't want you or I to see each other either in case we recognise each other."

A thought then struck Luna. "Mother, we've worked out a plan that could rid us of Sniphle. The problem has been getting to the place where we can do it and being there at the same time as him. Guess what? it's on the South Seas Island of New Bismarck... well, strictly, it's on a boat off the coast of New Bismarck."

Luna then explained how and why it had to be in deep waters. "All that needs doing is for the dive cage to be dropped into the deep... the exceedingly deep!"

Salena looked at Luna. "Easy!" she said, and both collapsed into uncontrolled laughter.

34
First Send Off

NASA, along with the heads of the ESA, JSA, and other worldwide space agencies, welcomed the large Directors Organisation party with a tour of their ongoing projects before ushering them towards the restricted area. Alex Gordon directed the D.O. party to sit in an auditorium, joined by almost seventy other guests. After a brief address regarding the progress NASA and the other space agencies had made on their relocation project, Gordon continued his speech while, on an enormous screen, NASA relayed the meeting to other space agencies via video links worldwide. He explained the developing story of the completion of the Mars outpost, and the expected completion of its Europa twin in the next week.

After his presentation, he waited a few moments for the applause to die down. He then shifted to the side of the stage, turned, and began to discuss the primary motive for the meeting. "Ladies and gentlemen, the primary reason all of you are here is to meet the first of our volunteer space settlers." There followed a round of applause before he continued, "You've all heard the rumours, but now I can reveal the method these brave pioneers will use to get there. As you saw from the video presentation, we've completed the Mars outpost's first-phase 3D-printed buildings, and at present they can accommodate up to one hundred people." Again, a spontaneous round of applause rang out. "Once our brave pioneers are there, we'll expand the facility to hold at least a thousand. Ultimately, the plan outlines a city of one hundred thousand within the next ten years. Initially, we have chosen surveyors, engineers, doctors, and construction operatives versed in the specialised 3D-printing techniques we're using. To put some of your concerns at ease, in the beginning, life at these new outposts will follow much the same routines as life on Earth. In the second phase, these outposts will require a broader section of the 'normal' Earth types serving society: teachers, artists, nurses, miners, farmers, administrators, etc. You name it, if there's a need, we'll utilise them." Gordon paused, looked down, then back up to his audience, and, smiling, said, "Perchance, even a midwife and a lawyer or two." He grinned in acknowledgement of the humour and held up his hand. "Now, let me introduce you to the first batch of twenty... can I say, genuinely brave pioneers? We'll follow them on each Martian day with another twenty of their compatriots until we complete this first phase."

He stepped back a little, waving for the volunteers to come forward. One by one, they filed in line to extended applause, with the audience rising to their feet. The slightly overweight Alex raised his voice a little, dousing the applause. "Now, these are very brave people, and have put themselves forward to be euthanized." He smiled at the attendees, who were aware of what was about to happen. "The Directors Organisation has given us their assurances they will restore them to life..." He smiled again and waited a moment. "... on Mars, each housed in a suitable pristine

DNA-shell body selected by each individual taking part." The applause rang out again as the NASA administrator invited the D.O. team onto the cramped stage. "Director Sniphle, we all want to thank you and your Director Organisation team for helping humankind make this giant step to not just the planets of the solar system but eventually, we hope, the stars."

For Sniphle, this was the crowning moment of his life. Although he basked in the praise, others within the team knew who the genuine heroes were, and were, inwardly, genuinely ashamed. As part of the contract, it was to be each individual space pioneer who was responsible for their own passing, not the space agencies.

With families gathered for their last face-to-face words with their kin, all congregated in a large aircraft hangar with suitable coffins enclosed in small cubicles. On a trigger from Alex, the administrators and nursing staff began their gruesome task of attaching the infusion lines to the twenty volunteers. Although the administrators had arranged the occasion to give each individual and their families a sense of quiet, curtained privacy, the hanger became filled with a hubbub of lowered voices and abundant sobbing. It was the volunteers themselves who released the toxin into their own drip lines. Some acted without thinking, almost as though stepping through a door. Others had to force themselves, while bravely rethinking what they were doing.

Within thirty minutes, the initial process was over, and a cloud of silence hung over the hanger, eventually broken by NASA staff reopening the gigantic doors, revealing heavy unproductive rain clouds. The noisy opening prompted the grieving kin to make their last anguished farewells, and reluctantly, each group dispersed.

Two days later, the Specials readied themselves to gather any initial spirits. Within the next 24 hours, Ariel and Arche had gathered the spirits of all 20 volunteers before relaying them to the female specials, Charon and Rhea, who took to their task of encouraging their charges to begin the journey to Mars.

Apart from a few fears from one or two of the volunteer spirits, the Specials excitedly gathered the sometimes-wayward spirits. Then successfully herded their charges to Mars. Once at the new colony, Triton, accompanied by Luna, began the almost effortless task of encouraging the volunteers into their new bodies, one by one.

Celebrations began when the first of the Volunteer Pilgrims contacted Earth with the report that she had made it. She then introduced the others as they arose and pushed their way forward to be recognised. Each bore a label showing their identity in its new body to the watching families, administrators, and Directors. Celebrations started on Earth as each confirmed that they had made it safely to their new bodies. The leader of the group stepped forward towards the camera, and after settling into a seat behind a table, looked both left and right at his comrades, then began a brief speech. "Houston, you watched twenty leave. I can confirm that twenty have landed on Mars."

Following this, they made a public announcement to people on Earth who looked farther in their lives, no longer tied to a place where their fate seemed predetermined. They saw an avenue to escape beyond their birthplace, similar to the era when Europeans had discovered the Americas over six hundred years earlier.

Following the Mars' success, the Director Organisation became world famous. But soon there came unscrupulous companies trying to sell their own versions of the D.O. methods without understanding how it worked. They searched the world for clairvoyants to replicate the Specials' abilities, but try as they might, none could reproduce the process. Although some of their psychics could contact ephemeral spirits, none could replicate the process of escorting spirits into their DNA-shells. The problem appeared to be contacting the new spirit specifically. They found that when the medium had entered a state in which they were receptive to the spirit world, the quantity of other existing spirits clambering to be reborn, overwhelmed them. The countless angry spirits prevented the recently dead person who had paid their life's fortune for a fresh new life from contacting the psychics. Although there was the occasional success, they were inconsistent, and virtually all the start-up companies trying to cash in on the phenomena failed after being sued by grieving families pining for their deceased loved ones.

It was during this time that they inundated the Director Organisation with calls to retrieve these lost souls. It also built pressure from both the space agencies and those running the D.O. Centurion program to increase their numbers. Sniphle knew this was coming, but all his attempts to overcome the problem had so far come to nothing. Pressure mounted, and he knew there were few options. He knew he had to increase the rate of turn-round.

To do that, he needed more Specials... and that would be a gamble. He had also considered trying to repeat his first experiments and remake the DNA concoction given to his original specials. However, he remembered that while creating his original unregulated mix of DNA strands that there was something, some other presence hovering close to him, nudging his mind to push his experiments further. Although taking the prescribed medication regulating his depression, it also seemed as if there was another force inside his head guiding, prodding him to do outlandish cutting and mixing. But he'd put it down to tiredness and the medication.

Now, with hindsight, he knew his youthful playing with the three billion letters of DNA code had turned out to be extremely fortunate. His great weakness had been his innate lack of record keeping. Only now, and with greater historical knowledge, did he realise they couldn't easily repeat his experiments. It reminded him of the old story about how long it would take to get a hundred chimpanzees bashing away at keyboards to reproduce the entire works of Shakespeare. Reproducing the Specials DNA code would be a similar impossible task.

His next possibility was to take copies of the Specials code and grow replicas, but he had doubts holding him back at first. However, faced with mounting pressures, he eventually replicated the Specials DNA. Initially, he gathered cells from all those present at the D.O. headquarters, the six females and the two men, Arche and Arial. He already had a Triton shell in its growth stage, and didn't want to develop two separate Tritons at the moment.

He realised he couldn't use the approach of using snippets of DNA from the Specials and grow a new DNA-shell. This would give him a shell, but he needed the functional article. He therefore knew he had to go the long-term route by using a DNA snippet and implant it into new embryos. The outcome, however, was that the new Specials wouldn't be of any use for at least another fifteen or sixteen years, or whenever the active part of the Special abilities triggered. He thought, *Teenagers... that's when those nice little children answer back.*

His mind made up, he gave the order to go ahead for the long-term solution. The thoughts of the psychotic Sniphle became simple. Time and urgency to get the Specials in place didn't matter anymore. *My life is as long as I want it. I can have a Keno´ T Sniphle Dou, 3, 4, or as many as I like. I can live forever, provided there's at least one special available.*

But for now, he would have to work the Specials harder, until the new teens came along.

35
Faster Than Light

The NASA administrator smiled across the desk, after showing Sniphle in to sit in the chair opposite him. When settled, he said, "Director Sniphle, once again we must thank you for coming to see us at short notice. The reason we've asked you to attend is not because of the three volunteers going missing for a week during what you call the gathering stage—although it *is* a wake-up call. I understand the three met with your gathering specials a day late, with no harm done. So, all seems to be progressing well with the interplanetary DNA-shell program."

Sniphle frowned with a shake of his head, breathing deeply. "Oh, they turned up for the couriers to escort them to Mars, so no problem." Then, in his usual suspicious, domineering manner, Sniphle raised his voice, repeating, "So there isn't a problem, then?"

Administrator Gordon, very aware of Sniphle's bristly manner, replied coolly, "Oh, no, we're pleased with what you have done so far... But."

Sniphle intolerantly broke in, grumbling. "There's always a 'but' when payment is due."

Gordon, still calm, replied at once, "Oh, no. I think you'll find we've paid everything up to date as of this morning."

Sniphle looked round to his financial director, Roger Ganley, who was still nervously standing near his assigned chair. His damp hand began pawing his tablet, and he answered without being asked. "Yes sir, it arrived in the account this morning."

Turning back to the patient NASA administrator, Sniphle halted a moment before forcibly repeating what Gordon had said: "So ... what is this... 'but'... then?"

Gordon gripped the table to relieve his annoyance at having to deal with Sniphle. He ignored Sniphle's distrust, knowing he would delight the D.O. with his next offering. "We want to start a couple of extra projects. This time we'll need exploration prior to establishing any kind of physical presence." He stopped for a moment as he read the alarm in Sniphle's face. "Is there a problem, Director Sniphle? You seem a little put out. Is it money?"

Once again, Sniphle allowed his discomfort to surface. "No, it's no longer a monetary issue. I have to come clean with you." He hesitated and looked back at his team, knowing that not all knew what he was about to tell. "It's a case of supply and demand. The Specials are at full stretch already, and a couple aren't as reliable as we would like. What you're implying is that you want them to travel to other planets and other moons to gather and return with data, yes?"

Frustrated, Gordon tried to interrupt, but Sniphle continued. "If, as you say, you want them to explore fresh territories, they'll have to be trained to do so. This takes time, and as you know, not everyone is able in all subjects." He looked over his shoulder at his chief finance officer, pointing a thumb at him. "Roger here is good at financial numbers, but if I asked him to do load calculations for differing materials in a roofing truss, or control calculations for the frequency of a simple car spring damper, he would be out of his depth. Ask me why I keep him on. It's simple. He's excellent at his job and knows accountancy numbers better than anyone else I know." Sniphle looked around at blank faces before he went on. "What I'm saying to you is, the Specials are like us all—good at some things, but not in the specialist fields you have in mind." Again, Sniphle looked up and could see blank faces, then restarted his explanation. "What I'm trying to get through to you is that my Specials are not geologists, geophysicists, or planetary experts. Therefore, can't provide the detailed information you want from these places."

Alex painted on a false smile in an attempt to relieve his increasing frustration. Under the table, he stretched out his hands and closed them into fists; then he drew a deep breath and stood. "Director Sniphle, thank you for pointing this out to us. Over the past decades, since the middle of the last century, we've been sending missions to almost all reaches of the solar system, and pretty much have a handle on how it's made up. What we want is for your people to look for the possibility of life on planets *beyond* our solar system... in systems around other stars." He waited until the thought struck home to the D.O. group, and before they responded, he said, "We've done quite a few calculations regarding the travel times of your," he hesitated, "Specials. We've found in repeated situations they travel faster than light in astral form."

He reached over for a folder, opened it, and pulled out a sheet of paper; then, after a quick scan found the item he was looking for. "Ah, here it is! At its closest, Europa is about 5.2 light minutes from Earth." He looked directly at Sniphle. "We've timed your Specials, and they can do it in well under three minutes without trying." He held up his hand as a sign that he had not finished before he started again. "We don't want to spend time, people, and hardware on an exploration trip to probable life-supporting worlds circling another sun, only for them to find these worlds to be toxic. Our calculations tell us these expeditions would take 80-90 years each way, at a minimum. We believe your people can do it in a much shorter time."

Sniphle could see the enthusiasm on the administrator's face. He enjoyed the warmth it generated and, while understanding NASA's desire to explore, realised its problem. "I'm very sorry, but we don't have the resources, and won't for at least another fifteen years or more."

Gordon smiled before casting his eyes to his colleagues, then back to the D.O. team. "You don't understand about time, do you? But think about what I've told you. If you come up with a way of testing one of your Specials to see how fast they can travel, we would be extremely interested in helping."

Defensively, Sniphle leaned back, his eyes darting, protecting his thoughts. There was someone in mind whom he could spare for the task, but he kept quiet and thought about how he might gain in this new endeavour.

36
Budget Cuts

The journey to New Bismarck in the company plane took longer than she had expected, tiring her both physically and emotionally. Although she had ceased using the medication to depress her advancing illness, Salena needed the pain-reducing meds to help relieve the physical effort of life itself.

The social openness of the islanders helped relieve her mental stress until the arrival of Sniphle two days later. When he arrived, for once he appeared relaxed, and it seemed he'd shed the aura of menace he had while in the D.O. headquarters. His first task was to show Salena around the complex. Although he acknowledged Salena's obvious pain, he didn't relent with his tour, his only comment being, "Bear with me. Once you have your new body, this old body of yours will only be a fading memory."

He next guided her to a viewing station, where she could see into the ultra-clean environment where the new DNA-shells were being grown and stored. In a controlling way, he prolonged the tour, enjoying watching the agony she endured as she was being shown around. Eventually, she gave in to her pain and requested they cut the tour short. Only then did Sniphle acknowledge her discomfort by calling for a wheelchair to help her finish. Once settled, he took her through into a small room with a large viewing glass overlooking three nude bodies, all similarly featured, all with the light-olive colouring of the islanders. However, the Island's new DNA techs had been playing with their freshly gained skills, and had given the shells unique features. They differed significantly from Salena's own European features. All had vaguely higher cheek bones, with an almost oriental shape to their eyes, coupled to marginally broader nostrils—but most interesting was their red hair. Their body features were like the islanders', but during their 600-day growth, they had not been subject to the locals' love of rice and fatty, sugary foods, and so were a little more slender.

In his chosen aura of superiority, Sniphle said in his dominant way, "Choose!"

She looked at the three, noting a very slight difference in the centre one, which to her eyes wasn't quite right. Otherwise, they were all very similar. Burdened by the thought that there could be dozens or even thousands who looked the same, she asked, "Will I meet up with a range of them who look the same as me in the days or even years to come?"

In an offhand, irritable tone, Sniphle replied, "The choice is yours. However, remember, of the billions of people in the world, the chances of meeting another with exactly the same features as these again are negligible. For your information, there were only five of this model's run, built as part of this facility's test program... Do you want one or not?"

She heard menace in his voice and knew there was something behind his insistence, so she decided on a double bluff. Not wanting the one in the middle, she said, "The middle one, then."

Following her choice, Sniphle directed her to be wheeled away to the laboratory for preparation for euthanasia. True to his devious nature, he directed the technical team to take the DNA-shell body on the left instead of the central unit. "That one will do her; let's not give her all she wants."

As with so many before her, two female Specials met and guided Salena's spirit-self to a transfer point. They then escorted her to New Bismarck, where she was met by Arche rather than Triton. Reassuringly, he helped her to settle into her new body.

She awoke aware of the absence of painful discomfort, the first time in as long as she could remember. The effort of tensing her muscles was pain free. Initially, restraints held her back, but the islander nurses reassured her these were only temporary. "We just need to carry out a few checks until you're completely aware of your surroundings," they told her. Once Salena acknowledged their questions and calmly answered their queries, smiling, she asked them to release the bindings. The cheerful, attentive nurse reassured her, "It's only for everyone's safety, until you're aware of what has happened to you." After waiting a further five minutes again, the nurse looked at the new Dou body, seeing nothing other than a bright-eyed, calm patient. Carefully, she released the bindings without further delay. "It looks like you are okay. How about some breakfast? We have been told some come out of the switch thinking they are someone else. Some seem to think they have two or more people within them. But from the way you have answered the questions, all seems fine. Once you go through the physical tests we must conduct, we can let you go."

There followed a range of tests and bodily inspections, revealing that three of the small toes on her left foot were joined. There was also a problem with the pulse on her right wrist. It followed a path down the outside of her wrist instead of the inside. After consulting with the D.O. doctor and a consultation with Salena herself, they agreed the oddities were acceptable. Satisfied, the chief technician duly signed the applicable papers and said, "So, let us go to see Director Sniphle. He asked if you would join him on the boat."

The NASA administrator responsible for the next range of space exploration received an alarming call from his financial tormentors. Public sentiment towards space travel had taken a hit because of the outcry from voters wanting politicians to support the opportunity to 'live forever.' The regular cycle of elections was pressing politicians to give voice and monies for research into ways for the not-so-rich to extend their lives with new bodies. However, the research expenditure would eat into other scientific projects—the major loser being space research and the settlement of pioneers on other worlds, of course.

With his budgets cut, NASA's Alex Gordon needed to lean on the world's other space agencies to take up the slack until NASA's funding renewed. His other possibility was to cut current costs, the major expenditures being the Director Organisation. Hesitantly, Alex made his call, knowing polite conversation about money with the D.O. chief would be fraught with difficulty. "Director Sniphle, something has come up and we need to talk."

Sniphle replied in a sharp tone, "I'm in New Bismarck completing and commissioning one of the DNA-shell manufacturing facilities." Sniphle, though, picked up on the urgency of the Administrator's voice and, after a slight pause, asked, "Alex, do I detect a problem? Why are you calling at this hour?"

Gordon replied with a stock answer when in this position: "We need to talk face-to-face. Something has come up." Allowing no reply, he repeated, "Face-to-face."

Sniphle knew it was important and knew the conversation was probably being monitored and recorded. Given his political awareness, he resolved to make light of the administrator's tone and urgency. "Let's meet at my facility; it's away from the winter in your part of the world. I'll send the company jet to pick you up. Listen, it's Friday evening where you are. Why not stay over here for the weekend, and I can have you back at your desk by Monday morning?"

Gordon thought over the ramifications of accepting a vendor's invitation and instantly turned round the conversation. "What an excellent idea. I can also look over your new plant and report back to my team here."

Sniphle could hear that there was an underlying agenda, and went along with it. "I'll get my crew ready for you. We'll have an aircraft ready for you before 7:00 pm tonight." With that, the pair said their goodbyes and began their individual preparations for the meeting.

The condescending Sniphle greeted the new, fresh-bodied Salena on board the company yacht. "Ah, Salena, welcome aboard. How do you like your new self?" Sniphle was in his smarmy phase, recognisable by most who had met him before.

She acknowledged his welcome, but kept her genuine feelings to herself. "Director Sniphle, thank you once again for all you've done for me, but remember, my name is now Salena-Dou." Both she and the Director genuinely smiled together, and any atmosphere of confrontation melted.

"Salena-Dou," he smiled again, "do you scuba dive?"

"No, not really. I did a Discover Scuba when I was in my teens but have been so busy with the rest of my life, I never continued."

"Well, if there's time and the weather isn't too harsh, maybe we can get you wet. I'll get you fitted out just in case. In the meantime, something has come up and I have to entertain a NASA representative for a day or so. If you don't mind, I'll leave you in the competent hands of the crew until I've finished with him. Then, with any luck, we can show you some big fish." With that, he introduced her to one of the qualified dive instructors and bade her good luck.

The NASA administrator stepped off the plane following an uneventful journey and greeted by Sniphle himself. "Alex, welcome to New Bismarck. It's good to see you once again. What's on the agenda? Better still, why the urgency?"

An islander stepped forward with the local polite reverence to those of higher status. "Sir, let me take your bag." Alex acknowledged the junior man, noting his reddish hair as unusual compared to the other island men. He looked into his eyes and saw a bright intelligence, before handing over his overnight holdall, keeping a data-file case. Sniphle, seeing the look on Alex's face at the somewhat strange features of the young man, said with his false smile, "He's one of our locals, one of the trial units built in this facility. Unfortunately, his original self died, falling from a roof while working on site here. As an act of goodwill, we donated a DNA-shell to him."

Alex, without understanding local protocols, came straight to the point. Backing off from Sniphle's cosy tone, he said, "Director Sniphle, we must talk. Is there somewhere private?"

There was something about Gordon's tone that Sniphle picked up on, and in an immediate and powerful way he replied, "Yes, follow me." Once ensconced in Sniphle's office with the drinks and titbits flapped away without words, the door was closed behind the pair. "So, Alex, what's the grim news?"

Coming straight out with it, Gordon replied, "We're going to have to shut down the colonisation project for now. I don't know how else to say it." He waited for a response, knowing there would be an eruption. Sniphle though, remained calm as he digested the implications of the announcement. On the one hand, it would eat into his profits, but there would be cancellation charges. On the other, it would help ease the logistical problems of overworking the Specials.

He went into his act of seeming to express an eye-popping facial expression of anger. Then he covered his face with his hands in a show of disappointment that hid his thinking through the ramifications. Seeming to recover and still acting out his disappointment, he looked up at Gordon. "Hmm, let's have those drinks now."

There followed a lengthy explanation from Gordon as to the reasons, and how other subcontractors were taking the soon-to-be-made-public announcement. Sniphle followed this, labouring on the great losses his company would incur, although pleased at the timing. He also knew there would be time now to enhance all aspects of the D.O. organisation, and to smooth the rough edges off the recently commissioned New Bismarck facility. He also knew that, given time, the space agencies would recommence the projects. *There are many lifetimes to come*, he thought, smirking to himself.

He then thought about the small offshoot of the project and said, "What about the deep space mission you had mentioned? Surely you have enough funds for that?"

Alex thought for a moment. "You mean the FTL tests? That shouldn't take too long. Maybe a week by the time we get the technical guys set up. Yes, we should be able to squeeze researchers and monies for that."

Sniphle dropped his angry tone and replied, "Good. In that case, I'll arrange for a Special to visit your labs. You must give me the location." He settled back behind his desk, almost satisfied. He waited a few moments after the drinks were served and then, taking a leaf from the New Bismarck PM's book, change the subject completely. "How about scuba? Do you dive?"

37
Trips Away

Ngoosi entered Luna's room and could see the girl was in a deep sleep. She thought about waking Luna, but her knowledge of the Special made her hang back. Instead, she took a book and read aloud in a low tone. It was an old book written in a time unknowable to Ngoosi or her generation, but there were similarities to the current world: hunger, poverty, rich and poor, greed and kindness. *Oliver Twist* had always been a favourite of her grandmother, who had read it to her many times. Ngoosi had no children of her own, but she felt an affinity with the girl and felt a need to protect. While reading to the sleeping Luna, she was expressing herself, hoping the vulnerable girl wouldn't feel so lonely.

From far away, Luna stirred into waking, the flickering eyelids no longer apparent, with a calmness flooding over her frown. Soon, there were slight body movements, and at last she opened her eyes. "Ngoosi, I think my inner self has grown further. I've moved on. But I also travelled, just taking in the trees bending in the wind, and the birds busying themselves making nests. Then I heard your story of the little lost boy, at first sad, and then happy just to be with family around him."

Without addressing Ngoosi further, she looked beyond the open door. "I see more now... all." Sitting up, she asked, "What have they in store for us today, I wonder?"

Ngoosi, now up and animated, busily addressed the small cupboard for clothes and said, "Luna, remember the festival. We must get you, Mr Triton, and Mr Denzel to a festival in France. It will be a long day, so let us have you up, showered, dressed, and ready for transport."

The limo eased the party to the company aerodrome, where the crew ferried them onto a twin-engine plane. On arrival at the festival, the organisers had planned for them to enjoy the privileged box position to both view and hear the entertainment. Although the loose-limbed Denzel was unfazed by the events surrounding the journey, it exhausted both Triton and Luna, with both needing the help of their carers to get them into their seats.

First, there were introductions to the others in the box. The organisers introduced Denzel and the two Specials to high-earning contributing members of the Centurion Project, all of whom seemed to know each other.

All waited, and eventually a silence seemed to radiate from the musicians, progressively finding its way to the entire audience. The performance began with a quiet hum that broke out into a series of melodic notes. All the while, the volume grew. To Luna, it was a revelation. Instead of the jingly loudness blaring from individual shop stores in the malls, here was melody. But there was something else, a vibration seeming to fill the booth. Initially, it came through the flooring, rising through her feet and through the chair itself. The vibrations emanated through her while she sat, bringing a buzz through her tissues, rising via her thighs. They passed up through her spine into the base of her head and hairs of her scalp. She was hearing music as if for the first time. Luna was seeing dancers performing in harmony. She was seeing and hearing singing groups vocalising different, distinct notes, yet complimenting each other, orchestrated tones touching deep within the listeners. Melodies were reaching into her for a moment, then replaced instants later with notes matching a greater theme, only to fade away, giving way to further levels.

The others in the group sometimes continued their conversations, almost oblivious to the reason they were there. But the performers were unaware and continued their concert, locked into contributing to the whole. Sat outside the others' conversation, Luna regarded each performing artist and piece they were playing. She was overwhelmed. It lost Luna; it enthralled her. Her growing mind had gone a step farther and understood more. She followed the musical themes farther now, back through the rhythms into the composers' thought processes when writing these themes. She saw back to when they had written their music, of how they had sometimes written the combinations of notes in fits of melancholy, of fire, sometimes in the afterglow of making love and occasionally, to relieve a build-up in their minds.

A brief interval allowed one set of musicians and performers to clear a way for a single, slightly built young man to step onto the open stage. In clothes seeming too big, he addressed the microphone. In a quiet, unrehearsed speech, he spoke of the passing of his mother only a few days before. This type of performance being new to her, Luna concentrated and saw farther. She found she could enter his thoughts and saw the depth of feeling he had for his lost mother. With that, Luna knew she had climbed another step beyond humanity. Now she could see into the minds of others.

The young man sat at a white piano and began. At once, the audience quieted their hubbub as the first notes of a sombre version of Debussy's *Clair de Lune* began. It held the entire audience enthralled as the music continued its solemn theme. But Luna saw more. There, hovering beside the tearful player, lingered the ethereal figure of a smiling woman in rapture at the emotional performance. In a revelation, Luna saw back into the minds of the player and his mother, adding to her hope.

Another step had taken place. Luna could now see the authors of the music as they wrote, reminding Luna of her time with the dolphins. But this was different. Luna knew the step towards becoming unique was beyond all that lay around her.

At intervals, differing foods were offered and again, all was new to her, bringing marvels to her taste buds. Perfumed scents flooded through her as she saw back from their births—from the farmer's seed to flowering, from the squeezing of its petals to the scented mist surrounding the bodies of pretty people. To Luna, this was a day of wonder, not only toward the performances or the foods, but of visiting people who dressed in a range of clothing she had never seen before. *How do they stay clothed with such minimal support? These women seem to need little, yet I have all this strapping to hold me together.*

While the music, food, and differences of the others were washing over her, she knew all. People of all shades and colours visited, and in their own foreign languages, spoke to the booth organisers on a variety of subjects. Self, music, dance, the excellence of the food, then on to a variety of everyday subjects. Luna understood all—not always through her ears attuned to the music, but comparable in her mind to how she had appreciated the dolphins. She was reaching back to those writing the music; to farmers planning the materials; to cooks preparing the food. She now understood everything they were expressing.

Eventually, the day ended, and their minders herded the D.O. group once more into their limousine and back to the plane home. It freed the previously unenlightened Luna, as if from a sealed dark container, its lid removed, allowing in light. Both Triton and Denzel did their best to draw her out from her dazed state as they extolled the differing modes of performances, but could see they had lost her to the day's events. She knew now that her change was faster, growing stronger, deeper, with more dimensions... while knowing also that she had time.

The following morning, one of the senior Directors came to see Luna while she was having breakfast. "Luna, Director Sniphle has sent us a note from New Bismarck. He says you're to go with one of the NASA administrators to their labs in the USA. Apparently, they're supplying the transport and will return you here within the week. So, can you get yourself ready? A nurse will help."

With a loaded spoon held midway from the bowl and with a passive face, her eyes rounded on him, then she said,

"I want a nurse with me at all times when I go, or I'm not going."

Director Cunningham, shocked at her abrupt statement, knew there had been a change, noting to himself that the incident needed reporting. Recovering, he nodded. "Of course, Luna, I'll arrange for Nurse Jillian to accompany you."

"No! I want Ngoosi."

"Ngoosi, it will be," he replied in the manner of Sniphle himself. She looked at him, knowing he had little or no thoughts of her welfare, only an instruction to do as Sniphle directed.

"Good," she said, and while feeling his disdain, thought to reciprocate by extending a feeling of sharp venom that disquieted him. Cunningham, without understanding, felt a dread and knew he should escape her and the room as soon as possible.

The NASA team collected and transported the pair to their Ames Research Center in Silicon Valley and met by the Centre Director, Harvey Baxter. Asked if she wanted a tour, Luna replied she had already visited the Research Center, and knew the functions of each of the departments already. "But thank you Harvey, for the offer."

Harvey accepted her explanation, knowing the Specials were Outliers, having done his research. Then, with no outward slight, he moved ahead with the reason for her visit. "In that case, let's get on with it. We want to get this part over and documented before the bean counters start pulling the plugs."

Ngoosi questioned all that was taking place, and although understanding little, she knew Luna would do her "travelling thing" and would need someone to help her when she returned.

The calm-faced Harvey stepped in once more. "So, Luna, if it's okay with you, what we want you to do is to travel from here to our Mars facility. Note the letter and two-digit code number written on the whiteboard in the chief administrator's office. Then return here and report."

Luna nodded.

"We'll hook you up to monitor your brain functions to find out if and how long you're travelling."

Again, she nodded.

Harvey, expecting more than the nods, continued, "We'll repeat these runs several times once you identify where the Chief's office is. When you know the location, we want you to repeat the process, so it won't hold up your speed because of the initial searching time made on the first run... Is that all okay with you?"

Again, Luna nodded before she looked to Ngoosi and back to the research officers, who were trying to be as friendly as they could. "Okay, let's do it."

The wired Luna sat on a comfortable bed similar to her own back at the D.O. facility. Then, when wired up, she told them Ngoosi should sit beside the bed before she closed her eyes. The operators surrounded their monitors and watched as her brainwaves changed and showed new rhythms.

Luna found her trigger point easily, and mentally rose from the bed, looked down at the monitoring team, and headed out and up. She left Earth far behind. Now there was Mars, and towards its southern hemisphere she saw the just-built facility contrasting with the barren landscape.

In through the roofing shell, she toured the complex with its multi corridors connecting the uniform buildings and found the office with its whiteboard. There, printed on the board, was a simple, "T43." Briefly she saw the Chief Officer as she addressed her work-tablet, having no inkling of Luna's presence. She smiled to herself; the Dou's here all seem to be remarkably similar in build, and apart from subtle changes in skin hues and features, they all looked the same.

"Uppercase T43," Luna said as she opened her eyes to the waiting team on Earth.

Ngoosi smiled. Her charge was back. Feeling a sense of relief, she took a backseat as the NASA team began questioning the Special.

The slim Harvey, who was in his early thirties, came forward. "Yes, you're right, T43. At the moment, Mars is almost at its farthest point from us, 12-light minutes distant. You made it in less than seven minutes, even though you had to search for the whiteboard." He smiled at her, a genuine smile of appreciation for someone who had achieved something impressive. His bright warm eyes, behind a pair of old-fashioned horn-rimmed glasses, were new to Luna when being addressed by those in authority. "Are you ready to repeat the experiment again, or do you want to rest?"

"Let's do it. Let us see how fast we can do it this time."

Harvey, warming to her, smiled and looked at the other members of the team. "Okay, let's give it half an hour to analyse any subtleties in your brain patterns during the search and return journey. We'll contact Mars, confirming the whiteboard has been re-written and that they're ready."

Luna repeated the journey six times that day; and after returning from the last, she said, "Okay Harvey, I've almost had enough. Maybe just one more."

He smiled. "Good, we'll stop for the day after that. I'll just get Mars to do the changes to the whiteboard." When that was taken care of, once again, she settled back into her bed, blinked back to the watchful Ngoosi, and closed her eyes. Almost immediately, she snapped her eyes open and said, "BCG33793 written in alternating colours, yellow, red, blue."

"Nineteen seconds! Wow!" The rest of the NASA team applauded as they read out the figures. Harvey came forward, beaming. "At first, we thought it was some kind of magician's trick when you came back with the letters and numbers on the past trips. So we thought we would colour-test you out." He smiled into her eyes. "Wonderful! You are very special."

Outwardly, Luna was very calm, like a parent home from work to a houseful of excited children. She waited a moment before asking, "Harvey, what now? Is that it? Are there other tests that you require of me?"

His eyes were wide with wonder at what had occurred that day, knowing he was in the presence of someone utterly unique during an event that might never be repeated. Respectfully, he said. "Luna, we'd love to have you here full-time, but I know it wouldn't thrill the D.O. for us to hold you here."

The NASA team began clearing up their gear and slowly made their way out of the Lab, leaving the permanent recording equipment behind. Luna looked to Ngoosi and blinked her eyes as if asking if she was okay, to which her friend blinked back with a subdued smile. Luna then turned to Harvey. "So, I can go?"

He looked pensively at both Ngoosi and Luna, then raised his eyebrows, took a breath, and said, "There's one more set of tests tomorrow, if you're game for it. To prove the timings, we'd like you to do the same as today, but this time going to a moon of Jupiter, Europa. If you say yes, I can arrange it for tomorrow, and we'll do a maximum of three runs." He waited with a half-open mouth, like a child expecting Christmas gifts.

She thought only for a moment, looked up at Ngoosi, and nodded to him. "What are we having for dinner? I'm starved."

38
Rebreather

Salena quickly made friends within the New Bismarck community, who responded to her as though she were one of their own. After completing her first PADI scuba course, she took to it like a duck to water. At once, she started the follow-up advanced course. But like most new divers, she thought she was ready for anything, not knowing how little she knew. In the back of her mind, her thoughts were to get friendly with the boat crew, hoping to find a weakness in Sniphle's cage-diving escapades.

Her thoughts turned to Sniphle, but to her disappointment, he had returned to the D.O. facility in the UK, his team advising her his island trip had been cut short following the visit by the NASA administrator. Hopefully, he would be back shortly. Briefly, they explained that the impending NASA cancellation needed preparation for some important financial planning prior to the NASA press release. His team advised he couldn't go with her on a dive, but suggested she stay for a week there, enabling her to take in her body changes and to get some dives in. When he returned, she was to remind him of his invitation for one of his "big fish" cage dives.

She approached Kai, one of the older D.O. cruiser crew members. "Tell me, Kai, when are you next going to sea in the *Simiram?*" Kai thought for a few moments, and told her they were going to test out the capabilities of the new cage at depth within two days. He explained that the new eight-by-four-metre cage needed sea trialling before Sniphle's next visit. Interested, Salena asked, "What tests are to be done?"

Kai, always one to please, explained. "The new cage has to be big enough for up to six divers to freely move around. It's also three metres high, so the divers can accommodate each other if they want to observe a particular fish or shoal. When we are current-running, or they instruct us to sail to another location with the divers down, we must ensure the cage remains stable. Therefore, sea trials are needed."

She took in what he'd said and asked innocently, "What about depth?"

Again, he was ready with his answer. "We take it to its max depth of 100 metres to ensure its stability. In practise, the divers won't be going much deeper than 30 meters, because, as I am sure you're aware, dive times are reduced and the light at depth is not good."

She charmed herself onto the *Simiram* easily, as most of the crew regarded her as both one of their own and one of the D.O. hierarchy to keep in with. On the two-day trip, they spent most of the time observing the streamlined modifications to the cage. They also noted how it behaved in the sea currents at typical dive locations. As predicted, it was hard to keep the cage from spinning back and forth when the current was running at its highest. But at slack water, it hung stable, as designed. They carried out other tests to check its performance when the craft was moving at "dead-slow speed." This followed by accelerating speeds, and finally as the craft matched the sea currents. However, while conducting the trials, they had not accounted for undersea currents running different directions to those at the surface.

While she spent her time acting as an unofficial D.O. company onlooker, Salena made it her priority to study the *Simiram* and its crew for any weak points during the diving operations. Following non-specific conversations with various crew members, she homed in on any weaknesses of the cage. She found the cage system to be robust, with no clear weaknesses, even though she had been earlier told of the clutch being a possible weak point. As the chief engineer told her over breakfast on the second morning. "Salena, even if the clutch should fail and allow the cage to run away, when the cable system gets to 100 metres, the cable itself stays fixed to the cable drum. It most definitely would never come loose. The cage would just hang there at 100 metres until we hauled it up again by other methods."

Her idea of putting pay to Sniphle through a deep-water accident was becoming more difficult than she had expected. She was disappointed, but kept her eyes and ears open as the crew went about their normal maintenance routines. She watched as they cleaned everything. She watched how they would oil and grease all the exposed surfaces. Then she noted an enormous swivel chair housed within the cage, and asked what they used it for. The crew member, Peter, smiled and explained that Director Sniphle wanted a captain's seat housed within the cage. Here he could just sit and watch while other divers would have to attempt to hang on to keep their level and position within the cage. Peter explained the chair within the cage could swivel around 360 degrees, but to do this required a great deal of maintenance. Nontoxic oils and grease were necessary after each dive following surfacing.

Salena also watched the dive maintenance crew, who were busily maintaining the dive gear when, during her outwardly casual tour, she visited the dive equipment area. Here she saw the air compressor in its own room, and a separate room for the hung-up dive wetsuits, fins, BCDs and weight belts. "Which set is mine?" she asked. The crew member responsible then showed her that each diver's equipment was given its own cage locker. On hearing this, she pricked up her ears as a possibility passed through her mind. With a frowning but interested expression, she asked, "What about Director Sniphle? Which one is his?" The crew member directed her to one of the cage lockers. Here, she saw that his was not an ordinary Buoyancy Control Device with its provision for an air tank, but a much neater unit. She frowned, puzzled, and asked, "What's this he has?"

The crew member smiled. "Ha! He has a rebreather set instead of the BCD. This is superb; it uses the exhaled CO_2 from the diver. The unit automatically processes it, then adds pure oxygen from a small tank instead of a large, cumbersome air tank. The downside is, it's expensive for the casual diver, and of course there's more training involved."

39
Chish-and-Fipps

Harvey sat at his desk with his eyes fixed on the figures on his screen, studying Luna's travel times from the previous day. Then, looking up at the two arriving visitors. He said, "Ah, Luna, Ngoosi, welcome back." Homing in on Luna, he inquired, "Luna, how did you feel yesterday's visits to the Mars complex went? What I mean is, did you do or see anything other than trying to find the Chief's Office, or was it a concentrated effort just to find the office and code number?"

Luna's deeper understanding had allowed her an appreciation of people other than those at the D.O., and her appreciation for Harvey and his NASA team was growing. She could see an in-built enthusiasm in their manner as they looked for her input rather than just ordered her and the Specials to do their bidding. She looked at Ngoosi, always bringing her to a smile, seeing her also appreciating these eager individuals as they tried to make them feel at home. First, she eased loose, the buckle on her belt, knowing it would pinch her middle as she tried to relax onto the upright, comfortable padded chair, and said, "Harvey, first, may I thank you and the team? I think I can speak for both myself and Ngoosi. You have made me understand we are not all the same, and there is good and not-so-good all around us."

She glanced around and saw the team members look to her almost in surprise, but realising she was genuine in her words. "But Harvey, to answer your question, did I see anything other than corridors and differing rooms in my search? Yes, there were many things. For example, were you aware of just how much fungus, mould, and insects there are in the Mars complex?" This brought the NASA team members to frown in astonishment. "Also, may I comment that the DNA-Dou's running the place all look very much the same? It's as if they were all honeybees, busy but nearly identical. Surely most people would like something different occasionally!"

He rubbed his face, trying to hide his expression. At first, thinking she was deviating from the reason for her visit, he said, "I'm sorry, Luna, but we're here to do a feasibility study to see how long it would take you to travel to the stars. We're not actually part of the Mars or Europa settlement program."

Disappointed with Harvey's answer, her enthusiasm somewhat dampened, she said, "Okay, let's get started."

Harvey could see the dip in her enthusiasm, and said, "Luna, I'll pass on your observations, thoughts, and comments. In our line of business, it's always good to get a new prospective." With that, he looked at Ngoosi. "What about you, Ngoosi? Have you any input as to what you've seen or heard so far?"

A little protective of her charge, Ngoosi replied, "No, you have all made us very comfortable; it's all we could ask for.

But please, take to heart what Luna is saying to you. Hers is a fresh pair of eyes."

Harvey nodded in acknowledgement. "Yes, we can see that."

Over the next hour and a half, the team fussed around her, attaching the brain sensor cap until one of the team came forward. "Harvey, Europa has sent us the first codes."

Once again, Luna settled back, making herself comfortable, then closed her eyes. The team checked their displays of her mental activities, then one by one, intercommed their readiness to Harvey. Without being told, Luna noted all taking place and, as if by a signal, searched for her trigger.

Aware that her spirit-self had opened, she looked out as if from a forest canopy after emerging from deep jungle. Now with life and possibilities all around, she mused to herself, *Not now; first, Europa*. There she saw Ngoosi sitting beside her, always watching and aware, her eyes flashing from one team member to another as they made their comments, then back to Luna's quiet physical self, relaxed in the chair.

Luna travelled up and away, noting the clouds as they tried to hide the NASA complex far below her. Dark now, she moved to the night section of Earth before eyeing Jupiter, and soon its moon, Europa. Luna homed in on the region of Europa earlier depicted by Harvey's team and made her way to the outpost offices of the complex.

Oh! She smiled, spying the whiteboard displaying, 'Hello, Luna!' and beside it a large honeybee drawn on the board: ✸ She also saw the code neatly written nearby. After taking it all in, she looked around and saw one of the Complex members looking around as if trying to glimpse her presence. This brought with it an uncontrolled feeling of joy—but now it was time to return.

She awoke, announcing, "232 minor case t, capital R, and a honeybee symbol." Looking around at the team on their AI consoles, she said, smiling, "That honeybee was a nice bit of humour from the Europa team." Then, glancing up at the waiting Ngoosi's broadening grin, she said, "I'm okay, don't worry."

A pony-tailed, eager young man pushed forward and said, "Three minutes and nine seconds; wow, you did it again! At present, Jupiter is close to us, and we've calculated the distance as 31 light minutes and 43 seconds, give or take a few milliseconds."

Luna seemed sharper in thought and, looking to Harvey, said, "Set it up again. I'm in the mood. I'll do one more now that I know where the office is." She looked around and found Harvey looking over the figures on one monitor. Aware of her stare, he said, "Don't worry Luna, I'm with you, I was just going over the figures again... unbelievable." He looked up, "Okay! Let's send the results to Europa and tell them to set up another. It will take at least an hour and a half, so while they do that, let's have an early lunch."

After the lunch break, she settled back down into her comfortable position and waited for her trigger. In the back of her mind she was thinking, *speed*. Without waiting to look at her resting physical body, she sped away. Knowing precisely where the office was, she eyed the whiteboard, collected the written code, and turned back towards Earth and Ames.

Surprising everyone still around her, Luna opened her eyes only moments after she had closed them. "Easy this time. 'Sugar 53–keep talking,"' she announced, almost breathlessly. The NASA team looked to each other, some looking back to their instruments and displays, and then back to Harvey with worried expressions.

Harvey's key assistant came forward, handing him a printout. "Twenty-two seconds." Harvey stared at it as if reading it over and over, trying to contain his disbelief. Without speaking, he handed her the sheet. He turned to the other members and announced. "Luna, this is unbelievable—it's over 170 times the speed of light. We— that is my team and I—need to look over these figures and contemplate what's happening here."

Without acknowledging his words, Luna began, "Harvey, that's it. I want to go home now." She rose from the bed and unsteadily held onto Ngoosi's reassuring arm. "Can you arrange our transport?"

The stunned NASA team only started moving when Harvey's assistant broke the silence. "Sir?"

Harvey broke away from his static state and told Luna, "Yes, of course. I'll get the flights arranged right away, although I'm sure they won't be until tomorrow morning. In the meantime, let's have dinner this evening with the team." He paused, trying to get his thoughts in place. "I think we're all in shock."

Later, Harvey and the team rose as one when Luna and Ngoosi arrived at the venue. With a brief smile, he said teasingly, "There's a nice range of distinct types of foods here. I'm not sure what you Brits eat any more. Anyway, we have just about everything, including Chish-and-Fipps." Again he smiled, as she looked up and saw the humour in his jibe.

While the evening conversations centred primarily on the differing research and development routes the Mars and Europa bases were taking, the topic finally rounded onto the timings of Luna's Mars and Europa journeys. Harvey's assistant approached and asked a question, playing with his logic following the last two journeys. "Luna, when we do the calculations, it appears the Europa trip was far faster than the Mars trip. Have you any idea why?"

At first, she seemed quizzical, then understood, saying, "You didn't take into consideration the fact that I had to slow down on the end of each trip so as not to overrun. On each occasion, slowing down took the same amount of time; only the travel time was different. On looking back, I suppose it took two or three seconds for each trip, so I believe my speed was far faster than what you measured. Harvey, when your people do the calculations, remember I also had to first get up to speed, then slow down when getting back to Earth each time."

The assistant, fumbling to get his calculator while hurrying through the numbers in his head. "That's over 220 times the speed of light. With that kind of travel speed, you could get to Alpha Centauri in about a week!"

Luna kept quiet and thought a bit. Without the self-adjustments of having to first accelerate, then slow down at the end of each trip, she was sure she could travel much, much faster.

When Luna and Ngoosi arrived back at the D.O. complex, Sniphle met them but ignored Ngoosi, greeting just Luna in an overtly gushing way. "Luna, welcome back. We have much to talk about. I've arranged a meeting in my offices in about an hour, so please make yourself comfortable, and I'll send someone to collect you when I'm ready." Although his inner self tried to get him to spend a little longer on pleasantries as an act of courtesy, his psychotic need for dominance overruled any politeness. He bade her good day.

Luna was no longer in any mood to be pushed around by the D.O., and while all too aware that they had control over her physical body, she resolved to make a new beginning. She arrived early for the meeting with Sniphle. When greeted by Janice's expressionless, icy stare, Luna snubbed the overprotective assistant and entered Sniphle's office unannounced. There sat Triton, who turned and greeted her with smiling eyes. Sniphle froze in his chair, but otherwise seemed comfortable with the incursion, and invited Luna to a seat. "Excuse me, Luna, I was just discussing with Triton his up-and-coming DNA-shell transition."

Luna collapsed into the comfortable seat and said, "Go on with what you were doing. Remember, Director Sniphle, you asked me to come here."

For once, Sniphle felt a little uncomfortable when talking to Luna, reminding him of similar occasions with Triton. "Okay, just let me finish what we were talking about." He turned to Triton, sitting opposite him across the desk. "Where were we? Ah, yes! Triton, of the original team of Specials, you're the only one who hasn't taken a Dou body. Not that we didn't want you to, but we thought it best if your Dou body was the same as yourself... that is, in the flesh as you were when 25 years old." Sniphle shifted in his seat a little and reached for a folder, opened it, and produced two photos of Triton's Dou self in its current state of build. "As you can see, it's you, but!" After pausing a moment, he said, "Except for your essence, your intellectual self... you." He waited to see if there was any reaction, but there was none.

Unknown to Sniphle, both Triton and Luna, in their spiritual forms, had already visited the DNA-shell labs and had seen his new body. Together they were witness to the 600-day gestation, from its small seed to its fully developed, muscular frame. Together they had also witnessed the progress of other DNA-shells, much like children waiting at a fairground candyfloss machine completing their stick of floss. Now, knowing the new body was almost complete, they waited for Sniphle's call.

With a nervous eagerness, Sniphle shuffled his chair further towards his desk. "So, Triton, the Triton-Dou DNA-shell will be ready at the end of next week." Sniphle looked for a thank-you, but none came as the pair deliberately kept the insecure man on edge. His nervousness showed a little, and he released more than he had planned. "I also have a new Dou shell in progress as well... for myself."

Luna couldn't help herself. Unhurried and emphasising her words, she asked, "Does... it... have... hair?"

Sniphle's eyes sharpened a little before relaxing. "Luna, you're still full of those little jokes, aren't you? But to answer your question, yes, I bowed to the male ego thing and specified black hair." Then, almost in a sneer, he continued, "Not that ginger stuff that you have."

Triton could see what was happening and sought to calm the situation by changing the subject. "Director Sniphle, when do you want to make my change? There are two Centurions to be settled, and NASA has a new batch being sent to Europa. From memory, I should be free in about 10 days."

Sniphle appreciated the question and pulled up Triton's file on his screen. "That's good; we can't hurry the progress of the Dou shell, so you'll have two day's rest before we call you in."

Sniphle turned to Luna to break the growing tension between them. "So, Luna, I heard about your exploits."

She remained silent, but Triton broke in with a frown, as if he were unaware of the NASA deeds. The proud parent within him brought a smile, though, and he asked, "What have you been up to, Luna? I hadn't heard from you since the French festival."

Sniphle selected another folder on his screen and scanned through it. Then he read aloud the NASA report on her travels to and from both Mars and Europa. When finished, he screen-printed the last of the report and placed the copy on his desk before saying. "Luna, what they've been discussing with me is for the Specials to pioneer a way to the stars. It will be like your achievement in our solar system, but they want someone to investigate other star systems and their planets. They want to see if life exists there, and if it would be possible for human life to exist there as well. They say sending a manned ship, or in fact a ship with AI modules, would be too long for all involved."

Again, Triton broke in. "Travelling to the stars will take years!"

Luna broke her silence. "It's not just to the stars... optimistically, it's to the stars and back."

40
First, What Is Your Name?

J anice knocked at the door and entered without waiting for an answer. "Sir, it's NASA again... it's Alex Gordon."

At the mention of Gordon's name, Sniphle replying said, "Put him on speaker. For him to call this early, something's going on." He clicked the speaker button. "Alex, hello, how are you? How can we help?"

Although normally on first-name terms, the Administrator, replying in a flat tone, said. "Director Sniphle, I understand the tests we conducted with one of your specials were exceptionally productive. We want to bring forward the actual mission if you can spare the Special any time within the near future."

Sniphle was at once on his guard, knowing Alex would not normally have used his formal title, thinking, *This conversation is being monitored.* Aloud, he said, "Administrator Gordon, of course we can come to some arrangement. Shall we talk terms, or shall we leave the finance to others?"

The Administrator disregarded Sniphle's friendly voice. "We at NASA have to make extra cuts. There will be no more projects starting as of Monday coming. So if we want this to go ahead, it's better we start now."

Sniphle glanced at Luna, knowing it was her decision. She thought first of the journey alone. How long—weeks, months? But where; to which star system? Her lack of expression was because of intense thought rather than worry or shock. Turning back to his monitor, Sniphle said, "Administrator, I have Luna with me at the moment." He turned to her; she was no longer slumped on the soft seat, but alert, staring through the window to the horizon. "Luna, are you okay?"

Triton was aware of her conflict and spoke up. "Alex, it's me, Triton. Please give us some time; we'll get back to you as soon as we can. But don't make your plans just yet. What you're asking is without parallel. It needs thought."

That Alex understood, but with outside pressures weighing on him, said, "Sure, but please get back to us as soon as possible. Oh! By the way, we're talking Proxima Centauri b, which is about 4.2 light years away."

Luna, disregarding Sniphle, responded with a question: "Mr Gordon, is Proxima Centauri b the best option for life as we know it?"

Confident, Alex replied, "No, so far that would be Kepler 452b, but that's about 1,200 light years from Earth. Even at your fastest, it would take you five and a half years each way."

Luna ignored the impatient, mouth-opened Sniphle, saying, "Mr Gordon, let me think about this; I have other thoughts about travelling. Please have Harvey set out a list on his white board of the preferences in his conference room, with laid-out star maps. I'll study them and will let you know my decision. If you require a speedy answer, ask Harvey to do it now so that I can respond."

The NASA administrator, who realised she had given him an order, responded without hesitation. "Yes, Luna, I'll get Harvey right on it. How do I contact you?"

"You don't have to; I'll be there. Therefore, if Harvey is doing it with his team, ask him to speak up as if I'm in the room. It may give me more insight." With that, she stood and bid farewell to Triton, ignoring Sniphle, and headed for her room.

After she left, the avaricious Sniphle asked, "Alex, what about the payment if she does what you ask?"

Understanding more than Sniphle could know, Alex Gordon replied, "I'm not sure she wants payment." Then, after clearing his throat a little, he noted, "It seems to me she's on her own on this one. Is this in her working contract with you?"

Sniphle didn't respond at first, looking up to see Triton glaring back at him. With a darting look away, then a look back at his monitor, he said, "Alex, I'll talk this over with Luna and get back to you ASAP." With that, he switched off the link.

Within Sniphle's damaged ego, his psychotic self moved to another level.

With no further discussion, Triton left the office and headed for Luna's room. On arrival, he could see she'd already bedded herself down and was in a deep sleep. He knew what she was doing; his eyes lit up. Taking on his role as a proud parent, he sat by her bed and waited for her return.

Sniphle, his heart pounding, stressed by the conversation, knew Triton could make trouble. But he also knew the Specials relied on the D.O. medicines to survive.

Contemptuously, he reasoned to himself that if Triton caused any problems, it would all blow over, given time. He pressed the intercom button and stated, "Janice, book me for a week in New Bismarck. I need some R&R".

"When for, sir?"

Sniphle felt his vindictive ire gathering following the departure of Triton and Luna, after he had become a mere side-member of the meeting. He knew he needed time away to regain his self-esteem; almost shouting, he told Janice, "Today... today!"

Sniphle's plane arrived in New Bismarck in the late evening, local time, and they ferried him to the company accommodations with its extraordinary views over a quiet sea. Even though his body clock was 10 hours behind, the trip exhausted him enough to fall into a deep sleep, only to be woken by the housekeeper in the next room. He showered and dressed in his progressively relaxed style: shorts, T-shirt, and flip-flops, accompanied by a worn baseball cap to protect his pate from the sun. While breakfasting, Tupaia, the PM's son, arrived, telling him of the dive cage's progress. Sniphle asked when the tides would allow them to set out; Tupaia's expression changed to one of wrinkled concern, and he began filling Sniphle in on the progress of his father. The PM had lately shown signs of forgetfulness that had other members of the ruling council worried. Quiet for a moment, Tupaia wiped the sweat from the back of his neck, and with a worried expression said, "I think it's time we implemented the PM-Dou process. Our nation's father is failing. It's time for the D.O. to step up and complete its part of the agreement."

Sniphle knew he had to start the process, and at once set in motion the retrieval of the PM's specified DNA-shell via a series of calls. He turned to Tupaia. "Okay, it's done. We now have to explain to the grumpy old man that it's his turn."

Relieved, Tupaia laughed. "That will not be easy. We *may* have to get two of our girls to give him an incentive to renew his marriage tackle."

Tupaia accompanied Sniphle to the D.O. offices, to make arrangements for the PM to begin his body-swap preparations, while the cage boat, *Simiram*, was fuelled and readied for a trip.

Early the next morning, Sniphle arrived at the quay with Tupaia, and welcomed aboard by the captain while they ferried his luggage to his quarters. After making his way to the bridge, it surprised him to find Salena chatting to the chief engineer. Wanting to maintain control, he said, "Ah! Salena, I had forgotten you were staying on for a time." In his most irritating, strutting superior pose, he asked, "How do you like your fresh, unfamiliar face and its lovely little upturned nose?" Then, with a sly look, he remembered how he had left her. "Is it what you were expecting?" Without waiting for an answer, he added. "How was the scuba course?"

Salena ignored his first question, answering with a smile, "I did the Basic open-water course followed by the Advanced. Your friendly crew also allowed me to do a few more dives to give me more experience and prepare for a cage dive."

This reminder of his forgotten promise to her annoyed Sniphle at first, but relented, and figured he would give her a fright by going deeper than she had expected - possibly getting the crew to arrange the cage spinning while she was down. Anyway, he would think of something to upset her day.

The crew, as usual, were ready and waiting for the divers. Salena, like her instructor, also along for the ride, kitted out in 5mm wetsuits with the normal BCD arrangement. When Sniphle arrived, they could see that he had plastered himself with sun protection cream, covering his exposed skin and oozing out from under his suit. On seeing Salena's pointed gaze, he commented, "When you have skin as old as mine, you have to protect it."

Salena-Dou changed the subject with a smile. "I thought you had a Dou body ready for you."

He thought back to his last visit to the DNA facility, remembering his overtly masculine new Dou self, and in a show of superiority said, "Yes, ready in two days!" Then, answering her earlier query, but speaking down to her, he said, "The oil helps me with the wetsuit; it just slides on." Then, in one of his unprotected thoughts, he added, "Besides, I enjoy the local girls plastering it on this old body of mine."

Salena suppressed her genuine feelings and smiled falsely, as if it were a normal thing to do.

The *Simiram* set out for the dive site and made good time on the calm early morning seas. As they arrived near the site, the captain ordered the satellite-controlled bow thrusters to engage. Once done, the divers entered the cage, where Sniphle assumed his position in the captain's chair and strapped himself in. Salena and her instructor stood by, holding onto side rails, steadying themselves against the mild swell. The crew, meanwhile, worked on positioning the bottom of the cage a few inches under the mildly lapping waves. The instructor, taking control, said, "Okay! Before we start, let's do our buddy checks to make sure all is working before we descend." Turning, he positioned himself to face the others. His face adopted a serious, patient look. "Let's start. B. W. R. A. F." He held up one finger and began, "First B... Buoyancy Control Device." Per normal protocol for an instructor, he stepped before Salena and began checking Salena's BCD, as she did similarly to his outfit. Looking up, he said to Sniphle. "I'm sure you checked your rebreather arrangement in the locker room, didn't you?" Sniphle replied he had. Salena wasn't sure that was true, but she said nothing.

"W... Weights!" On seeing Salena's well-positioned, he turned to Sniphle.

"I have integrated weights," was the call from the almost-disinterested, bad-tempered and bored Sniphle.

The instructor held up a third finger. "R... Releases." Once again, both Salena and the instructor went through the routine, began checking the BCD quick release clips.

Following this, the scowling Sniphle seemed to become increasingly angry; sweating freely, he shouted, "Let's get on with it, let's get wet," and began calling to the crane operator.

However, the instructor was not to be denied. He Held up a fourth finger. "A... Air." Sniphle turned on the oxygen valve on his rebreather, which, unknown to all, had a small but significant leak from the oxygen hose.

No one knew what happened next. Some said there was a small spark that ignited the abundant O2-oil mix. In reality, the oxygen escaping from the leaking hose generated enough heat at its source to ignite and burn the oil on Sniphle's hands. The fiercely escaping jet of oxygen fed the initial small flame, creating a blowtorch effect with the fire feeding on the escaping oxygen. The flame next caught the sun oil-soaked wetsuit. With flaming hands, the screaming Sniphle fumbled with his chair's seat belt. Fighting through the pain, he eventually freed himself. He sprang out of the chair and eyed the cage door, but as he tried to run in his oversized swim-fins, he tripped on the welded cage floor, falling headfirst into metal grating, tearing a gash on his cheek. The small oxygen tank continued to force-feed the blue-flamed blowtorch fire as the neoprene and oil burned, now cutting into his stomach. Bravely, the instructor, acting on instinct, stepped forward at once with his sharp dive-knife, cut through the strapping holding the O2 tank, and flung it off the flaming Sniphle.

Sniphle's piercing screams could be heard from the farthest reaches of the boat. But those dealing with the flaming man had to ignore them, concentrating on easing his still-smoking charred body through the cage door into the sea, dowsing the partially molten neoprene wetsuit. Without thought. Salena jumped into the water beside the now-unconscious Sniphle and began ensuring that his face was out of the water, allowing him to breathe.

They hauled his burnt body from the sea and housed him in a convenient cabin close to the unmoved cage; by then, the ship's captain had the vessel heading for port at full speed. On instinct, Salena, with her nursing skills, kept him alive while monitoring his vital signs.

The two-and-a-half-hour journey seemed to drag on for the crew. But to those ashore, arranging quayside pickup and the standby staff to be ready for his hospital care, time was too short. All the while, the hyper-focused Salena remained by his side before handing him over to the doctors standing by. She later reflected, "With the pain he was in, should I have let him go during that journey instead of keeping him alive?" But within her was a caring instinct that not even Sniphle could douse.

Throughout the next three days, his body was in an agony unknown to anyone other than a burn victim. The painkilling medications did little to ease the pain for more than a few minutes at a time. Parts of the centre of his body were burnt away, and his lungs partly scorched. His respiratory system was being driven by an AI, and as a result, he couldn't talk through the incumbent tubes. When the effects of the painkiller drugs wore off, his conscious self tried to call for someone to let him die. But unfortunately for him, he remained in a semi-conscious state of absolute pain.

Eventually, he died, despite the considerable efforts of those around him.

When his personal assistant, Janice, arrived on site at the New Bismarck hospital, she brought with her his personal file, with its directions for what to do in case of his sudden death. As predicted, it directed that they should prepare his new Dou body and that the Specials should help his spirit to enter it.

Arial and Arche were there to detect his spirit almost three days later, and led his unsure spirit, as they had done with many others before, to Elara and Ananke. Together, and with little affinity to Sniphle, they led him to Triton. True to Sniphle's malice-driven nature, when meeting up with the first of the Specials he said, "Ah! Triton, here to greet me and take me to my new self, as you have done and will do for the rest of time. I have you, and you are in my pocket, and there is absolutely nothing you can do about it. In just a few moments, I will be in my strong new body. However, although I promised you a new body that I know you have viewed many times over its gestation, I have decided otherwise. Now you'll get another, weaker body, one body unable to copulate. You can't meet up with Salena as you had planned, because the body I have chosen for you suffers from many mistakes and deformities. Only its brain is like yours. Therefore, when you die, you will be kept alive for only one purpose... to ferry spirits to their newly completed bodies."

Triton felt the thoughts of the malevolent spirit, and did not react. Instead, he couriered the menacing spirit to a place beside a bed, where a still DNA-shelled body lay. As he had done many times past, he gave his farewell words: "I believe this is where we bid our goodbye to the spirit world."

Sniphle's spirit hovered over the body for a few moments, looking up and around at the beautiful nurses and his shapely personal assistant in attendance. *Things to come, things to come indeed.* Then, on Triton's quiet recommendation, he settled back into his new body.

His eyes flickered open and took in the lovely figure of one of the local nurses sat by his bed, lost in a ream of papers. His new, unlined face glanced around the room. He saw a chatting pair of doctors, and to one side, Salena. As he moved his head, it triggered the nurse to flap the papers shut, calling to the doctor. While trying to move, he was at once reminded of the precautions he had put in place for all awakening Dou's, with straps restricting movement. Grumpily, he barked out to the timid duty nurse, "Okay, it's me. You can undo these and let me up!"

She looked to the junior doctor for guidance, who promptly approached the bed. "I'll take over from here," he told her.

Nodding, she replied, "I'll call the senior duty doctor." Nervously reaching out, she pressed the call button.

The junior duty doctor began, "Sir, your instructions were that all spirits returning to their new bodies should answer a few questions and get checked over as a matter of routine. It will only take a moment. The senior doctor is on his way. But in the meantime, let's complete the questionnaire before he arrives... Are you ready?... Sir."

Still in a slight haze after waking, and with sweat showing on his unlined forehead, Sniphle relenting, said, "Okay, if you insist, fire away."

His horizontal body appeared to twitch a little as the duty doctor approached and sat beside him. Then, opening the touch-screen program, he began reading from the top. Smiling, almost in embarrassment, he began, "First! What is your name?"

There was an uncharacteristic, almost gentle smile across the face of the muscular male body as it lay there looking clearly at the Doctor. "My name is Doctor Vanessa Trokker. What's yours?"

"No, it's not," came another voice with an unfamiliar accent. "My name is Charles Taylor. My son is Triton Taylor." Another voice broke through, unmistakably a woman's. "No it's not! My name is Bethany Linden. I'm his aunt."

Other voices chimed in, each claiming unfamiliar names, before a sharp, barking voice, unmistakably that of Sniphle, shouted, "Get out of my head!"

The shocked duty doctor called to the open-mouthed, dumbstruck nurse, saying, "Quick, get the sedatives, we need to shut him—*them* down until we get the senior D.O. doctors here."

Both Director Vernon and Director Dr Ranghan arrived and positioned themselves close to the waking but secured Sniphle. Vernon began by saying, "Sniphle, Director Sniphle, sir, if you can listen for a few moments, try to concentrate. I have something to tell you." Senior Director Vernon, sat by the Dou body appointed as Sniphle-Dou, pulled his chair up a little and in a clear voice, said, "Director Sniphle, sir." He then spoke up a little, and beginning again, said, "To all of you inside this Dou body, I have to inform Director Sniphle of what has happened. It will affect none of you, but some or maybe all of you maybe pleased with what has happened. Therefore, please give us a lull in your chatter to allow me to get my message to him."

The Dou's body seemed to relax a little, no longer as tense. Director Vernon, feeling more confident, continued in a less-respectful tone, "Sniphle, do you remember the Dou body you were preparing for Triton?" He paused only a moment before he continued, "Of course you do. Well, what you didn't know was that while you were playing, it was with another body, not Triton's. It seems the local lab techs didn't trust you much, and all they allowed you to do was to play with a substitute shell. They hid the real Triton-Dou away, safe from your occasional visits."

An uncharacteristic and genuine smile slowly appeared on Sniphle-Dou's face, and all those present knew it was not his own.

41
No Way Back

Luna knew there was little she no longer understood about her body and knew the task she was about to try was merely for new knowledge, not profit. During her spirit-self visit to NASA, collecting the presentation of star maps, she carefully took in Harvey's running commentary. She now knew which key parts of the sky would function as her directional pointers once her journey began. Now back inside her physical body at the D.O. facility, she contacted the NASA Ames staff on screen. "Harvey, thank you for the star maps and your commentary. They're just what I needed. I plan to go to both targets as soon as possible." On the screen in front of her, she could see frowning faces, but continued. "That is, Proxima Centauri b, 4.2 light years away. Then on to Kepler 452b."

Harvey's eyes rose in open-mouthed concern, and he protested, informing her as best he could about the distances and, importantly, the time needed to achieve her intended goals. But she had decided. Luna knew he could have little understanding of her new nature, and to explain to him was impossible and now irrelevant. She simply informed him she would ensure he was the first person notified of her observations. Then, in a kind voice, "Harvey, in due time you'll get my reports, in some form or other."

Almost as an afterthought and pushing out the warmth of affection, she told him, "Harvey, thank you. In the brief time I knew you, you showed me your inner self; and with it, a hint that humanity may well have a future."

With that, she switched the comms off and turned to her ever-attentive protector. "Ngoosi, I will leave shortly, and may not come back. I've talked to Triton; he will find you and your mother a residence where you will both be happy for the rest of your lives." Wrapping an arm round her former carer and smiling as if to a child, she said, "If I return, we'll get together once more. But my journey will be lengthy, and I'm not sure if I *will* return."

As her nature directed, Ngoosi's eyes filled with tears. Her face drawn; she knew Luna was telling her this was the end. "But who will look after you?" she asked, hinting that while travelling, Luna's physical body would require attention.

Luna knew that once she was travelling, she no longer needed her physical body; but even should the journey be long, its eventual demise would not be important. A hint of humour sparked a broad smile creeping across her face. "Don't worry, Goosi, the AI will monitor me for a time." After a brief pause, Ngoosi saw the joke and, turning, looked into Luna's eyes as recognition, remembering other times when the AI had fumbled the same routine. The tearful relief of humour helped Ngoosi as Luna added, "Well, let's hope there are no power cuts and hiccups, shall we?" Both saw behind the black humour and went into fits of repeated giggles.

Salena-Dou settled into her old house and was greeted tentatively by Pan, previously cared for by Jillian during Salena's stay in New Bismarck. Although pre-warned by Triton and Luna, Pan still found it unsettling to have the olive-skinned, younger Salena-Dou going through her normal daily routines. However, he settled back into their life patterns quicker than all had expected, but now treated Salena more as a sister than house mother. He too had made a phase change, an extra step, becoming more independent.

It was during a visit by Luna, who was saying her goodbyes to everyone she cared for, that she noted the interest Pan was taking in her proposed journeys. Her mother, no longer the matronly woman she had known, was now an energetic, youthful woman with the learned lessons of a full life driving her duty of care. To Luna, she was no longer Mother; Salena was someone else now. She tried hard, but it was difficult to call her Mummy any longer and resorting to how others referred to the new edition, said. "Salena, where is Triton now? I need to say my goodbyes to him before I go on my travels."

A little put out by her daughter no longer calling her by her maternal title, Salena replied understandingly, "Luna, my love, your father is finishing the last of his duties in his ever-older self. He's finishing the last of the latest batch of Europa transfers, then in four days, he'll transfer to his new Dou body."

Salena looked up from the large, comfortable settee with its plumped-up cushions and patted the seat beside her. "Luna, come sit with me for a while. As I understand it, your journey may take a long, long time." She stopped herself, as if remembering something especially important. "Oh! Did you hear what the D.O. board has decided now that Sniphle-Dou can no longer carry out his duties?"

Luna knew, but allowed her mother to tell her anyway, "I heard some of it, but remind me."

Salena's eyes creased into a smile. "The remaining Directors, now without Sniphle's evil direction, have appointed Triton as head of the organisation." She opened her arms as an invitation. Emotion fought itself forward, and despite trying to keep her cool, Luna fell into her mother's arms in a burst of tears.

Pan, who had been listening as always, spoke up, surprising the two emotional women. "Luna, can I come with you on your travels?"

The two women looked at each other, and in a look of excited recognition, each raised a hand and slapped them together. Pan had changed. Luna saw now how much brighter he was. Maybe it was part of his growing up, delayed for all these years, but maybe something else. She answered. "Pan, I'm first going to Proxima Centauri b, and it should take me about a week. If you want to come along, we must stay together, or I may lose you." She waited until she could see if he understood.

For almost the first time in his life, Pan seemed calm. Taking in all Luna was implying, he said, "Luna... While I've been here in this house. I can sometimes disappear within myself for weeks. Only Salena seems aware, and she accommodates my lost times." Wide-eyed, Salena nodded. He pleaded once more, "Please let me come with you!"

Salena rose from her seat, smiled, and nodded. Then, blinking tears away, she took him into her arms, knowing her time with him was nearing an end. Luna saw him differently now; and on seeing the poignant scene, she gave a slow blink of her eyes in approval. "Good, let's do it!"

With a calm expression, Luna took in her surroundings, as she had done for many years: the white walls and bedcover, the ill-designed electrical outlets in the middle of the wall, with cables dripping toward her AI panel. She delayed her next step. She just lay back, taking in all she could see while waiting for the trigger point, sometimes interrupted by thoughts of others. Her mother Salena. Her father, Triton, now in the throes of being prepared for his last days in his current body. The AI machine watching her bodily functions, Ngoosi sitting beside her sobbing, still gripping Luna's hand. Her mind's eye wandered to the star maps. When at last the trigger point was there, almost like a dream flickering to life. *First, I must collect Pan, and then away.*

Pan, who had taken a room within the D.O. facility and was being watched by the staff, lay waiting for his own trigger. As if responding to a knock at his door, he found the point as Luna made her presence felt. "Come, let's go."

Out the pair travelled, away from Earth, passing the outer planets and towards the outer perimeter of the solar system.

A voice came to Luna, reminding her that somebody, that something, was watching. It reminded her of her beginning... her spirit-self travelling those many years before.

"Luna, my butterfly, my first. You have at last reached a threshold. To go farther is up to you! But if you do, I may not

allow you to return. You must now find your own worlds... You must realise the solar system is mine, and only one of us may exist here."

Luna, unbothered, no longer afraid of this unseen being, answered as an equal. "Who are you?"

"You will remember if you try. Try... yes, it was me whom you felt on your first conscious travels all those years ago. It was I who prompted this Earth you just came from to evolve you. It has taken me billions of years to produce you, but here you are, travelling into an unknown future to enlighten new developing stars."

Without understanding all that the voice had told her, she thought of Pan, but before she could gather her thoughts into words, the invisible presence pre-empted her.

"No, Luna... Pan doesn't know of me, and doesn't know of our conversations; only you do. He has not reached the stage you have, and never will. But don't worry, I will not harm him if you let him return to Earth... soon."

There was a lull before Luna grasped that the address from the mysterious being was over. Worriedly, Luna reached out and called, "Are you still with me, Pan?"

Still in awe from their journey so far, he replied, "Yes, but which way?"

Relieved, she answered, "Just stay with me."

Together, they travelled toward their first goal. But Pan found it difficult to stay with her, and when asked if he was okay, he replied. "Yes, but you're so fast I find it difficult to keep up."

Kindly she replied, "I know; I've been helping you, but don't worry, we're almost there. Look, see the large star there in front of us now?"

Together they homed in and roamed around the reddish star Proxima Centauri, with its interesting planets, Proxima Centauri b and c. Visiting both, they noted that Proxima Centauri b, was especially attractive, with its oceans, in some places ice flows, and in other places steamy fumes rising. But was there life?

The pair travelled below the sea's surface, and there was indeed life, in great abundance and diversity. However, they could see little to encourage this as anywhere near a next step for humanity. To live in this place, humans would have to develop both mind and body to accommodate these strange environments.

"Pan, we've seen enough. We cannot recommend this place yet. The system has many millions of years to develop before it becomes habitable for humans, or for the peoples on Earth to evolve to accommodate this planet... We must move on!"

While contemplating her next step towards the Kepler 425 system, Pan entered her thoughts. "Luna, I can't do this. You differ from me. I need to go back." He waited a moment for her comment, but she remained silent. "I can't make this journey with you to the Keplar system. I was struggling to stay with you on this simple journey to Proxima Centauri. I'm sorry, but I must return to Earth." Again, Luna remained quiet before he said, "Let me give all that we have learned to Harvey and the guys at the space agencies. The expedition you're about to take is beyond anything I can do."

Luna knew it would come to this and had tried to help him, but she felt it was like taking a toddler on a marathon run—that she would have to carry him most of the way.

Between them, they agreed on what they should convey to Harvey on Earth. Importantly, Pan should inform them that Luna would travel on to Kepler 452.

"Pan, I'll accompany you back to the Sol system and make sure you can find Earth from there."

As they approach the outer region of the solar system, the being once more entered her thoughts. *"Luna, don't worry about him. I know Pan is fragile, but I will escort and guide him to Earth safely. Remember though, I cannot allow you to enter... This is my realm."*

"But what of my physical self, back on Earth?"

"Luna, my butterfly, that physical body is merely a shell... a chrysalis. It is empty, and you have no further need of it."

Shock and an emptiness hit her. If she'd had a physical body, the new realisation of what she had become would have collapsed her. Even without her physical form, she felt heavy. Time had slowed. A clumsiness started blanketing her thoughts, but fighting back, she threw off the almost overwhelming shock.

A new door had opened, but she remembered her fragile companion. "Pan, my special one. Thank you for being with me. But... I must leave you now, but don't worry about finding Earth, a guide will show you the way."

Without remorse or conflict, remembering her task, she turned and looked to the stars. Thinking back, remembering Harvey and his star charts she looked further, deep into the cosmos for her next star goal. Her deep mind elsewhere, she disregarded the Presence and Pan's half-worded reply and set out once again.

42
Carrots

Salena noted movement from the bed and knew he was recovering, reconnecting, reliving. She waited, carrying on with her duties, allowing him to focus, to watch her movements as the fuzz of reconnecting his mind to his new body adjusted.

She moved away from the chair, bending forward toward the monitor as she had done those many years past, now with her back at forty-five degrees to him, pretending to be unaware of his watching eyes. Her breasts hung forward a little as she reached to change the monitor screen aspect. She turned her head and watched as his eyes followed her form from ankle through to her breasts, which were lightly touched by her loose clothing, until his eyes caught her looking at him. Then smiling, "So, you're coming alive, are you?"

This time he didn't look away as his teenage self would; but he turned away to catch his surroundings, away from her gaze. As in those earlier days, he glanced back once again to catch her smile of sympathy. Light-heartedly, she said, "You're embarrassed. Most men can't help themselves, and as far as you're concerned, I know you mean no harm. I'm here to look out for your needs while you're here, so just relax, and we'll both enjoy your stay."

With a broad smile rapidly spreading across his face in acknowledgement, and remembering that far-away time, he asked, "What's your name again? There were so many at the introduction, I didn't catch it."

They both looked into each other's eyes in recognition of those past words, both with an uncontrolled smile before taking in the changes. He, now older than his late teenage frame those many years ago. She now with light olive-coloured skin, striking red hair, and green-black, sparkling eyes.

With memories still engrained and with an openness for children, she looked deep into his clear eyes. "We need to catch up on those lost years." Recognising his pending desire and its effect on her. Mouth half-opened, she paused a fleeting moment with a twinkle in her eyes, then approached him. "Come on, let's get those restraints off you." First, in a downward glance of false shyness, she looked up into his eyes, revealing her true thoughts. "Let's not waste time. Let's make some babies."

Her cheeks blushed, Salena's bright eyes slowly blinked; then, bending forward, she kissed him and smiling, "A couple of little carrot-tops will be just what we need."

43
Maybe

Doubts invaded her thoughts after almost a week when she thought of sleep, food, people. Luna delved back into her earlier times of loneliness, of no one to share with, but was now overwhelmed by the vastness. But that soon passed; she saw nebula nurseries giving birth to myriads of young stars. Revelling in the vast wonder, she saw how the changing aspect of her view overtook how the clouds of dust and gases appeared, much like simple, yet colour-filled cloud formations on Earth. Her deep understanding allowed her to envision miniscule molecules gathering to form dust and onward, toward larger bodies. She took in the wondrous views of the stars she passed with their individual planetary systems.

Gone was her gnawing loneliness. Luna became filled with the vastness and wonder at the birth of star systems as she passed through them, helping give her further resolve. Once more, she had a drive, and while she entertained the thoughts biting into her psyche, there was something else driving her forward. Something unresolved.

She experimented with her senses as the weeks piled on, now crawling like a baby, now learning better control, to clamber and eventually to walk... and now to fly. She travelled farther and faster, then faster still as she realised her goal was near.

"What is your name?"

To Luna, the shock of hearing a voice breaking her concentration, entering her head, was frightening. She stopped and began searching her inner self to see if it was herself in sleep. But no, the question came again.

"What is your name?"

Luna, in her distinctive way, replied, "And who are you? How are you inside my head?" She paused, gathering more to her senses. "Where are you?"

"We do not have names, and may I point out, you do not have a head... you have no physical form. But we detect your spirit, your memories... you, and it is this we are addressing."

Defensively, she replied to the voice, "My name is Luna, and I am here to observe this star's planets." She paused a little, waiting for a reply, but none came. Reasserting her bravado, she said, "What about you? Why are you here? How can I detect your thoughts?"

"Luna, we have always been here, as we have been in all star systems. You are the first of your kind to enter this system." The voice paused before beginning again, changing its tone and slowing its speed. *"From now until its sun fails, these planets around Keplar 452 are yours."*

The voice waited for her to respond, but when she did not, it continued. *"There are good signs of life here, and it is you who shall direct all that life's future."*

'What are you talking about?'

"Luna, this system is yours now. We know you are young and still growing; we know you will make mistakes, but

whatever you do, we believe you will help this system rise as others have done. Remember, your own ancestors rose and developed on Earth under Sentinel guidance. Creatures on Earth were helped and guided, from the first single-celled organisms to what they are now. You, Luna, are at the next level... a Sentinel level, and it is now your turn to help this system's development."

Luna's realisation that all she was being told was truth brought her to recognise that this system was to be hers. "But I know nothing. How can I help guide this system? I'm but a baby with a blank mind as far as this responsibility goes."

"We know that. You will make many mistakes. But you will also learn as your worlds develop sapient beings. Luna, you have known many evil things during your brief life, but you recognise good."

Luna was in shock, and it seemed she had opened a door to infinity. "I can't change or mould anything - how can I?"

There seemed a change in the thoughts entering her, as if another being, part of a group of others, began, *"Luna, we know what you have been through. We know your reactions to those events, some with anger, some with thought. We do not know how you will govern this planetary system. Whatever you do, this system is yours to guide now."*

"How can I change and mould things that are part of the physics of nature? I have no physical form."

"Luna, we are leaving now. We are about to re-enter our home, what your scientists call Dark Matter. It is all up to you. You will find a way as you grow. As you said to us, you are but a baby, but you are still evolving. You will develop and find extra powers to fulfil whatever changes your new planets

need."

The first of the voices arose again. *"Luna, it is time for us to go. Be patient with your worlds and be helpful to them."* A silence grew before the voice returned. *"Farewell, young Luna."*

In desperation, Luna cried out to the spirits, "Wait... Which way?" But there was no reply, and she felt a new hollowness within.

Luna gazed down on her new worlds and chose first, the closest. 'I'm growing; I can feel it in me. It's not quick, but I've been aware of the changes since my first days of Travelling back on Earth.'

She looked down at Keplar 452b once more, seeing now the emerging single-celled creatures in tidal pools, and smiled. Remembering her time on Earth, its seas and land, its flora and fauna, new horizons for the living, and a new hope for the dead.

'I see everything below me much clearer now.' Then pleased with her new world.

"Maybe I can... Maybe I can."

Epilogue

The choking foam-like fuzz his mind encountered, arose and subsided on each pulsing day. A warm glow lightening his eyelids until a vague physical disturbance, then the regular infusion into his arm put him into the deep once more. The day wore on until dusk when the warm glow faded once more into the dark.

Keno' T. Sniphle lay where he had been held for the last year and a half, housed within the secure wing of the Director Organisation building. They kept him in a chemically reduced state ensuring, both he and his accompanying vocal spirits remained subdued. The DO staff were instructed to keep giving him his regular four daily doses without failure. But things were changing as both his physical and mental self gradually accommodated the chemical toxins, allowing longer cognisant daily thoughts.

A further six months passed before he was able to open his eyelids and glance around his white walled room. Luckily for him, while the duty staff were otherwise engaged, there was the shadow of another trying to reach into his thoughts. "Keno' my little prince, where are you."? But while trying to fathom an almost forgotten term of endearment, his Artificial Intelligent module kicked in and released its programmed dosage. Images and thoughts dissolved and Sniphle soaked back into his induced sleep. Almost six hours later, the process repeated itself. However, Sniphle was ready and recognised the directed thoughts as someone dear from his past. Aunty Beth! Then, once again, the AI released its programmed dosage, and he fell again into its induced sleep. But his thought remained.

Once again, the soft thoughts entered through the fuzz, "Keno' my prince, talk to me."

The lapses in the medications affect grew longer, and Sniphle was able to respond. "Aunt Beth, it's been so long since we last talked. How are you?" A little fire in her response helped his recollection of the events. "Keno' my naughty boy. Remember well, how it was you who had me killed. But within me, I cannot help myself. Inside you is something I cannot resist and after searching your thoughts I know you did it for a greater reason."

Within his memory, he smiled at the remembrance of those brief years with his aunt. Him as an underaged student and her subsequent conviction as a menacing paedophile. Then when she was released from prison, his mixing of chemicals to bring about her death and any further association with her. But that time had passed forty-four years ago until his own chemical induced subjugation almost two years ago. Now he felt good again at the news, as she seemed to have forgiven him.

For once, he felt the infusion of chemicals enter the intravenous drip in his arm, and the glow within his eyelids dimmed once more.

Almost six hours later, his thoughts came full once more. This time, not only Aunt Beth, but another spirit made its presence felt. "Director Sniphle. You bastard! I get to meet you at last without your minders." His malevolent thoughts raced for who these new thoughts could be. But the numbers were large, and he let them play in his head until they revealed themselves. "Remember me and your laughter at me going into spasm and your minder beast throwing me to my death 20 floors below." Oh yes, he remembered now, Dr Trokker. He recalled the mix he had fed to her, the spasms, her narrowly missing him with a glass in hand. Then her squirming in his minders arms as he squeezed her through the window.

Another voice entered, trying to babble through Trokker's screaming attempt at inflicting verbal damage into Sniphle's mind. Mat Phillips had been the instrument Sniphle had used to kill Triton's parents. It was a simple task to get rid of Mat by supplying him with an extremely potent dose of his favourite pleasure. With the police writing off the death of both Triton's parents by Mat as *'another'* addicts unpleasant accident. The continuing babble in Sniphle's head did little to deter him from anything other than his own thoughts. The main one being the need to escape this cacophony of noise.

In the weeks that followed, the periods of clear thoughts became longer. He still had Trokker, Aunt Beth, Matt and a dozen more constantly babbling at him, but his paranoid, psychotic inner thoughts allowed him to focus on his own agenda and not of others. Away from the fug of the regular six hourly paralysing AI administered infusions, the clear periods of thought were mostly prior to, and here, he sometimes caught echoes of speech from doctor's and carer's happening to be close by. With malevolent cunning he realised there may be a way out of this bedlam he had made for himself. Purposely, his conniving plans formed; first to separate his babbling adversaries, and then... to combine them.

Acknowledgments

I would like to acknowledge the great patience and support of my wife, Janette.

In the time it has taken to complete this tale to printed work. I also must thank Sue Black for her suggestions, Andy Leak, for his insights, Michelle Dunbar for her enormous technical prompts and Alexa Whitten for her visionary imagination.

Thank you all.

About the Author

After leaving school, Ken travelled, and continues to do so. First spending 12 years with the British army, serving in Germany, Cyprus, Libya, and finally at a research and development facility in the UK.

With itchy feet, he spent his next 5 years in Iran and Iraq before returning to the UK to catch up on his college education.

Armed with a little more Ed, he worked for a tech company, travelling throughout Europe before living in, and managing their overseas operations in Africa, the Middle East, and the Indian sub-continent.

The endless time spent in airports and hotels allowed him to make copious notes observing the peoples and places which now express themselves in much of his out of world expression.